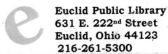

Also by Beverly Jenkins and available from
Center Point Large Print:

The Blessings Novels:
  Bring on the Blessings
  A Wish and a Prayer
  Heart of Gold
  For Your Love
  Stepping to a New Day

The Destiny Series:
  Destiny's Surrender
  Destiny's Embrace
  Destiny's Captive

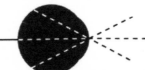

FORBIDDEN

Center Point
Large Print

FORBIDDEN

Beverly Jenkins

CENTER POINT LARGE PRINT
THORNDIKE, MAINE

This Center Point Large Print edition is published in the year 2016 by arrangement with Avon Books, an imprint of HarperCollins Publishers.

The text of this Large Print edition is unabridged. In other aspects, this book may vary from the original edition. Printed in the United States of America on permanent paper. Set in 16-point Times New Roman type.

ISBN: 978-1-68324-191-1

Library of Congress Cataloging-in-Publication Data

Names: Jenkins, Beverly, 1951– author.
Title: Forbidden / Beverly Jenkins.
Description: Center Point Large Print edition. | Thorndike, Maine : Center Point Large Print, 2016.
Identifiers: LCCN 2016040396 | ISBN 9781683241911 (hardcover : alk. paper)
Subjects: LCSH: Large type books.
Classification: LCC PS3560.E4795 F674 2016 | DDC 813/.54—dc23
LC record available at https://lccn.loc.gov/2016040396

To Sarita, Bette, the Ladies of Ca/Az
and the rest of the Rhine Whiners:
Rhine Fontaine is finally here. Enjoy!

Prologue

Georgia 1865

WEARING THE BLUE uniform of the Union Army, Rhine Fontaine tethered his horse to the post and surveyed the charred piles of rubble of the house that once anchored the largest plantation in the county. It had also been his home. The sight of the destruction pleased him even though the bitter memories of his life there would follow him to the grave. The former two-story mansion with its Romanesque columns, wide front porch, and well-kept grounds had been set afire by his great aunt Mahti. She'd died in the flames along with his crippled, bed-ridden father, Carson Fontaine, who'd ruled his three hundred slaves with all the cruelty of a medieval king. Rhine hoped Carson was rotting in hell, but he mourned Mahti. She'd raised him, loved him, and helped him try and make sense of the harsh unfeeling world he'd been born into. With her gone, he and his younger sister Sable were the last living ties to their mother, Azelia, the descendant of an enslaved African queen. Rhine had been so young when Azelia died he could no longer recall her face, voice, or touch, and that, too, fed his bitterness. Slavery had been an abomination. Rhine hated it and this place so

7

deeply that were he not seeking information on Sable's whereabouts, he would never have come back.

He walked past the mansion's remains to see if the rows of slave cabins were still out back and maybe find someone with news of Sable. Although the war was over and slavery was dead, many of the enslaved had chosen to remain with their masters. He couldn't begin to understand their thinking nor did he judge, because he'd made what some would consider an equally unthinkable choice.

The cabins were there but in such terrible disrepair he doubted anyone lived in them anymore. Entire sections of the wooden walls were gone and many had no roofs. Weeds had grown tall enough to fill doorways, and as he stood in the eerie silence memories flowed back of slave children running and playing after a long day in the fields; their mothers cooking and mending, their fathers tending the small gardens that held beans, corn, yams, and collards to supplement the lean rations Carson grudgingly supplied. Those remembrances also brought back the sounds of mothers screaming helplessly while some of those same children were dragged off and sold.

From behind him a woman's voice snarled, "There's nothing left to steal here, Yankee, so, get off my land."

He turned to see his father's wife, Sally Ann

Fontaine, standing in the doorway of one of the dilapidated cabins. Her ragged dirty gown, unkempt hair, and shoeless feet were shocking. The last time he'd seen her she'd been queen to Carson's king. Now she looked worse than any of the slaves.

"Hello, Mrs. Fontaine."

She studied him for a brief moment before recognition widened her brown eyes. "You! Where's my Andrew?"

Andrew was his half brother. They'd gone to war together to fight for the Confederacy. "I don't know. After the first battle, Drew deserted. Said he was heading west."

"You're lying!" And as if the hope of her son's return was the only thing keeping her sanity intact, she leapt upon him screaming obscenities and pounding him with ineffectual fists. "No, you lying bastard! Where's my son!"

He grabbed her wrists. "I don't know." And he didn't. He also didn't remind her that she and Drew had been estranged when they rode off to war because Drew refused to treat the slaves the way their father did.

As she crumbled and began weeping, he released her wrists and asked, "Have you seen my sister Sable?"

The tears stopped and the hate in her eyes seared him. "She ran off the morning after that old witch Mahti set fire to the house. Heard she was in one of the camps, so I sent a man to bring her back, but he said she'd taken up with some fancy French Black who refused to hand her over."

Rhine assumed she was referencing Major Raimond LeVeq. When Rhine last saw his sister a year ago, he'd already switched his allegiance to the Union army, and she'd been a laundress in a contraband camp. LeVeq, a ranking officer at the camp, had been taken by his beautiful sister. Sadly, after only a few days Rhine's unit had moved on and he'd had to leave Sable behind. Hearing that LeVeq had kept her out of Sally Ann's clutches pleased him, but he had no idea where she was now. He also wondered about the fate of his half sister, Sally Ann's daughter, Mavis.

"What are you doing in a fancy Yankee uniform?" Sally Ann asked.

Rhine didn't reply. As the silence lengthened, she offered a bitter chuckle. "Passing again, are you?"

Rhine's ivory skin, jet black hair, and green eyes made it easy for him to pass as someone he wasn't. He was ten years old when he first realized he could do it successfully. In his role as Andrew's slave, he'd accompanied the Fontaine family to a hotel in Atlanta. When their father Carson walked into the hotel's restaurant and saw Rhine eating at the table with Andrew instead of in the back with the other slaves, he waited until they returned home and whipped Rhine until he bled. Ten-year-old Andrew had been whipped as well, but not as severely.

In a voice dripping with disgust, Sally Ann sneered, "Andrew turns his back on his race, and you turn your back on yours. What a wretched pair you are. Get off my land and don't ever come back."

Riding away, Rhine trusted that the old African queens whose blood ran in his veins would reunite him with Sable in the near future. With that belief settled firmly in his heart, he headed to his own future; one he planned to live out as White.

Chapter One

Denver
Spring 1870

"STOP HIM!" EDDY Carmichael screamed, scrambling to her feet from the mud. The man who'd snatched her purse and shoved her down was now running away down the dark Denver street. Taking off in pursuit, she called for help, but there were no policemen about and the few people on the walks nearby gave her no more than a passing glance. Up ahead, the thief turned a corner. Not wanting to lose him, she ran faster, but by the time she reached the spot, he'd disappeared. Frantically casting about for clues as to his whereabouts, she saw nothing. Anger turned to frustration and then to despair. Inside the purse had been her paltry month's pay and the train ticket to California she'd purchased less than an hour ago. She'd been saving for the passage for months in hopes of starting a new life in San Francisco. Now, penniless, angry, her skirts and cloak covered with mud, she set out for home.

Eddy dreamed of owning her own restaurant. It was a common belief that women like her, the descendant of slaves, had no right to dream. Yet, she knew from the articles she'd read in the newspapers that members of the race were pursuing theirs in spite of the disenfranchisement being ignored by Congress and the bloody lawlessness of Redemption ravaging the South. Colleges were being built, land was being purchased, and across the nation Black owned businesses were springing up like columbines in the spring. At the age of twenty-seven and unmarried, Eddy saw no such opportunities for herself in Denver, and now thanks to the thief those dreams were in peril.

Her home was a room she rented above a laundry owned by her landlady, Mrs. Lucretia Hampton. Eddy had been so sure of leaving town, she'd already given the woman notice and the new tenant was due to move in tomorrow afternoon. Although Mrs. Hampton would show concern over Eddy being robbed, the laundress was first and foremost a businesswoman and would likely not alter the agreement.

Putting her key into the door lock of her room, Eddy stepped into the darkness. As always, the acrid scent of lye wafting up from the laundry below filled the air. The room was so tiny even a mouse would have difficulty turning around, but on her meager salary it was all she could afford. Having worn the mantle of poverty since the death of her parents twelve years ago, she was grateful to have it. Making her way through the shadows over to the pallet that served as her bed, she struck a match and set the flame against the stub of candle in the old tin saucer that sat atop a battered wooden crate. While the wavering light filled the room, she removed her mud-stained cloak. Rather than attempt to clean it with the small bit of water in her basin, she hung it on the nail protruding from the back of the door with the hope that once the mud dried it would be easier to remove. She put her last pieces of kindling into the hearth. The resulting heat would be minimal but at least the flames held beauty, another element her life lacked. Warming her hands, she thought about her plight. She supposed she could remain in Denver and start saving again. Choosing that route meant finding another room to rent and a new job, because she'd given her employer notice, too. Six months ago, the hotel where she'd worked for the past three years as a cook had been purchased by a new owner whose first act had been to remove Eddy and every other person of color from the kitchen. He offered her a new job scrubbing floors for less money. The demotion was both infuriating and humiliating, but knowing how blessed she was to still have employment, she'd swallowed her anger and scrubbed the floors until they shone. Even then, he constantly found fault with her work and routinely docked her pay for what he termed inferior effort. She knew for a fact he'd never offer her the job back, and there was no way she'd be able to rent another room without one.

She ran her hands over her eyes and sighed. She didn't want to stay in Denver, not even for another day. Her future lay elsewhere and she knew that as sure as she knew her name, but how could she could get the money for another ticket? Mrs. Hampton didn't give loans. The Colored community was small and most were as pinched by poverty as she. Those who weren't certainly wouldn't loan her money even if she had the gall to ask. Her only relative in the city was her younger sister Corinne, and asking her for money made about as much as sense as asking the new owner of the hotel. After the deaths of their mother Constance and teamster father Ben in a blizzard, Eddy did everything she could to provide for herself and sister; she took in laundry, cooked for the wealthy, looked after their children, and swept their floors. But her beautiful baby sister chose to fall back on her looks and figure and took up with a pimp in the city's red-light district. Although the pimp was long gone, Corinne still resided there along with her two young daughters. Eddy knew her sister would laugh in her face for having the audacity to ask for money. Corinne had nothing but derision for Eddy's desire to better her life, but Corinne was her last resort. It was too late to pay her a visit at the moment, but she'd planned to stop by on her way to the station in the morning to say good-bye to her nieces anyway. Now, her visit would be about something different entirely.

"At least I won't have much to pack," she said softly. She'd sold what little possessions she'd had in order to help pay her rent and purchase the train ticket. What remained was her mother's locket, a cast iron skillet, her small cookstove brazier, and a few meager changes of clothing. She had nothing else. Were she not so accustomed to having to claw her way through life, she might have collapsed and wept, but being made of sterner stuff, she'd learned long ago that weeping changed nothing.

The following morning, Eddy gathered her things, took a bittersweet look back at the place she'd called home, and closed the door. After handing Mrs. Hampton the key and being told, "Godspeed," she set off. Her clothing and the skillet were stuffed in an old carpetbag and the cookstove was balanced on her head. It was a chilly April morning and the city was just coming to life.

Most of the residents of the red-light district were sleeping off last night's excesses, so the streets were quiet. The seedy area with its cribs, saloons, and bawdy houses looked tired and worn-out under the dawning light of day. Eddy guessed her sister would be asleep, too, and would probably not welcome the early morning visit, but it couldn't be helped. Setting the cookstove on the ground by her feet, she knocked on the shack's door.

Her twelve-year-old niece Portia answered the knock and her dark eyes brightened. "Aunt Eddy!"

She threw herself into Eddy's arms, and Eddy held her tight and kissed her brow. Eddy loved the girls and hated the circumstances they were being raised under. She dearly wanted to offer them a home with her, but going from a destitute mother to a destitute aunt served no one. Although Corinne swore she loved her daughters, Eddy worried about them constantly, especially now that they were growing into young ladies.

Portia's baby sister, ten-year-old Regan, appeared and also met Eddy's appearance with joy. Both girls had inherited their mother's great beauty. Eddy assumed Corinne knew who their fathers were but had never shared the identities with Eddy.

Regan asked, "Did you come to spend the day with us, Aunt Eddy?"

The hope in her eyes twisted Eddy's heart. "No, sweetie. I came to talk to your mama. Is she sleeping?"

Regan nodded. "And if we wake her up she'll whip us. Won't she, Portia?"

Portia didn't respond verbally but the tense set of her chin affirmed it.

As if cued, the angry Corinne entered the room belt in hand and snapped, "How many times have I told you not to wake me up?" Seeing Eddy, she paused. "Oh, it's you. What do you want?"

"My purse was stolen yesterday. My train ticket to California was inside."

"So?"

Eddy held onto her patience. "I came to see if I could borrow enough to buy another. I'll pay you back once I'm settled."

"Why are you going to California?"

"To look for a job. There's nothing here for me."

Portia looked mortified. "You're leaving Denver, Aunt Eddy?"

Eddy knew she should have told them about California before now, but she and Corinne were like tinder and matches, so she kept putting the visit off. "I'm hoping to," she said softly. "I'll come back to see you and Regan as soon as I can. I promise."

Portia, so stoic for someone her age, raised her chin stiffly. "Okay."

Corinne said coolly, "Portia, since I'm up, go strip the sheets off my bed, and pump some water so we can start the wash."

"Yes, Mama." She hurried from the room and disappeared into the back.

Regan laced her thin arms around Eddy's waist and pressed herself close. She whispered through her tears. "Please don't leave Aunt Eddy. Please."

Eddy felt awful.

"Regan, stop that sniveling and go help your sister."

"Yes, Mama."

Eddy caressed her cheek in good-bye and Regan left the room.

"You didn't have to be so mean, Corinne."

"Don't tell me how to raise my children. When you get your own, you can treat them any way you like. And, I don't have any money for you or your highfalutin dreams. I told you years ago, you'd make more money down here than you'd ever make uptown. You had the bosoms and the looks, but no, you thought you were too good."

"No, I didn't want to become a whore, Corinne."

"Yet here you are begging help from a whore."

"I'm here begging help from my sister." Corinne's legendary allure had faded; too many men, too much whiskey, too much hardship. Now, instead of features that could've launched ships like the fabled Helen of Troy, she looked as tired and worn-out as any other women of her profession. Eddy was saddened by that.

"I have nothing for you. Guess you and your dreams will have to walk there."

"I guess so." Eddy thought back on how much she once loved her sister, the giggles they'd shared in their bedroom at night, the way they'd played as girls, and the sense of family their parents always tried to instill. Standing before her now in a ratty, faded green wrapper was a woman she didn't know and it broke Eddy's heart. "Good-bye, sister. I'll write when I get settled."

"Fine."

Eddy left.

Setting aside the sadness of the painful visit, Eddy set out to see an old friend of her parents, an aging teamster named Mr. Biggins. He rented wagons for tradesmen and sometimes for people traveling. It was possible he knew of someone going west who might let her tag along in exchange for her cooking skills. Thanks to her father, she also knew her way around wagons and animals. Although it had been years since she'd driven a team, it wasn't a skill one forgot.

When she entered his establishment his old blue eyes brightened in much the same way her nieces had.

"Morning, Miss Eddy, you finally coming around to accept my marriage proposal?"

Chuckling, she said, "No, Mr. Biggins, but I do need your help."

His smile stretched the gray beard on his cheeks and showed his missing teeth. "Guess I'll have to settle for that. What can I do for the prettiest little lady in Denver?"

She told him about the thief and explained her dilemma.

He blew out a breath. "I'm so sorry. Set you back, did it?"

"Quite a bit. I'm wondering if you know of anyone going west who will let me go with them? I can pay my way by cooking."

"As a matter of fact, I might. Got a wagon out back belongs to a drummer. He's on his way to Fort Collins. I know it's north and not west but a lot of travelers pass through there, so you'll probably find someone heading west. He's a nice, easygoing man. Pretty sure he'd like some company, especially if you're willing to cook along the way."

Even if she wasn't going directly west, Eddy was elated. Leaving Denver was a start.

"He's due to pick up his wagon any time now. You had breakfast? Got some eggs in the skillet on the stove."

She hadn't eaten, so she sat and ate with Mr. Biggins while they waited for the drummer to make his appearance.

The drummer, a portly middle-aged man named Abner Pickerel, looked Eddy up and down after hearing Mr. Biggins's proposal. "Only going as far as Fort Collins, miss."

"I understand but if I can ride with you I'd be truly grateful."

"How many trunks do you have?"

"None. Just a carpetbag and my cookstove."

He eyed the stove where it stood on the floor by the door. "You sure you can cook?"

"Abner, why would she have a cookstove if she didn't know her way around one?" Mr. Biggins asked, sounding exasperated.

Eddy sensed the drummer still wasn't sure.

After all, she was a stranger, but she prayed he'd say yes.

Finally, he said, "Okay. Come on then. I suppose there's no harm in helping you out. Give me somebody to talk to on the way."

She wanted to kiss him. "Thank you. I'll not be any trouble."

"Good. Let me pay my bill and we'll be on our way."

Mr. Pickerel turned out to be an excellent traveling companion. He made his living selling patent medicines that according to his boasting cured everything from stomach ailments to foot pain. He and his mule Rebecca had been traveling from St. Louis to Fort Collins for decades. While he and Eddy traded off driving, he shared a wealth of stories about the people he'd met, the towns he'd visited, and how much he missed his late wife, Edna. Eddy, in turn, shared her hopes of opening her own restaurant.

"A restaurant, huh? You certainly cook well enough."

"Thank you. I learned from my mother. She was even better."

"You've a long way to go to get to California though."

"I know, and having no money makes it even more of a challenge, but I'm determined."

"What are you going to do when we reach Fort Collins?"

"Hopefully find someone as generous as you've been to help me travel farther."

"My sister-in-law, Winnifred Davis, lives there. Sometimes places around town have news boards set up where people leave notes for travelers. Might be able to find you someone on one of them."

She thought that a great idea. "Thank you."

Because he had to stop and sell his medicines at farmhouses and in small towns along the way, it took more than a few days to travel the sixty plus miles to reach Fort Collins. Eddy found him to be respectful and considerate, and his hunting and fishing skills allowed them to feast on rabbits and fish.

Eddy had never been to Fort Collins. Mr. Pickerel told her it had been erected in 1864 to protect the Overland Trail mail route and travelers during the Indian wars of the mid-1860s. The fort was decommissioned in 1867 and the area around it was now bustling with farmers and businesses.

When they reached the city, he stopped his wagon in front of an old house. "This is my sisterin-law's boardinghouse. She might be able to put you up until you find another ride."

"Since I can't pay her for the room, do you think she'll let me cook or clean in exchange?"

"Let's go in and see."

Eddy worried his sister-in-law would be wary of her, but when Abner explained about the robbery and why she was traveling with him, Mrs. Davis fussed, "My goodness. Gotten so decent women can't even walk down the street. So you're on adventure to California?"

"I suppose you can call it that." Eddy liked her.

"I always wanted to go on an adventure. Closest I ever got was the long wagon train ride from Kansas to here with my late husband Bill. After all the trials and tribulations of that, I was cured. Been rooted here ever since."

"Mr. Pickerel said you might have a room to rent, but because of the thief I don't have any money."

"I am one boarder short. How do you plan to pay me?"

"I'm an excellent cook and I can help with laundry, scrub floors. I don't expect you to take me in for free."

"I would like to have my floors scrubbed," she replied as if thinking aloud. "The girl I used to depend on recently moved to Colorado Springs."

"Then may I do them in exchange for a room for a few days?"

"Yes, you may."

"I can start now if you wish."

"You just traveled all the way from Denver. You need to eat, rest up, and get your strength back. The work can wait until the morning."

Eddy was grateful for the boon. She was bone tired from the travel and the days of sitting on the hard wooden seat of Mr. Pickerel's wagon and could certainly use the rest.

After dinner, she was given a tour of the house. It wasn't a particularly large one but Eddy knew doing the task in the manner she was accustomed to would take most of her day.

So the next morning after a hearty breakfast, she began. By sunset the floors in all the rooms had been scrubbed and waxed. It was backbreaking work, and when she was done her knees ached and her hands were red and chapped from the hot soapy water.

Mrs. Davis gushed over how beautiful the floors looked. "Oh my, look how they shine! Are you sure you don't want to stay here and work for me, Eddy? I could really use a hand. I'm willing to pay. It won't be much though."

Eddy thought the floors looked mighty fine, too. "I thank you for the offer and for allowing me to stay, but I really need to find a way west if I can, and the sooner the better."

"But, Eddy, think about it. You could start saving again and maybe by next year this time have enough for the train ticket."

She was right of course. The ticket stolen from her had cost almost seventy dollars. Depending on how much Mrs. Davis was able to pay, it could take a year to save that amount. In the meantime, she would have a nice place to stay. However, California was her goal, but having been raised to be polite, she said, "Let me sleep on it and I'll give you an answer in the morning."

"That's fair. Go get cleaned up and help yourself to dinner. You've earned it."

After dinner, Eddy sat in the small upholstered chair in the room she'd been allowed to use and yawned tiredly. Deciding to prepare for bed, she searched through her carpetbag for her nightgown and was about to remove her clothing when a knock sounded on the door. Walking over to it, she found Mr. Pickerel on the other side.

"Can you come to the parlor for a moment? Got some people I want you to meet." He must've seen the confusion on her face because he explained, "Met a man and his wife going to Salt Lake City. His wife is carrying and they're looking to hire a woman to drive one of the wagons."

She was stunned.

He smiled. "Told you I'd help you out."

Once again she wanted to kiss him.

When Eddy entered the room, the young White couple looked surprised. Eddy wondered if it had to do with her race but decided to give them the benefit of the doubt and to keep an open mind.

"This here is Miss Eddy Carmichael," Mr. Pickerel said, introducing her. "She helped me drive from Denver."

"Pleased to meet you," the husband said. "Name's Henry Cates. This is my wife, Candace."

26

Eddy noted the skepticism in his gaze as he assessed her, but said, "Pleased to meet you as well. Mr. Pickerel said you're looking for a driver?"

When he didn't respond, Candace spoke up, "Yes, we are, and if you can drive a team of mules, we'd be real pleased to have you come with us. Right, Henry?" she asked pointedly.

His face reddened. Nodding, he stammered, "Um, yes. Real pleased. Can you drive a mule team?"

"I can."

"How many?"

"I've never driven more than four."

"You know how to hitch, unhitch, and put 'em up for the night?" he asked.

Eddy nodded. "I do." She was never more thankful for being the daughter of a teamster. "My daddy was a teamster. Did overland hauling. He taught me to drive."

Candace smiled. "Will you be able to leave first thing in the morning?"

"I will."

They discussed where to meet, what time, and how much they were willing to pay. Upon hearing the amount, Eddy did her best not to kick up her heels with glee.

Henry added, "Probably take us a month or more to go through the mountain passes and all."

"That's fine." Eddy knew that driving mules was even more backbreaking than scrubbing floors, and until her ride with Mr. Pickerel she'd never driven such a long distance. This journey would be a tremendous challenge, but to earn the fee they'd promised, she'd drive those mules smiling and standing on her head. After a few more moments of discussion to clarify her duties and such, the Cateses departed.

Eddy said to Mr. Pickerel, "Thank you so much."

"You're welcome."

Mrs. Davis groused, smiling, "Abner, if I didn't love you so much I'd take a switch to you for finding a way for Eddy to leave me, but I'll forgive you."

He grinned.

"Mrs. Davis, thank you for your hospitality," Eddy offered.

"Thank you for my floors. Go on up and get some sleep so you'll be ready to leave on your next adventure."

Up in her room, Eddy changed into her nightgown. Thanks to Mr. Pickerel, she was that much closer to her goal. Still smiling, she crawled into bed.

Chapter Two

JUST AS SHE'D predicted, the journey was arduous. The first three days her arms hurt so much from the strain of holding the reins, she had trouble raising them, but as time went on they became stronger. The Cateses were Mormons. They'd been married less than a year and had been driven from their homestead in Iowa by persecution that had hounded the sect in many parts of the country since the 1830s. According to them, there were communities of people who shared their faith in Utah Territory and they were looking forward to living there and raising their child in peace. The baby was due to be born by summer's end.

As they crossed Colorado, Henry Cates didn't have much to say to Eddy, but Candace with her smile and grace more than made up for his terse company. Henry drove the main wagon, which was filled with farming equipment and some of their household furniture. Eddy, riding with Candace, drove the wagon filled with clothing, bedding, and Candace's precious trove of books.

"I want to start a lending library once we get settled," she explained one morning as they drove through a chilly fog-shrouded valley accompanied by birdsong. "Henry and I had

29

quite a disagreement over them. He wanted me to leave them behind, but I told him if I couldn't take my books, he'd be going on without me."

"May I ask why you wanted a woman driver?"

"Henry's got a lot of jealousy inside. He didn't want me around another man." Then she laughed. "Look at me, I'm as large as a sow. What man is going to want a woman carrying? But he was as adamant about finding a woman as I was about my books."

"So, you drove all the way to Colorado from Iowa?"

"Yes, but our driver was Henry's cousin, who lives in Fort Collins. He took the train to our homestead to help us. I told Henry we stood little chance of finding a woman to drive all the way to Salt Lake City, but we found you." She turned Eddy's way and said earnestly, "God was with us, and with you, too."

Although Eddy had never been a churchgoer, she had to agree.

The journey was filled with long tiring days and cold nights. They crossed rivers, got lost on a few occasions, and were forced to double back. They heard wolves howling at night, saw bighorn sheep, deer, and lots and lots of birds. Eddy used her stove to cook stews made from the rabbits Henry snared and the root vegetables the couple had stored in her wagon. When travel took them near small streams and lakes, fish and water fowl was added to the fare. Throughout it all they were surrounded by the most beautiful expanse of country Eddy had ever seen. Other than the drive with Mr. Pickerel to Fort Collins, she'd never ventured very far from Denver and had no idea Colorado and its mountains and valleys offered such spectacular views.

As Henry estimated, it took a bit over a month to reach Salt Lake City. After receiving her fee and thanking them, Eddy paid for a room at a local boardinghouse and savored sleeping in a real bed, even if the mattress was not the best. The next morning, she got directions to the train station from the lady owner of the boarding-house and set off to buy herself a ticket west. Being closer to her goal filled her with excite-ment. She was pleased to learn that a westbound train was due in a few hours, so she paid the agent the price for a ticket and sat down to wait.

While seated, she thought about all she'd experi-enced since leaving Denver and wondered how her nieces and sister were faring. She planned to keep her promise to Portia and Regan about returning to visit once she got herself settled in California, and thought maybe they could train out and visit her if Corinne agreed. Eddy also wondered what her parents would think of this. Her mother would worry as she always did about her girls, but her father would be proud that she'd taken her life by the horns in an effort to better herself. Were they still alive, she'd probably be married with children of her own by now because that was what the future held for well brought up young women. Her younger self had often dreamed of finding someone who loved her as much as her parents loved each other, but their deaths caused her to set aside all fanciful thoughts and concentrate on the reality of finding food and shelter. Now, she was far past the age of being sought after, and although that saddened her, she had her dreams, and if she could make them come true by working hard and never giving up, that would be more than enough.

When the train arrived, she and the handful of passengers boarded. She chose a window seat to take in the sights. After placing her cookstove and carpet bag at her feet she made herself comfortable. As the whistle blew to signal the departure, she wanted to cheer. Eddy Carmichael was on her way to California.

According to the conductor's announcement, the route would take them across Nevada then south to a city called Reno. There she would change trains to one that would take her into California and on to San Francisco, her final destination.

The ride was uneventful. She'd never seen desert before, but Nevada seemed to be filled with it. As the train chugged its way over the land-scape, she took in the mountains on the horizon and the wide-open land that spread out beside the tracks. At Reno, she left the train, and with the help of the kind conductor got in a long line of people bound for California, but when the ticket agent informed everyone that due to problems with the track the train wouldn't arrive for another three days, she was crestfallen.

Seated on a bench in the station, she was once again weighing her options. Something bumped her foot. A child's ball. A little boy ran over. Having only a limited knowledge of small children, she guessed he was five—maybe six. He had straw gold hair and bright blue eyes. "May I have my ball back, ma'am?"

Smiling at him, she handed it over.

"Thank you," he replied shyly.

A man dressed in all black and wearing a clerical collar walked up. He was tall with sandy brown hair and appeared to be middle-aged. Although his eyes were as icy blue as a winter sky, his face and smile were kind. "I'm sorry, ma'am. Didn't mean to bother you. The ball got away from us. Trying to entertain him while we wait for our wagon to be fixed."

"No apologies needed."

The little boy ran off to play with the ball in the field near the depot.

The man further explained, "Brought the boy here hoping to show him the train, but the agent said it's delayed."

"I know. I was planning on taking the train, but now I'm trying to decide what to do."

"We're on our way to Sacramento. My bishop has assigned me to a mission there. I'm a Catholic priest. My name's Father Nash."

"I'm Eddy Carmichael."

"Pleased to meet you, Miss Carmichael."

"Pleased to meet you as well."

"If I can be so impolite to ask, where are you bound?"

"San Francisco."

"You're not traveling alone, are you?"

"I am."

"It's not safe for a lady to be out here alone."

"I'm being very careful and so far have not had any problems."

"That's good. Some people make their living preying on young women like yourself. I have two sisters, and whenever I see a woman alone I become concerned."

He asked her how long she'd been traveling and where she was from while he kept an eye on the little boy with the ball. From their conversation, she learned he was an itinerant priest and the little boy, Benjamin, was an orphan he was escorting to an orphanage in Sacramento.

"So are you going to find a room here and wait for the train to arrive?" he asked.

"I suppose I'll have to." Although she hadn't

planned on dipping into the money she'd been paid by the Cateses so soon.

"Why don't you ride with Benjy and me?" he offered. "The agent said the train won't be here for three days, and in three days you can already be in Sacramento and have caught the train there for San Francisco."

Eddy hesitated.

"I understand the hesitancy but I'm a man of God, Miss Eddy. You'll come to no harm, and I could use the company and someone to help me answer the hundreds of questions Benjy seems to wake up with every morning."

Her smile met his. She'd been depending on the kindness of strangers since leaving Denver and he seemed to have been sent from heaven. "I'll accept, but you'll have to let me pay you and cook along the way."

"Benjy and I will accept your generous offer to cook, and if you want to pay me something, I'll put it in the collection plate at the orphanage. The sisters there could use the help. So are we agreed?"

Saved once more, she said, "Yes, we are."

"Let's round up Benjy and see if the wagon's ready."

An hour later they were under way.

It was mid-afternoon as the old Conestoga bumped along the rocky desert road. Eddy was glad for the shade provided by the aged and patched canvas. The heat was stifling. Benjy was asleep in the back and she was sharing the seat with Father Nash. They'd been traveling just over two hours when she sensed something not quite right. They were supposed to be traveling west, but from the sun's position in the sky they seemed to heading south. "Are we heading south?" she asked.

"As a matter of fact, we are, but first things first. What else do you have to offer me besides your cooking?"

She studied him. "I offered to pay you, too, remember?"

"I do but I'd like something a bit more substantial." The eyes she looked into were mocking.

"Meaning?" she asked, suddenly wary.

"You're a beautiful woman, I'm a healthy man. Need I say more?"

Eddy fought down the fear spreading up her spine. "You're not really a priest, are you?"

"No, just a healthy man who likes to prey on pretty little pigeons like you. You'd be amazed how many people fall for this priest getup and the story."

Eddy stiffened.

He glanced over. "How about you open that blouse and let me see what you got in there."

"No!"

"You sure?"

"Yes."

"Never been one to force a woman. I may be a scoundrel but I have scruples. Give me your money then."

"No!" she snarled.

He chuckled and pulled back on the reins to halt the team. "This isn't a discussion, girl." He reached beside him and brought out a knife. The large shiny blade glittered in the sun. "I'd hate to scar that pretty face." He beckoned with his free hand. "Give me your money."

Shaking with reaction and terrified about what he might do if she continued denying him, she reached into her handbag.

"All of it, honey. Benjy and I have to eat."

"And I don't?" she snapped.

"Lift that skirt and I'll let you keep half."

"No."

"The money then. We're wasting time."

She handed him all she had, and he smiled. "Now, hop down and start walking. This is where we part ways."

"What!"

"You don't want to be bedded, I don't want you riding."

She scanned the bleakness surrounding her. How could he do this? She picked up her brazier and carpetbag and climbed down. He tossed her a canteen. "If you ration it, you might make it to somewhere. Watch out for scorpions. They give a nasty bite."

He drove off without a word.

Eddy was horrified. She knew she was at least two hours from the train depot, but if there was a town or settlement closer, she didn't know. Vowing never to be so trusting again, she shaded her eyes to see the sun and started walking north back to the depot, hoping Nash—which was probably not his true name—burned in hell.

Eddy made good headway at first and sipped sparingly from the half-filled canteen. However, as time passed her progress slowed. After a while the stifling desert heat and the relentless blinding sun conspired with the vast open stretches of rock and sand to sap her strength so badly, it made her want to fall to her knees and surrender to whatever fate would bring, but she forced herself to keep walking. She could barely breathe. Her throat was raw from thirst. She'd taken the last precious sips of water from the canteen hours ago, or had it been days? Her brain was so fuzzy she couldn't remember. She did know that crossing the desert on foot was still better than offering herself to that snake Nash, but she also knew she'd probably die. Soon. The skin on her hands and face were blistered. She'd stumbled and fallen more times than she could count. Her skirt was torn and filthy. She'd given up trying to determine the time of day by the angle of the sun. All she wanted was water and shade, but there was none. Trying to keep the cookstove on her head took more energy than she possessed so she dropped it and stopped. Only sheer will had kept her moving until then and now it was gone, too. Black spots swam across her swollen eyes. She sensed herself swaying. When she dropped to her knees on the hot rocky ground, she barely felt it. It was the last thing she remembered.

"Is that someone walking?" Rhine Fontaine asked from his wagon seat. He pulled back on the reins.

His business partner, James Dade, shaded his eyes. "Looks like it."

Rhine picked up his spyglass for a closer look. "A Colored woman. What in the hell is she doing out here alone?" A person had to be feeble-minded to be walking across desert under the full day sun. Crossings were best done at night. A dozen questions filled Rhine's head. Had her horse run off? Had her wagon lost a wheel? He handed Jim the glass and quickly turned the team.

"Looks to be in pretty bad shape," Jim said, still eyeing her through the glass. "She just dropped to her knees."

By the time they reached her, she was sprawled on the ground and didn't appear to be breathing. Rhine grabbed the extra canteen and jumped down while Jim pulled a tarp from the bed and then joined him.

The first thing Rhine noted were her blistered

cracked lips. He could only imagine how long she'd been walking. He placed his ear on her hot chest. She was breathing, but barely. "Miss?" No response. He tried rousing her gently. "Miss!" he called louder. Uncapping the canteen, he poured a trickle of water over her lips while Jim held the tarp above them to provide some shade. Finally, her eyes sluggishly opened. Even though she looked disoriented, relief washed over him. "Here, drink. Slowly."

An urgent moan escaped her as she eagerly clutched the canteen and began drinking. He knew she wanted to gulp it down, but nausea and vomiting would be the end result, so he said again, "Slow. Drink slow."

He let her drink as much as he dared, and all the while scanned the area for a companion or clues as to how she'd come to be there. When he thought she'd had enough, he told Jim, "Let's get her to the wagon."

Rhine gently scooped her up and she began to fight. She had all the power of a gnat but she was flailing and twisting and crying out hoarsely. He backed out of reach of the ineffectual blows. "No one's going to hurt you, darlin', I promise. We're just trying to save your life." She continued to fight. Rhine, carrying her as best he could, looked over at Jim with disbelief.

Jim cracked, "Pretty feisty for a half-dead woman. Probably a hellion at full strength."

When they reached the wagon, Rhine laid her down in the bed. Jim placed the carpetbag and the cookstove they'd found near her. "You drive. I'll tend," Rhine said.

While Jim turned the team towards Virginia City, Rhine worked on their patient. The first thing needed was to cool her down. With that in mind, he began undoing the buttons of her shabby blouse, and she began flailing and crying out again.

Barely missing being punched in his eye, he told her, "I need to open your clothing so you can cool off. Stop fighting me now. Please."

But she kept it up. He ended up tearing the blouse in two, and she instinctively covered herself. A damp and much mended shift lay under the shredded blouse. Guilt rose within him but soon dissolved beneath what he knew to be necessity, so he poured water on the clean handkerchief he pulled from his coat and began sponging it against her bare shoulders and arms. He bathed her face, and in the process cleared away the mask of salt left behind by the desert heat. He removed the patterned head wrap covering her matted, sweat-wet hair and once again wondered how she'd wound up in the middle of the desert. Repeatedly soothing her with the damp handkerchief and his voice, he decided that once they reached town, he'd hand her over to boardinghouse owner Sylvia Stewart. She'd take things from there.

• • •

It was dark by the time they reached Virginia City, and Rhine looked upon that as a blessing. He didn't need gossip hounding him for playing the Good Samaritan. To avoid prying eyes, they drove through the city's alleys to Sylvia's place. Jim ran in and seconds later returned to say, "She's not home. Whitman Brown said she'd be back within the hour."

Rhine cursed. "Okay. Let's take her to our place. One of us can come back for Sylvia later. Hopefully she has room to take her in." Even though there was something about the fretfully tossing young woman that made him want to hold onto her until she was well enough to take care of herself again, he knew she needed to be cared for by a woman.

Once they reached his saloon, he told Jim, "Let me get her upstairs, and you go and see if you can find Doc Randolph."

"Will do. Do you need my help?" There was concern on Jim's broad face, too.

Rhine jumped down from the bed then reached in and gently eased her into his arms. The tossing and soft moans of protest started up again. "No, she weighs less than a baby rabbit. You go on ahead. I should be all right."

So while Rhine entered the silent saloon through the back door and climbed the stairs to his apartments, Jim drove away.

Chapter Three

RHINE ENTERED HIS shadowy bedroom and gently placed Eddy in the center of his large four-poster bed. Another man might fret over her and her dirty clothing being laid on the clean sheets, but he was more concerned with her well-being. Her breathing was so shallow and her skin still so hot he worried that she might not pull through. Taking a hasty look back at her over his shoulder, he quickly grabbed a basin and hurried down the hall to the washroom to fill it with water so he could continue wiping her down.

Luckily, it was a Sunday and the saloon was closed. Otherwise she might've been disturbed by the noise and revelry of drunk miners and card players from the floor below. He stuck the large sponge into the water-filled basin and slowly and gently slid it over her face, throat, and the tops of her breasts above the shabby shift. That she wasn't wearing a corset was a plus. More than likely she would've died in the heat had she been. To his thinking, she'd be better off nude and immersed in a tub of cool water, but he needed to wait for Jim to return with Sylvie—as she was affectionately called—or Doc. The questions surrounding Eddy's plight continued to plague

Rhine, but they had to be set aside until she was strong enough to answer.

A short while later, Jim entered with Sylvie and both came to the bedside. Concern filled Sylvie's face. "Sorry I wasn't home. I was out at the orphanage. Jim said you found her in the desert?" The middle-aged boardinghouse owner was a trusted friend.

Rhine stopped his ministrations for a moment. "Yes. And her skin's iron hot."

Sylvie placed her palm on her forehead. "She is very warm. Poor thing. I'd suggest a tub, but until she's fully awake I'm scared she'll slip beneath the water."

"I can hold her up if you think that will help."

She studied Rhine as if thinking that over. "It might. Do you know who she is?"

"No."

"Okay. Do you have a shirt or something for her to wear?"

"Yes." He walked to his wardrobe and took down a shirt. "Jim, were you able to find Doc?"

"He's in Reno. He'll be back in a day or two."

Rhine saw the exasperation on Sylvie's face. She had been a nurse for the Colored troops during the war and served in that capacity now for the city's Colored community. According to the rumors, she and Doc Randolph had been at odds for decades, but Rhine had no idea why.

Sylvie took the shirt from his hand. "Let me get

her undressed and I'll call you in to carry her to the tub. In the meantime start filling it with water."

Eddy thought she was dreaming about being carried down a dark tunnel. She knew a man was carrying her but she had yet to see his face. He eased her into a pool of water and she leaned back against his strong shoulder. The water lapped over her like a balm, magically erasing all her hurts and soothing her everywhere: throat, arms, breasts. It felt so glorious, she sighed with pleasure. Languidly opening her eyes, she stared into the deep green gaze of a White man. For some reason, she wasn't alarmed. His jet black hair and handsome, ivory-skinned features seemed familiar somehow. She gently cupped his unshaven cheek—something she'd never done to any man before—and he smiled softly. She smiled in return, and that was the last thing she remembered.

"I trust you'll be gentlemen if I leave her in your care for the night?"

Jim nodded.

"Of course," Rhine added, eyeing the woman sleeping peacefully in yet another one of his clean shirts beneath a light blanket.

"My cook, Felix," Sylvie said, "left to go back East yesterday, so I'll have to listen to my boarders complaining about my serving them burnt breakfast before I can come back here to check on her in the morning."

Rhine smiled. Everyone in town knew Sylvie had no cooking skills at all. He pitied her boarders. "Do you have a replacement for Felix in mind?"

"Not yet. Nor do I have a place for this young woman to stay, at the moment. One of the men will be leaving in a few days and she can finish her recovery with me. Will you mind looking after her until then?"

Rhine glanced over at Jim, who shrugged, so Rhine replied, "No." His fiancée Natalie probably wouldn't approve if she knew, but he'd cross that bridge if and when the time came.

"Okay, good. I'll bring some aloe for her sunburn tomorrow. When she wakes up, encourage her to drink, but not a lot all at once. Jim, cook her light food. Eggs, maybe some toast, and we'll see how things go. Let's hope she'll be in better shape after she rests up."

Rhine agreed.

Jim asked, "Do you want me to drive you back?"

Sylvie nodded. After glancing down at the young woman a final time, she said, "Keep an eye on her."

After their departure, Rhine surveyed his sleeping guest. He ran his eyes over the clear-as-glass ebony skin, the long sweep of her lashes, and her perfect mouth. While in the tub, she'd taken him by surprise when she opened her eyes, looked deeply into his own, and cupped his cheek as if they'd been lovers. The urge to turn her hand and place his lips against her damp palm had also taken him by surprise. He had a fiancée and was due to be married before year's end. He had no business thinking about kissing another woman. Deciding what he'd felt was nothing more than concern, he set the incident aside and took a seat to watch over her as promised and await Jim's return.

Eddy awakened in a four-poster in a large room barely lit by a turned down lamp. Having no idea where she was or how she came to be there, she shook the cobwebs dulling her thinking and noticed she was wearing a man's shirt! Perplexed, her eyes moved around the room to a well-appointed sitting area and then to the face of a White man watching her from one of the chairs. Panic flared. She snatched the blanket to her neck and she drew back fearfully.

"Don't be afraid. You're safe. I'm Rhine Fontaine. My friend Jim and I found you in the desert."

Confused, she tried to force herself to calm down so she could make some sense of this, but she couldn't. Watching him warily, she asked, "Where am I?" Her throat was dry as sand. She wanted water badly, but needed to solve the mystery of this first.

"Virginia City."

"And this place is?"

47

"My bedroom."

Her eyes went wide. "I need to go, I can't stay here."

"Maybe in a few days, but right now—"

Alarmed, she didn't let him finish. She swung her legs over the side of the bed. Her mind was so foggy she wasn't sure what was happening, but she knew she had to get away.

He stood and said urgently, "No! You'll fall!"

He was right. The moment she stood, she was hit by a wave of weakness so strong, her legs folded as if they were made out of cards. She cried out involuntarily as she hit the floor.

He walked over to her. "As I said, maybe in a few days. Are you okay?"

Drawing away again, she looked up and recognized the face of the man from her dream. She stilled. Had it been a dream? "I'll scream!"

He sighed. "If you feel that's necessary, go right ahead, but I'm not going to hurt you—in any way. When you're done, I can help you back into bed, or carry you to the facilities, whichever you'd prefer."

Heated embarrassment burned her cheeks. Her needs were not something she talked about to a stranger, and especially not a White man stranger. "I can walk."

"No, you can't, but if you want to try, I'll wait."

At that moment she saw her bare legs sticking out from beneath the long-tailed shirt, and also realized she had on no underthings! No drawers. No shift. As quickly as her weakened state allowed, she reached up and pulled the blanket down. Ignoring him as best she could, she covered her bare legs. This was getting worse and worse.

"As I said, my name's Rhine. And yours?"

"Eddy. Eddy Carmichael."

"Pleased to meet you, Miss Carmichael. You gave my partner Jim and I quite a scare out there in the desert, but I'm pleased to see you are recovering."

Then her muddled brain remembered Nash's perfidy and her walk across the desert, but nothing else. "How long have I been here?"

"Four or five hours."

Lord, she was thirsty. "May I have some water please?" she croaked. She felt so weak. It was not a state she was accustomed to.

He poured her a glass from a pitcher on the nightstand and handed it to her. "Slowly," he advised softly. "Just a little for now."

She nodded and took a few short swallows. The water tasted so good and she was so thirsty she wanted to down the entire offering, but heeding his advice, she took only a few more slow pulls. Done, she handed the glass back and her parched throat savored the relief. "Why am I so weak?"

"Walking the Forty Mile Desert under a full sun takes its toll. So, Miss Eddy—facilities or back to bed?"

She hated to admit it but she really needed choice number one. Thoroughly scandalized, she confessed softly, "The facilities, but I can walk. Just point me in the right direction." Looking around, she didn't see a screen of any kind.

"It's at the end of the hallway."

"Oh," she said disappointedly. Still bent on getting there under her own power, though, she wrestled with the blanket in an attempt to fashion it around her waist. Trying to get it out from under her hips and secured without treating him to another show of her legs was a struggle, however. He'd seen more of them than any man ever before.

"Do you want to go today?" he asked in a tone of muted amusement.

She shot him a glare. Reasonably certain the blanket was secured, she said, "Yes." Now she just had to get up. No small task. The fullness of the blanket made it difficult to get her feet planted so she could stand. She decided she'd use the side of the bed to give her the leverage she needed. She scooted closer.

"You always this stubborn, Miss Carmichael?"

"It's called determination, Mr. Fontaine."

"I stand corrected."

Giving him another withering glare, she grabbed hold of the bed's wooden side panel and began working herself to her knees. She made a bit of progress, but her weakened state conspired against her efforts. Refusing to surrender and breathing harshly, she slowly inched herself to a standing position, careful not to get her feet fouled by the swath of blanket, and promptly keeled face forward onto the mattress.

Chuckling softly, he picked her up from behind and placed her gently into the cradle of his strong arms. He smiled softly. "It's called stubbornness."

Rolling her eyes, she allowed herself to be carried from the room.

Rhine came from a long line of determined women, and the little lady presently in his wash-room could have been one of them. While he stood waiting in the hallway a short distance away from the closed door to give her the privacy she needed, he had nothing but admiration for Miss Eddy Carmichael. He wondered again what she'd be like at full strength. Those withering looks she kept shooting him had probably brought more than one man to his knees, but he was finding them amusing.

The door opened and there she stood, upright but panting from the exertion. She appeared to be wobbly on her pins and on the verge of toppling, so he went to her and picked her up. She didn't protest but he could tell by her tight face that she wasn't enjoying being carried as much as he seemed to be enjoying offering the assistance.

He set her gently back in the center of his bed. "Would you like more water?"

She nodded.

He poured again from the pitcher.

When she'd had her fill she handed the glass back with a shaking hand. "Thank you."

"You're welcome."

"And thank you and your friend for rescuing me."

"You're welcome for that, too."

"I had a carpetbag with me. Did you find it?"

"Yes."

"Can you bring it to me." No matter her condition, she wasn't going to go without underwear.

"Yes, I will. Now, lie back."

Again a nod. He waited while she undid her cocoon. From the slow pace of her movements, she obviously had very little strength, but rather than offer to help and draw her ire, he let her handle it alone. Finally free of the blanket confines, she slowly spread it out, seemingly careful to keep her lovely legs hidden from his sight. Content, she snuggled in. If she had any lingering worries or misgivings about being in the room with him, she didn't voice them. "Rest now," he told her quietly. A blink of an eye later she was asleep. Shaking his head at her determination, he went back to his chair for some rest of his own.

The next time Eddy awakened she was alone. The drapes on the windows were drawn, giving her the sense that it was night and making her wonder how long she'd slept. Finding herself alone was a relief. Seeing her carpetbag on the nightstand was a relief as well. Her rescuer had been caring and attentive, but a woman like her had no business in the home of a White man, let alone his bedroom. So far, he'd lived up to his pledge of not harming her, but would it last? She would have to trust him at least for now. For her own peace of mind though, she needed somewhere else to recover, but her still weak state made that a problem. She knew no one in Virginia City. Was there a Colored community? If so, did he know someone who'd be willing to put her up until she got back on her feet? For a woman who'd always depended upon herself, being bedridden was maddening. That she had no idea how long it would last only made it worse. Struggling up, she retrieved the carpetbag and after puzzling over the torn blouse she found inside, she took out a clean pair of drawers. It seemed to take a lifetime to get them on but she managed. She didn't have the strength to add a shift so she left it off.

Hearing the doorknob turn, she raised the blanket to her chin. Fontaine walked in.

"Good evening, Miss Carmichael."

As he approached the bed, she offered a hesitant nod. She wanted to ask about the blouse but was still leery.

"Feeling better?"

"Somewhat. What time is it?"

53

He pointed at the clock hanging on the wall. "Nine in the evening."

She felt like a ninny for not having noticed the clock earlier. "How long have I been asleep?"

"Since about midnight."

"Last night?"

"Yes."

She'd slept away almost an entire day!

"Do you need my help?"

He was referencing the facilities, and she was embarrassed all over again. "Yes."

Without a word, he gently scooped her up, blanket and all. He glanced down into her face. Holding her eyes, he asked, "You don't like this, do you?"

"No." The faint scent of his cologne and the heat of his body whispered to her softly.

"You'll be on your feet again soon. I promise."

She dearly hoped so. As for the whispers, she attributed them to being unwell and shook them off.

When she was back in bed, she asked, "Did I really hear music just now or is it in my head?"

"No, it's the piano player."

She cocked her head. "Piano player?"

"Yes. I own a saloon. We're on the floor above it."

"A saloon!" She didn't think her situation could get any worse.

A slight smile curved his lips. "I'm afraid so.

It's called the Union Saloon. Jim and I own the place."

She fell back against the wealth of pillows. "I shouldn't be here."

"I've made arrangements for you to move into Sylvia Stewart's boardinghouse, but she won't have room for another few days."

"Is she a Colored woman?"

"Yes."

That relieved her somewhat. *I'm in the bedroom of a saloon owner!*

"We run a respectable place here, Eddy. There are no prostitutes on the premises, and no one knows you're here but Sylvia, Jim, and myself. We plan to keep it that way."

Lord. A saloon! "Thank you."

"Hungry?"

"A little."

"I'll have Jim fix you something. Sylvia's a nurse and wants you to eat lightly. She also sent over some aloe to help your skin heal. It's in that small jar on the table there."

Eddy eyed the brown jar.

"She says you're to rub into your face, arms, and hands."

"What's aloe?"

"Cactus. Out here we use it for burns. Where are you from?"

"Denver. I was on my way to California when I was robbed."

"By whom?"

"Man named Nash. He told me he was a Catholic priest and offered to let me ride with him in exchange for my cooking, but he wanted more than that." She didn't elaborate. From the way Fontaine's jaw tightened, she was fairly certain he knew what she meant. "When I said no, he took my money, set me down, and drove away." Thinking about it made her enraged all over again. She wondered if the little boy Benjy was really an orphan or a part of the scam.

"You could've died."

"I don't think he cared."

"When you get on your feet, we'll have a talk with Sheriff Howard. This Nash needs to be found."

"I agree." And when he was, she wanted to be the one wielding the bull whip.

"Enough questions. I don't want to tire you out. I need to get back downstairs. I'll bring your food up directly."

"Thank you." She watched him depart. *A saloon! Good Lord.*

Rhine entered the kitchen. Jim Dade was not only his business partner but the Union's cook as well. He'd learned his trade at a fancy hotel in Saugatuck, New York. Like many men in Virginia City, he'd come west hoping to make his fortune in the mines, but on his first day underground he was so overcome by the terror of being in a confined space, he never returned. It was Rhine's gain because the man cooked like a god.

"She was robbed."

Jim looked up. "The little lady upstairs?"

"Yes." Rhine related the story.

"And he was posing as a priest? This Nash sounds like someone I'd like to meet."

"Agreed. I'd like to teach him the error of his ways. What a bastard." Like Eddy, he doubted that was the man's true name. "She says she's hungry. Can you make her some eggs?"

"Sure. Just give me a few minutes."

Rhine left Jim to do his magic and stepped into the loud, raucous confines of the saloon. The place was filled with the usual evening crowd. Miners were at the bar unwinding after their shifts belowground, day laborers were drinking and playing dominos at a table to his left, and throughout the room various card games were in progress. He moved among the men, sharing greetings and laughter, listening to the latest rumors about everything from new mine strikes to who might run for mayor in the next election, and buying drinks for those who'd had a particularly bad day. Rhine genuinely liked his clientele and they liked him. The Union, a typical western saloon, was atypical, too, in that it led the competition when it came to the quality of the food served. No other place offered better cuts of meat or stocked a wider or finer variety of spirits.

He and Jim recently installed a new gaslighting system that didn't fill the air with the noxious fumes usually associated with the old system, and the Union was the only saloon to have it. The Union was also the only saloon in the city that welcomed Colored people. Although he'd made it known that his doors were open to everyone, the Whites refused to patronize the Union because he didn't discriminate. It stuck in their craws like fish bones that such modern elegance would be offered to a race of people they deemed beneath them, but he didn't care because bigotry was the only reason that kept them from partaking of the elegance as well.

Kenton Randolph, Doc Randolph's eighteen-year-old son, was the Union bartender. "Things seem to be going well tonight," Rhine said.

"Yep. Everyone's behaving themselves, so far, even Ethan Miller."

Rhine turned his attention to the only white face in the room. The blond-haired Miller, twenty-two-year-old son of wealthy mine owner Crane Miller, was playing poker at a table by the window on the far side of the room. Because of his rowdy reputation, only a few saloons in the city allowed him entrance. He also had a penchant for cheating at cards, which accounted for his slightly crooked nose, broken in a fight with an old miner a few years back. He tended to behave at the Union. "Keep an eye on him."

"Will do."

Rhine returned to the kitchen. Her food was ready.

Carrying the tray, Rhine entered the room. Eddy sat up slowly, giving him the impression that he'd awakened her, and he was instantly contrite. "I didn't know you were sleeping. My apology. I can take this back."

She dragged herself up to a sitting position. "No. Please. I didn't know I'd fallen asleep."

"Are you sure?"

She gave him a nod.

He walked over. "Where do you want this?"

She eyed the tray with its covered dishes. "Here on my lap, I suppose."

He handed it to her and she gingerly set it atop her blanket-covered thighs.

"I'm sorry for taking over your bed, and your clothing."

"Don't worry about it. Getting you better is the only concern."

"You've been very kind. Once I get back on my feet, I'd like to repay you in some way. I can scrub your floors or launder the shirts you've let me borrow. I'm also a very good cook. Maybe I can make your favorite sweet. Do you have one?"

Rhine wondered what was wrong with him. When he first entered the room, the sight of her looking all newly awakened and soft in his shirt played havoc with his insides. He was supposed to be taking care of her, not wanting to slip beneath the blanket and explore her sleep-warmed ebony skin. "Uhm, no. Not really." She was a beauty, and not even the near fatal trek through the desert that left her wan and weak and her hair an unruly mess could hide it. He reminded himself again that he already had a beautiful woman in his life.

"I've never met anyone who didn't have a sweet tooth, Mr. Fontaine."

"Then I suppose I'm your first." There was more drawing him than just her beauty. He found the brief flashes he'd seen of her determination so intriguing, he wondered what it might be like to know her better, learn her hopes, dreams, likes, dislikes, and where she'd gotten the courage to set off for California alone. He shook himself free and found her staring up curiously.

"Is something wrong?" she asked.

He shook his head. "No."

Eddy had no experience with men, but there was something in his gaze that gave her pause. He was without a doubt the handsomest man she'd ever met, but she knew a man of his race and wealth wouldn't be interested in a near destitute Colored woman, at least not legitimately, and yet . . . "I—should probably eat this before it goes cold."

In a voice as quiet as the room, he replied, "Yes, you probably should."

For a moment she was unable to look away, and he seemed equally held. Whatever was happening lengthened until she finally forced herself to break the contact. "Tell Jim thank you," Eddy said, needing to say something. Focusing her attention on her plate, she fought to concentrate on picking up her silverware and not on the rising draw of Fontaine's nearness beside the bed. She dipped the tines of her fork into the steaming scrambled eggs.

"I'll look in on you later."

"Thank you." Eddy watched him leave. Only after he exited and the door closed behind him did she realize she'd been holding her breath.

Outside in the hallway, Rhine exhaled, too, and told himself that the best way to handle whatever this was would be to ignore it.

Chapter Four

WHEN EDDY AWAKENED next the room was shadowy but faint lines of sunlight played along the edges of the drapes. A look over at the clock showed its spindly hands set at twelve and six and she hoped it meant six in the morning. She didn't want to know she'd slept away the balance of yet another day. She paused and listened for sounds from the saloon below but heard nothing. Back home in Denver saloons were usually closed during the early hours and she assumed the same to be true here. The chair Fontaine had been sleeping in during her stay was empty, and although she wondered about his whereabouts, she was glad to be alone. She felt better than she had in days and was determined to make it to the facilities on her own this time. Moving the blanket aside, she drew in a deep breath, swung her legs over the edge of the bed, and eased her bare feet to the floor. Her legs shook a bit but held her weight. Pleased, she took a few steps. To her disappointment she was still weak, but decided if she went slowly she could make it to the wash-room and back without collapsing.

The plan went well, sort of. By the time she made it back to the bedroom, she was sweating profusely, her breathing was labored and Rhine

Fontaine was standing in the room looking like a parent ready to scold his child.

"You have to be one of the most hardheaded women I've ever met."

Using the edges of the furniture in the room to guide her back to the bed, she said, "I'm sure that isn't true, but thank you for the compliment." Because wrapping herself in the blanket would have impeded her movements, she'd left it behind. The hem of his long-sleeved white shirt fell past her knees but the bottoms of her legs and her feet were bare. "And no looking at my legs."

"They are quite lovely."

She turned to glare at him but the ghost of a smile playing across his lips made hers peep out of its own accord. "You are no gentleman." She slowly climbed back onto the bed and fell back. "Mercy." She felt like something newly born.

"Learned your lesson?"

"Probably not." After catching her breath, she angled her head his way. "I've worked six days a week since I was twelve years old, and I've never been bedridden in my life. This lying around is hard for me."

"Your recovery will take longer if you don't let your body rebuild its strength."

Frustrated, she turned her eyes to the ceiling and blew out a breath. "I suppose."

"Are you hungry?"

"Famished."

"That's probably a good sign. Jim's in the kitchen. I'll be bringing you breakfast shortly."

"Thank you."

"In the meantime, let's get you a fresh shirt."

She watched him open the large wooden wardrobe. The number of shirts hanging inside was impressive and spoke to his wealth. He took down one and a dressing gown and walked them over to her.

Sitting up, she took the garments from his hand. "May I have a basin and some soap so I can wash up a bit before I put these on?"

"Would you like me to run you a bath?"

"I'd love a bath, but as weak as I am, I'm likely to slip beneath the water and drown." The dream she'd had of being in a tub swam up from her memory, but she refused to share it. He didn't need to know he'd been in the dream and she didn't need any whispering this morning.

"I'll get you the basin."

He returned promptly with a pitcher of warm water, a clean porcelain basin, soap and towels. He set everything on the bedside table.

"Thank you. This shouldn't take long."

"I'll be back with your breakfast in about thirty minutes. Enough time?"

She nodded.

Once she was as clean as washing in a basin would allow, she donned his shirt and then the dressing gown. It was made of black silk and the most expensive article of clothing she'd ever worn. She rolled back the too long sleeves then ran her hand over her hair. It was such a mess. She wished she could do something about it but doubted he'd have anything she could use to dress it, so she'd have to let it be until she moved into the boardinghouse. Waiting for him to return, she picked up the small jar of aloe, undid the lid, and sniffed the contents. Finding it pleasant enough, she rubbed some on her face and pushed up the sleeves to do the same with the skin on her arms and hands. Her blistered hands ached, and if this would help dull the pain, she was all for it. She was recapping the jar when he entered. The Colored man with him made her pause.

"Eddy Carmichael. This is my business partner James Dade." Although she had expected the partner to be White, he was a tall muscular dark-skinned man with a kind smile.

She nodded shyly. "Good morning. Pleased to meet you." She did her best not to think about how appalled her late mother would be knowing she was entertaining two men while in bed.

"Same here," Dade replied. "Thought I'd come up and see how you were faring. Rhine says you're feeling better?"

"I am. Thank you for the rescue and for feeding me. The food has been delicious."

"I appreciate that. I don't get many compliments

about my food around here. People usually eat and leave without so much as a howdy-do." And he threw his partner a meaningful glance.

Rhine countered, "I compliment you on your food all the time."

"He's lying of course, but that's neither here nor there."

She liked Jim Dade. "Maybe when I get back on my feet I can repay you by cooking for you."

"You're a cook?"

"I am."

"So that's why you had that brazier with you when we found you."

"Yes."

Fontaine asked, "Would you care to have company for breakfast? Jim and I would like to join you, but if you prefer to be alone . . . ?"

"I know it isn't considered proper, but your company would be welcomed."

When Jim exited to go get the food, Rhine tore his eyes away from the sight of her swathed in his black dressing gown and concentrated on placing chairs around the small table. "Would you like to join us at the table or eat where you are?" He was glad Jim would be joining them for the meal because he needed the buffer.

"The table, please."

He made a move to cross the room to carry her the short distance but she put up a hand to stay him. "No. I can make it by myself."

Admiring her single-minded determination, he nodded. "Whatever the lady wants."

Draped in the too large dressing gown, she slowly made the short walk to the table and sat down. "See?" she said, showing him a small smile of triumph.

"You are moving better."

"Still not as well as I'd like, though."

"Give yourself time."

"Patience is not one of my virtues."

"I sensed that."

She cut him a look but there was a smile in it.

He sat and asked one of the questions foremost in his mind, "So why California? Do you have family there?"

"No. I was hoping for a fresh start. There was nothing for me in Denver. I'd like to own a restaurant, and from what I've been reading in the newspapers, California seems the place to try. I know I'll probably have to work for years doing something else like cooking or scrubbing floors until I can save enough money, but I'm not afraid of hard work."

The more Rhine learned about her the more impressive he found her to be. An urge to offer her the funds she needed rose up so intensely inside it almost spilled from his lips, but he knew she wouldn't accept so he asked instead, "Did your family in Denver try to dissuade you?"

She shook her head. "My parents are dead. They

died in a snowstorm when I was twelve. I have a younger sister, but she and I are estranged."

"My condolences on both."

"Thank you."

"So you set out not knowing anyone?"

"Yes. Do you find that odd?"

"Frankly, yes. I don't know many women who'd strike out that way alone." His sister Sable had set out towards her future alone, too. He thought she and Eddy might be cut from the same cloth and would probably get along. He just wished he knew where she was.

"I was doing fine on the journey until I ran into Nash—which I doubt is his true name."

"Whatever his name, the authorities will find him."

"I hope so. He had a little boy with him. He said he was taking the boy to an orphanage but I don't know if that was the truth or not."

"I'll let the sheriff know about the boy."

"Thank you."

Although they weren't talking about weighty matters, Eddy was enjoying their conversation. Her initial fears about whether she'd be safe with him were all but dissolved but the need to leave was still keen. Memories of last night's interaction returned, bringing with it the sensation of how time seemed to stand still while looking into his eyes, but it wasn't something she needed to be thinking about. A quick glance his way found him viewing her so intently she was caught yet again. Breaking the contact so she could breathe, she asked, "How long have you lived in Virginia City?"

"Since 'sixty-six. Came west after the war."

"Where's your home?"

"Georgia."

"Do you have family there?"

"Not anymore. I have a brother in San Francisco, and I lost track of my sister during the war. My parents are dead."

"My condolences."

He nodded.

She knew that many families had been torn apart during the war. Back in Denver she'd worked at the hotel with a man who'd spent two years walking across the South looking for his sold-away children and wife but never found them. "Is your sister younger or older?"

"Two years younger." The smile in his eyes made her think he cared for her very much. Eddy wondered if he'd fought on the side of the Confederacy and if his family owned slaves. She didn't ask. Such questioning was rude and he'd been incredibly kind to her. She didn't want his reply to the slave owning question to be yes because it would undoubtedly change how she viewed him, kindness or not.

Silence rose, and as it lengthened, Eddy searched for something else to talk about, only to have him ask, "Do you have a hobby or a favorite pastime?"

"Yes. Sleeping," she said with amusement.

"Sleeping?"

"I worked fourteen-hour days. I'd go home, grab a bite to eat, and go straight to bed because I had to get up before sunrise and do it all over again. There wasn't time for pastimes or amusements."

"I see."

She tried not to be moved by the gentle understanding he exuded and failed. "When my parents died, my sister and I had no other family. People from the church took up a small collection and they brought us food and wood, but they had children of their own and couldn't afford such generosity for very long, so I hired myself out." She thought back on how achingly weary she'd been day after day during that first year and how scary life had been. Her hands had cracked and bled from all the lye, and her knees had fared no better from being on them constantly, but her skin had toughened up and so had she.

"It must have been hard."

"It was. In many ways it still is, but if I don't work, I don't eat. It's pretty simple if you think about it."

He studied her silently for so long the air in the room seemed to still.

"If you could have one wish, what would it be?" he asked.

"To have two wishes."

He smiled at that. "Okay. What would they be?"

"One, to have my own restaurant, and two, to have my nieces come and live with me. They're my sister's girls. Ages ten and twelve. Life's very hard for them, too." She wondered how they were doing. On the few occasions that she prayed, they were who she prayed for. "I love them very much."

"They're back in Denver?"

"Yes."

"I could loan you the funds to bring them out for a visit."

Eddy shook her head solemnly. "No. I appreciate the offer but you've done more than enough."

"If you change your mind—"

"I won't, but thank you."

"Okay."

She was glad that he hadn't pressed her. He'd gone above and beyond in his generosity. She already owed him a debt she'd never be able to repay. The situation with her nieces would be worked out once she got back on her feet. Her situation with him was another matter, however, and in spite of trying to keep her attraction to him at bay, she was as curious about him as he seemed to be about her. Jim returned then carrying a tray filled with covered dishes, and in a way she was grateful for something to concentrate on besides Rhine Fontaine.

Once the food and tableware were distributed

they dug in. Her plate held scrambled eggs, a piece of toast, two strips of bacon, and applesauce. Theirs had eggs, too, but they were accompanied by fragrant, steamed potatoes seasoned with peppers and onions, large fluffy biscuits running with butter and honey, and thick slices of ham. Eddy looked between her scant serving and their huge helpings and the men must have seen the question on her face because Fontaine explained, "Sylvie said to feed you lightly."

And before she could protest, Jim added, "And we are far more afraid of her than of you, little lady, so eat up."

Pouting and chuckling, she did as told.

Which was a good thing because as they were finishing up a woman knocked on the opened door and walked in. "Good morning everyone. Eddy, I'm Sylvia Stewart. You must be feeling better." She had caramel skin and was of medium height. Eddy guessed her to be middle-aged, but like most women of color she wore her age well.

"Good morning," Eddy replied, smiling. "I'm pleased to meet you, and yes, I'm feeling much better. Mr. Fontaine and Mr. Dade were nice enough to eat with me and keep me company— even though I know it isn't proper."

She waved it off. "You'll get no lecture from me. Have you been using the aloe?"

"Yes, ma'am. It seems to be helping the pain."

"Then it's working."

Fontaine said, "We may have found you a cook, Sylvie." He inclined his head Eddy's way.

"You're a cook, Eddy?"

"Yes. Learned from my mother and spent most of my working life as one."

Sylvie clapped happily. "Hallelujah. But let's get you on your feet first before we discuss that. We can move you in this evening. My boarder left last night, but I want to get the room aired out and cleaned up before turning it over to you. Do you think you're well enough? My place isn't far."

"Yes," she said firmly, and shot a quick glance over at Fontaine and was snared by his expressionless eyes.

"Rhine, can you drive her over after dark? Apparently word is already out about you and Jim rescuing her. When I went to Lady Ruby's yesterday to get my eggs, she asked about it. I told her the young woman was at my place in my care."

Jim cracked, "No secrets in Virginia City."

Transferring his gaze from Eddy to Sylvia, Rhine replied, "I'm taking Natalie and her parents to dinner this evening, and then to Piper's, but I'm free to help out when I return."

"Okay, good. I'm going to finish up my errands. Eddy, I will see you this evening."

"Thanks for taking me in."

"You're very welcome." With a wave she departed.

Jim stood. "I need to get going, too, and start the day's food. Miss Eddy, it's been a pleasure."

"Likewise."

He nodded. "I'll send up something for lunch later."

"Thank you."

He gathered up their used dishes, piled them back on the tray, and left her alone with Fontaine. Eddy wondered who Natalie might be and her relationship to Fontaine. Not that it was any of her business. "Thank you again for taking me in, too, Mr. Fontaine."

"As Jim said, it's been a pleasure. More than likely Sylvie is going to confine you to bed for a few more days, so be prepared."

"I'm not at full strength yet, so that'll be okay."

"You two will get along well."

"She seems nice."

"If she hires you, you'll enjoy working with her, too."

"We'll see what happens."

"Her house isn't very large and the men she takes in are always respectable."

"That's good to know," Eddy said, watching him.

"She originally owned this place. It was much smaller back then of course. She and her late husband Freddy have been here since the first big Comstock strike in 'fifty-nine."

If Eddy didn't know better she'd think he was prolonging the conversation in order to delay leaving. She hoped she was wrong. That they might actually be attracted to each other was too outrageous to even contemplate. "You should go and do whatever it is saloon owners do. I'm a bit tuckered out. I think I'll get some sleep."

"Do you need anything?"

"No, I'm fine for now."

But instead of leaving he stood there silently, just as he had last night, his gaze holding hers, and the sensations shimmering over her were getting harder and harder to ignore.

"Rest up," he said softly.

After his departure, Eddy made her way back to the bed. Lying there, she thought the sooner she left Fontaine the better off she'd be. California was her goal, not exploring whatever was calling to her from a pair of smoldering green eyes.

Descending the stairs, Rhine wondered again what the hell was wrong with him. Instead of leaving her when Jim had, he'd stayed behind babbling inanely as if he hadn't wanted to part from her. Had she not politely sent him on his way, he'd probably be still there searching for something else to talk about. Frustrated, he entered the kitchen were Jim stood chopping vegetables for the evening's stew. "I'm going over to the orphanage."

"Will you be back in time for lunch?"

"Probably not." Limiting his contact with Miss

Carmichael would hopefully stifle this kernel of attraction that seemed determined to blossom in spite of his protestations.

"Okay. I'll look in on our guest while you're gone. Give my regards to Sister Mary, Willa Grace, and those troublemaking boys of yours."

"Will do." Confident that by the end of the day Eddy would be with Sylvie and he'd be returning to his well-ordered life, he stepped into his new Rockaway carriage, gathered the reins, and drove away.

The orphanage run by Mary Fulmer and her assistant Willa Grace was housed in an old mansion on the edge of town. Mary used to be Sister Mary of the Sisters of Charity, a local Catholic Order, until she locked horns with the Mother Superior over the Order's refusal to allow children of color into their orphanage. Mary found no charity in that, so three years ago, after much back and forth, she renounced her vows, left the Order, and established her own orphanage. The children under her care were of various races and ages. Over the years, she'd taken in as many as seven. Presently, there were four. Two of the four were eight-year-old twins Micah and Christian Sanford, the troublemaking boys Jim referenced. Rhine had come to care for them a great deal.

When he pulled up in front of Mary's place, the twins came tearing down the steps to greet him and his heart swelled.

"Did you bring us something?" Micah asked excitedly.

"Soldiers, candy, a yo-yo?" his twin chimed in.

"That depends. How much trouble have you been in since I saw you last?"

They went silent and shared a look as if deciding how much to confess. His last visit had been a few days before his trip to Reno with Jim and coming across Eddy in the desert.

Smiling, Rhine stepped down and tied the horse's reins to the post. He knew they'd gotten into some kind of mischief because trouble was their middle names. They'd arrived at the orphanage a year ago following the death of their father, and they were both so solemn and filled with grief Mary worried about their well-being. She asked some of the men in town like Rhine, Doc Randolph, carpenter Zeke Reynolds, and others to spend time with the boys in hopes it would help them adjust to their new life. Everyone pitched in. Doc helped with their lessons, Zeke Reynolds showed them the rudiments of carpentry, which they took to instantly, and Rhine concentrated on making them smile. He brought kites and drove them out to the desert to fly them. They hunted lizards, pitched horseshoes, played marbles, and had foot races. In many ways his times with them were reminiscent of the fun he and his half brother Andrew shared before assuming the roles forced upon them by slavery.

"Still waiting on an answer," Rhine prompted as the silent twins accompanied him up the steps to the front door. Much to Mary's delight, the boys did adjust to life at the orphanage, and there'd been hell to pay ever since. They were rambunctious and so bursting with energy that someone without Mary's patience and love might have taken them out to the desert, tied them to a cactus, and driven away. Which is exactly what Lady Ruby wanted to do the night they snuck over to her place in the middle of the night to play with the chickens in her coop and left the coop unlatched when they snuck back to the orphanage. "Were any snakes or lizards involved?"

They shared another look, and Christian admitted, "Maybe?"

Rhine knew that meant yes.

The interior of the cavernous place was cool. Thankful to be inside and out of the sun, Rhine pulled out his handkerchief and mopped at his neck. Even though he'd been in Virginia City for years now, he still found the desert heat oppressive.

"So where is Miss Mary?"

"Out back. It's wash day."

"And you're not helping?"

"She told us to stay inside so we wouldn't get dirty."

Ten-year-old Susannah Bird walked up. "Hello, Mr. Fontaine."

"Hello, Susannah." She was of Mexican and Paiute descent and smarter than some of the adults Rhine knew. He handed her the bag of penny candy he'd picked up on the way. "Will you put this in a safe place?"

Micah cried, "How come you gave it to her?"

Susannah answered, "Because I am the oldest and the most trustworthy."

When Christian silently mimicked her, Rhine struggled to keep a straight face. She was right though. In her hands the sweets wouldn't be hidden under her bed and eaten secretly, as the boys had done the first and last time they'd been entrusted with the bag.

She then added, "You two can't have any anyway. You're both on punishment."

Rhine swung his attention their way and they squirmed under his scrutiny. Before he could ask for an explanation, Susannah confessed for them. "They put a baby snake in Miss Willa's bloomers drawer."

The spinster Willa Grace was the housekeeper, and like Mary, had a heart of gold. Rhine said to the twins, who now looked like they wanted to disappear, "Correct me if I'm wrong but didn't Miss Willa Grace make you two a birthday cake a few months back large enough to feed half the town?"

Heads bowed, they nodded.

"And when you came down with those terrible

colds last winter, didn't she stay up three nights straight nursing you back to health?"

Shamefaced, they nodded again.

"So, do you think someone who cares for you the way she does deserves to be scared half out of her wits by a snake?" he asked pointedly.

They whispered in unison, "No sir."

"What's your punishment this time?"

They mumbled.

Susannah translated. "No sweets, desserts, and early to bed for the next three nights."

As much as they loved desserts, he knew they were very unhappy with their sentence.

"Mr. Fontaine. Do you want me to tell Miss Mary you're here?" Susannah asked.

"Please."

She departed, leaving Rhine with the guilty boys. "Have you apologized to Miss Willa?" he asked.

They nodded. Before he could interrogate them further, Mary appeared holding the hand of her youngest charge, a three-year-old girl named Lin whose parents had returned to China and left her behind. Mary was short and stocky and had a face weathered from the desert sun. Her gray hair was cut short as a man's. Having worn a nun's habit most of her adult life, she said she preferred it that way. "Mr. Fontaine, how are you?"

He met her kind blue eyes. "I'm well. I hear Trouble One and Two have been living up to their names."

The boys stared down at the toes of their brown brogans.

"They have, and unless they'd care for a full week of no dessert they will be on their best behavior while with you today. Is that understood?" she asked them.

Rhine was taking them into town for haircuts.

"Yes, ma'am," they said in unison.

Still unhappy with their prank, Rhine said, "Susannah told me what happened."

"Poor Willa," Mary said. "As always, she's the model of grace and forgiveness, but she did add a writing component to their punishment."

Since Susannah hadn't mentioned anything about writing, Rhine was confused. It must have shown on his face because Mary said to the boys. "Tell Mr. Fontaine what you are writing."

Micah replied, " 'Dear Miss Willa Grace. I will never play mean tricks on you again.' "

"And how many times do you have to write it?" she asked, turning to Christian.

He answered glumly, "One hundred times."

"That should keep you out of trouble for a while," Rhine said.

"We can only hope," Mary replied. "Now, go and wash your hands so Mr. Fontaine can take you to Mr. Carter's for your haircuts."

Once they were gone, Mary sighed. "May the Good Lord give me the strength to survive those two. I'm sure they didn't mean her any real harm, but they're like wild colts sometimes. Don't you want to do an old lady a favor and take them off my hands?"

Rhine laughed. He was sure she was pulling his leg but he wondered what his fiancée's response would be were he to suggest they add them to their family. He also wondered what the state of Nevada would say about a White man wanting to take two little Colored boys into his home. "How did the interview go with the couple who wanted Lin?" He reached down and gently chucked the girl's small chin. She smiled shyly and leaned into Mary.

"Not well. They wanted to raise her to be their housemaid, so of course I told them I wouldn't allow it."

She'd driven up to Reno to meet the couple. He found the outcome disappointing.

"So I guess my little family will stay intact for now," she said. "Not that I mind." She picked up Lin and nuzzled her neck. The child giggled.

The twins returned.

"Ready to go?" Rhine asked.

"Yes, sir."

Mary reminded them, "Best behavior, remember."

"We will," they promised in unison again.

Rhine told her, "We'll be back as soon as we can."

"There is no need to rush. Believe me."

Chuckling, he led the boys outside to his carriage.

They were indeed on their best behavior, but then again, Rhine rarely had to rein them in when the three of them were together. They seemed to enjoy his company as much as he did theirs. As always, they asked him a hundred questions or more about everything from how the gaslighting worked, had he ever seen Jesus, to how old they had to be to drive the carriage. They then speculated on what kind of dessert they wanted Willa Grace to make for them once they shook off the shackles of their punishment and she started speaking to them again. Listening to their happy and endless chatter, Rhine thought back on Mary's request that he take them off her hands, but he doubted the state would approve even if Natalie did agree to the adoption.

Inside the barbershop, Mr. Edgar Carter greeted them coolly. "What is this about snakes and Willa Grace's bloomers?"

As Jim noted, there were no secrets in Virginia City.

The boys stopped. Christian, the slightly taller of the two, asked, "Who told you?"

"Never mind who told me. Is it true?"

Eyes downcast, they nodded like condemned men again.

"I thought you'd learned your lesson the time

you used lamp black to give her new eyebrows and a mustache."

Thinking back on that, Rhine's shoulders shook with suppressed laughter. They'd altered her appearance one night while she'd been asleep. When she got up the next morning and glanced at herself in the mirror, she'd screamed at the sight of the heavy black brows and mustache. Mary had been none too happy and neither had Rhine, but once he reached home, he and Jim laughed until they cried.

"No peppermints today," Edgar said sternly. He always rewarded them with peppermints for good behavior. They looked crestfallen.

Rhine said, "See what happens to pranksters? Let's hope you've learned your lesson this time."

Edgar shook his head. "Be glad you don't belong to me, because if you did, you'd have to get your haircuts standing up." He held out the cloth bib that would be fastened around their necks. "Who's first?"

On the ride back to the orphanage they were uncharacteristically silent. Rhine wondered if they were thinking about the error of their ways. Micah, who had a small scar over his nose that allowed Rhine to tell them apart, asked, "Do you think if we stop playing pranks we could get a new pa?"

For a few moments Rhine assessed him silently.

Turning back to his driving, he said, "I don't know, Micah."

"We really miss our old one," Christian said.

Rhine's heart twisted. Their mother died giving them life, leaving their father to raise them alone. So far the only kin Mary had been able to find was an aunt in Reno who had five children of her own and couldn't or wouldn't take in her nephews. The aunt said there was a brother living somewhere near St. Louis, but he'd yet to be located. Rhine was reminded of his own futile search for his sister Sable. He also knew how it felt to want a new father because he'd desperately wanted someone other than Carson Fontaine his entire life. "I'm sure Mary will find someone. You just have to give it time." He had no idea if his response would ease their worries but he didn't know what else to say.

Upon arriving at Mary's, he watched as they climbed the steps to the porch. Before going inside they waved. He waved back, noting how quiet and empty the Rockaway seemed now that they were gone. *Am I growing too attached to them?* Once the door closed behind them, he thought maybe he was, but knowing there was no way for him to be anything other than a visitor in their lives, he headed to the saloon, and Eddy Carmichael immediately filled his mind. He wondered how she'd spent the afternoon but quickly pushed the question away. In a little over an hour he'd be meeting his fiancée Natalie and her parents at their home for dinner. Afterwards he'd drive them to Piper's Opera House for an evening of entertainment. Natalie was the woman he was supposed to be thinking about, not the one draped in his dressing gown and lying in his bed.

Chapter Five

TO HELP EDDY pass the time, Jim added a few newspapers to the tray of light fare he brought up for her lunch, and she was grateful. But once she finished both the food and the papers, boredom returned and she spent the rest of the afternoon willing the clock to move faster. She was tired of being alone, tired of the stifling heat, and ready to move to Sylvia Stewart's boardinghouse. Also vexing her was wondering where Rhine Fontaine might be, what he was doing, and who Natalie might be. None of the questions had answers of course, nor were the questions any of her business, so she turned her mind to other unanswerable questions, such as: What would it be like living in Virginia City, how long would it take for her to save enough money to continue her journey to California, and would she see Rhine Fontaine again after she moved to Mrs. Stewart's? Groaning over such futile musings, she fell back against the feather mattress and willed herself to sleep away the rest of the afternoon.

But sleep refused to come. Frustrated, she picked up *The Elevator*, a widely read Colored newspaper published in San Francisco, and was poring over it for the third time when a knock on the door sounded. "Come in."

It was Fontaine and he asked, "How are you?"

"Doing well. You?"

"I'm fine. I need to get my clothing for this evening."

She told herself the reason she was so pleased to see him had to do with how bored she'd been, but it was a lie. "Do you want me to sit in the hallway so you can get dressed?"

"Of course not. I can use one of the spare rooms."

"You have spare rooms?"

He reached into the wardrobe and took out a black formal suit and a shirt. "Yes, two, in fact."

She was puzzled by that. She'd seen the closed doors in the hallway but had no idea what lay behind them. "Then why didn't you put me in one instead of letting me take over your bedroom?"

"When Jim and I found you, you were so near death someone needed to be close by."

"And after?"

He shrugged. "Purely selfish really. I enjoyed being with you."

Her heart stopped.

With that, he reached back into the armoire and added a few more things to what he was carrying, like his shoes and what appeared to be a shaving kit. "Do you need anything?" he asked.

"No."

And he was gone. Eddy fell back against the pillows. *Lord!* Yes, she needed to leave the premises as soon as possible. That he'd openly admitted to being equally drawn to her was as startling as accidentally touching a hot stove. Even though he impressed her as an honorable man, were she to stay even a day longer there was no telling where this might lead.

He returned a short while later, dressed and ready for his outing. The tailored black suit, the snow white shirt, jet black hair, and vivid eyes all added up to a man as alluring as a god. "Presentable?" he asked.

"Your tie's a mite crooked."

He walked to the large standing mirror. Upon seeing nothing wrong with the tie, he glanced back at her in confusion.

"Just pulling your leg. You look fine."

He chuckled softly. "You are not right, miss."

She smiled in reply. In truth, she'd miss the few moments of light banter they'd shared. "So what is Piper's?"

"An opera house."

"Fancy clothes for a fancy place."

"Exactly."

She wanted to ask the question foremost in her mind but didn't.

As if aware of her thinking, he volunteered, "And Natalie Greer is my fiancée. We're to be married in October."

"Congratulations."

"Thank you."

She told herself she wasn't saddened by that

news because it was exactly what she needed to hear to put herself back on an even keel, but inside, she knew it was a lie. Taking him in in all his fancy glory, she imagined what it might be like to be the one he was escorting to the opera house, even though she knew how foolish the thought was. "You don't want to be late."

"I'll see you when I return."

"Have a good time."

"What is this about you finding a Colored woman out in the desert?" Beatrice Greer asked Rhine as they sat at the table in the grand dining room of the Greer mansion.

He waited for the Chinese maid to set down his plate and leave the room before replying. "She'd succumbed to the heat, so Jim and I brought her to town and left her in Sylvie Stewart's care."

"Has she recovered?" her husband Lyman asked. Like Rhine, Lyman Greer was on the town council and an influential member of the city's Republican party.

"Not yet, but I'm pretty sure Sylvie will get her back on her feet." And knowing what he did of Eddy, he was certain it wouldn't take long. Rhine had plans to travel to San Francisco the next day and he thought the trip would give him the distance he needed to get the determined little lady off his mind.

The next question came from Natalie. "Why on earth was she out there?"

"Apparently she was on her way to California, and the cad she was riding with robbed her, forced her out of the wagon, and drove away."

"She's not a whore, is she?"

Rhine stiffened. Natalie's disapproving tone was mirrored on her face. When he proposed to her six weeks ago, he'd told himself marrying the twenty-year-old, blue-eyed brunette beauty would give him the legitimacy he wanted for the life he'd planned, but the more he was around her, the more her true self came to the fore, and the more he questioned their compatibility. "She said she's a cook."

"I hope she's not lying. More whores is the last thing Virginia City needs."

Her mother glanced up from her plate and said pointedly, "Natalie, let's change the subject, shall we?"

"I'm only stating the truth, Mother."

"But it isn't something good women discuss, dear."

The 1859 discovery of the Comstock Lode with its rich veins of gold and silver brought miners to Virginia City from all over the world, and where there were miners there were whores. Eddy was a lot of things: fiery, stubborn, and hardheaded to a fault, but whore? No.

Rhine was glad when Lyman changed the

subject by asking his wife, "Now, who are we going to see this evening again?"

"A singer named Herbert Gould."

This was not the first time Beatrice had subjected them to one of her singing finds. Rhine just hoped he could sit through the performance without his ears bleeding.

Entering the opera house, Rhine saw that the auditorium was crowded as usual. All the well-to-do in the area were in attendance: mine owners, local politicians, and businessmen were accompanying their wives to their high-priced seats. Piper's Opera House could accommodate an audience of fifteen hundred. It was one of the most esteemed venues in the nation and built its reputation by showcasing everything from Shakespearean acting troops to world renowned singers. Infamous actor John Wilkes Booth appeared in the play *Apostate* only a month before assassinating President Lincoln. Mark Twain lectured from its stage in 1866. A deadly real life drama took place in 1871 when a vigilante mob muscled a murderer out of the town jail and hung him from the stage rafters. Rhine doubted tonight's offering would be that exciting.

He was correct. The singer he'd been planning to guard his ears against turned out to be a thin, mustached man reciting poems by Lord Byron. His high-pitched, nasal-toned voice and overly dramatic presentation resulted in many of the men in the audience quietly excusing themselves from their wives and making a beeline for the smoking room in the back of the theater. Rhine and Lyman Greer joined the exodus.

On the ride home, Lyman Greer said to his wife, "I thought he was supposed to be a singer."

"He is. He's all the rage back East but he has a case of the sniffles and didn't want to risk his voice."

"Men don't get the sniffles, Beatrice," he informed her drolly.

Rhine held onto his smile.

Natalie added in a petulant voice, "And I found it incredibly rude that you and Rhine left us, Father."

"We didn't want to catch the sniffles."

Finding that to be a perfect response, Rhine drove on.

When they reached the Greer home, Lyman and Beatrice thanked him and went inside but Natalie lingered. "So, how long will you be in San Francisco?" she asked.

"Just a few days. I'll be visiting my brother." Andrew was now one of San Francisco's most prominent bankers.

"Will you be discussing putting the saloon up for sale?" she asked, sounding hopeful.

"No, because it isn't for sale."

"I thought we agreed—"

"*We* haven't agreed to anything," he countered mildly.

"A member of the city council shouldn't own a place no decent person will enter!"

"My clientele are as decent as you and I. The only difference is the color of their skin."

"You're making me a laughingstock."

"You can always call off the engagement." And truthfully, one part of him wished she would.

"And let another woman in town have a shot at the most handsome man in Nevada?" Her smile caught the moonlight. "I won't be crying off. I'm determined to change your mind."

"And if you can't?" he asked, hoping he sounded nonchalant. For the past few weeks she'd been after him to sell the saloon, and she was as persistent as she was beautiful.

"I'm not worried. I always get my way. Now, give me a kiss before Mother comes out and starts fussing about me ruining my reputation by being out here with you in the dark."

He complied, and when he broke the seal of their lips, she whispered, "I'm not letting another woman have your kisses either."

He chuckled. "Come. I'll walk you to the door." Once there, he said to her, "I'll see you when I return from San Francisco."

She stroked his cheek with a gloved hand. "Good night, Rhine."

He inclined his head and walked back to his rig. As he drove home through the lamplit streets his thoughts involuntarily swung to Eddy. He wondered what she would've thought of Herbert Gould. According to the few things she'd shared about her past, she'd been working since the age of twelve, which meant she'd probably never put on a costly gown, fastened a jeweled necklace around her throat, and been escorted to a place like Piper's. Unlike Natalie, who had parasols to match every gown in her armoire, inside Eddy's old carpetbag he'd seen a few well-worn blouses, two skirts with fraying hems, and three threadbare shifts. She'd also been wearing an old pair of boys' brogans when they found her in the desert. Although Natalie had more materially, there was an underlying strength in Eddy's character that Natalie would probably never have. He also sensed that Eddy knew the value of what it meant to own one's own business and wouldn't badger him to sell simply because of personal prejudice. He was on his way to take her over to Sylvia's. Even though that saddened him, he knew her leaving him was for the best.

He drove on, and as always the night air was filled with the constant drone of the mines' machinery housed along the base of nearby Mount Davidson. The noisy pumps that kept the tunnels free of scalding water that flowed below the surface joined the cacophony set off by air compressors and the enormous hoisters that ferried caged miners underground and brought the newly found ore to the surface, twenty-four hours a day, seven days a week. Every now and then explosions echoed across the landscape from the black powder used to open up new veins that ran for miles around and below the city. Visitors and newcomers found the constant noise troublesome, but to men like Rhine whose wealth from the mines increased with each passing day, it was as soothing as a lullaby.

Dressed in her worn white blouse and faded dark skirt, Eddy sat in one of the chairs in Fontaine's bedroom and waited for his return. Her carpetbag and brazier were at her feet. She was anxious to get to Mrs. Stewart's home so she could recover fully and begin this new phase of her life even as she wondered how his evening had fared and what the fiancée looked like. For the hundredth time she told herself neither question mattered and that she should be more concerned with what her future held. It seemed like only yesterday that she'd left Denver, but in reality more than a month had passed and here she sat in his bedroom. The difference in their races notwithstanding, he'd gone out of his way to show her nothing but concern and kindness. Once she got on her feet and saved up her money so she could resume her journey to California, she'd remember him fondly.

"Are you ready?" he asked when he entered the room a few minutes later.

"I am. How was the performance?"

"Awful."

"I'm sorry."

"No sorrier than I."

She slowly pushed herself upright. Like this morning, she was moving easier but still not at a normal pace.

"Shall I carry you?"

"No." As she picked her way to where he stood by the door, he watched and waited.

"I can get you a cane," he said in a teasing tone.

"Ha, ha," she tossed back, and yes, she'd miss bantering with him.

He crossed his arms. "You know the sun will rise in about eight hours."

Finding it difficult to keep a straight face in the wake of his playful teasing, she countered, "Make yourself useful. Get my carpetbag and the brazier."

He complied and made it back to the door as she continued moving at a snail's pace.

"You're perspiring, Miss Carmichael."

"I'm fine," she said, breathing heavily.

Apparently he didn't believe the lie because he set down the brazier and carpetbag and picked her up.

"Rhine. Put me down."

"No. We want to get to Sylvia's tonight, not next week . . ." He paused. "That's the first time you've ever used my given name."

Looking up into his pleased and oh so wickedly

handsome face, she fumbled for a reply, "I needed to get your attention."

"You have it."

The whispering began again, but this time it was plainer and far more distinct. What in heaven's name was she supposed to do with an attraction to a man who was not only forbidden to her by law but engaged to be married as well?

His blazing gaze fixed on hers, he added softly, "If I deliver you all tuckered out and breathing hard, Sylvia will take a buggy whip to me."

"And we can't have that," she somehow managed to say.

"No. As Jim pointed out this morning, I am far more afraid of her than of you—or at least I was until now . . ."

Eddy's heart began a now familiar pounding. "We should go."

But for a moment he stood rooted, drinking her in, and she did the same to him.

"Eddy—"

She shook her head. "Let's just go, please." Whatever he intended to say would not negate the reality of who they were, nor their destinies.

There was now a hint of sadness in the eyes holding hers but he nodded understandingly. "Okay, but I owe you for telling me my tie was crooked."

That made her laugh.

Smiling, he carried her out of the room.

As they got under way, Rhine glanced over. "Are you comfortable?"

"I am."

It was a nice night and his mind played with the idea of driving out into the desert so they could sit, talk, and enjoy a few more hours of each other's company, but he knew that was impossible. "I'm traveling to San Francisco tomorrow. I'll be gone for a few days, so if you need assistance with anything have Sylvie send word to Jim."

"I will. What is that noise?" It sounded like a giant slowly beating a mountain-sized drum.

He explained the mining operations.

"And this goes on all day?" she asked.

"And all night, every day of the year."

"How do people sleep?" She wondered why she hadn't heard it earlier.

"You'll get accustomed to it." He could just make out her features in the dark but got the impression that she didn't believe him.

When they arrived at Sylvie's back door, he tied the horse to the post and came around to her side of the carriage.

She asked, "I suppose you're going to insist on carrying me again?"

"I am."

"I'm taking back my offer of sweets."

"I think I'll survive." After handing her the carpetbag and brazier, he eased her slight weight into the cradle of his arm and set out in the darkness towards the door. Because it would be the last time, he allowed himself to enjoy holding her near.

Sylvie appeared under the light above the door. "Good evening. Come on in. Glad you didn't make her walk, Rhine."

"She's been a perfect patient," he lied, and saw the smile on Eddy's face just before she turned away.

Sylvie ushered them through the large kitchen built onto the back of her place. "Her room is upstairs."

Once there, he set her down on a large upholstered chair.

"Thanks, Rhine," Sylvie said to him. "I know you have to get back. We don't want to hold you."

He only had eyes for Eddy while replying to Sylvia, "I told Miss Carmichael I'll be in San Francisco for a few days. When I return I'll stop by and see how she's faring."

Sylvie nodded. "That's very kind of you."

"Take care of yourself, Miss Carmichael."

"I will, Mr. Fontaine, and thank you again for your kindness."

Rhine wanted to linger, but having no legitimate reason to do so, he instead inclined his head in good-bye. "Have a good evening, ladies." And he departed.

Chapter Six

WHEN EDDY AWAKENED the next morning the unfamiliarity of her surroundings threw her for a moment, but it only took a few seconds to remember where she was. Sylvia Stewart's boardinghouse. Her first thoughts were of Rhine, and she wondered if he was thinking of her. She chastised herself for that. She was now back in the real world where he was a wealthy White man and she was as poor as a church mouse Colored woman once again relying on the goodwill of strangers. When he returned from San Francisco he'd resume his life with his saloon and fiancée. It made no sense to dwell on anything else.

Mrs. Stewart entered the room carrying a tray. "Here's your breakfast, Miss Carmichael, and I'm apologizing in advance."

Eddy had no idea what that meant until she pulled back the napkin covering the food. The plate held three strips of crisp black bacon, burned scrambled eggs, and on the edge, a pool of runny grits. Apparently Eddy didn't hide her reaction well enough.

"Sorry honey, I'm a really poor cook."

"No, this is fine. I'm grateful for the meal."

"You lie so beautifully."

Eddy dropped her head to hide her smile.

"My cook went back East. Until I can replace him, I'm afraid you'll have to put up with whatever I don't burn completely."

"Once I get on my feet, I'll help. I'm a cook, remember?"

"I do, and my boarders and diners are going to worship at your feet. Every time I lose a cook they swear my cooking's going to send them to their graves."

Eddy didn't wish to begin eating and appear rude but she was starving, so she dug in. Although the food tasted as bad as it appeared, her hungry stomach didn't care.

What sounded like a far off explosion filled the air. Startled, she asked, "What is that?"

"Black powder going off. It comes from the mines."

She remembered Rhine's explanation from the night before but had no idea there were explosions, too. "I thought I heard whistles last night. Does a train run through the city?"

"Yes, but the whistles mostly signal shift changes for the miners. It takes newcomers a little while to get used to all the noise, but in a week or so you won't even hear it."

Eddy still doubted that.

"So, how's our patient?"

The question was asked by a tall, statuesque red-haired White woman standing in the doorway.

She was wearing a beautiful white blouse and a fine-looking gray skirt.

"Morning, Vera," a smiling Mrs. Stewart replied. She made the introductions. "Miss Eddy Carmichael. Miss Vera Ford."

Eddy had had her fill of the charred breakfast and so set the tray on the nightstand. "Pleased to meet you, Miss Ford."

"I'm pleased as well. How are you feeling? Oh never mind, you've been eating Sylvie's cooking."

Sylvia drew herself up as if offended, then laughed. "Don't start, Vera Ford. You're not the best cook either."

"No, I'm not, which is why I run a dress shop."

By the fondness on their faces it was evident the two women were friends.

"In spite of Sylvie's awful food, are you feeling better?"

"I'm still a bit weak," Eddy replied. "But hoping it will pass soon."

"If anyone can get you back on your feet, it's Sylvie."

Sylvie asked, "I'm not meaning to be rude but how in the world did you wind up out in the desert by yourself?"

Eddy told them the story.

When she finished, both women appeared shocked and Vera asked, "He set you down in the middle of the desert?"

"Yes, ma'am."

"What a complete cad. Sylvie, we need to make sure the sheriff hears about this. We don't want this varmint preying on anyone else."

"Mr. Fontaine said the same thing," Eddy pointed out. She wondered if he'd already caught the train to San Francisco.

Mrs. Stewart's voice brought her back. "How awful that must have been for you, Eddy."

"It was." The only saving grace was that Nash hadn't forced himself on her, or killed her outright.

"Thank the Lord for Rhine and Jim," Mrs. Steward stated.

Vera agreed. "I wouldn't mind being lost in the desert if I knew the best looking man in the territory would find me. You couldn't have been rescued by a better man, Eddy."

Eddy agreed. Having no idea if Vera knew she'd been staying at the saloon, she didn't offer anything more.

Sylvia told her friend, "The handsome Rhine aside, Eddy's a cook, Vera. She's going to help me out here once she gets on her feet."

Vera nodded approvingly. "Good. Otherwise, your dining room will be closed inside of a week if the place has to rely on your cooking."

Sylvia tossed out, "And she calls herself a friend."

"Good morning, ladies," a cheery male voiced called out.

Eddy looked up to see yet another visitor. The brown-skinned man in the doorway was older, mustached, and carrying what appeared to be a black doctor's bag.

Sylvia's entire demeanor changed. "Good morning, Oliver."

Eddy noted the frost in the greeting.

Sylvia did the introductions. "Eddy Carmichael. Doc Randolph."

Eddy wondered what the story was between the two. She glanced at Vera and received a shake of her head loaded with exasperation.

"Nice to meet you, Miss Carmichael. Rhine Fontaine told me about you. Thought I'd come by to see how you're faring."

"Nice to meet you, too, Dr. Randolph. Other than feeling weak, I'm mending."

"Good to hear. Mind if I make sure?"

"No, sir. I don't have money to pay you though."

"That's quite all right. Think of it as a welcome gift from the community."

He walked to the bed and removed his stethoscope from his bag. He listened to her breathing then looked into her eyes and checked the blistered skin on her hands. He turned them over to view her palms. "You're putting aloe on her, Sylvie?"

"No, Oliver, I'm using lard," she replied sarcastically. "Of course I'm using aloe."

Eddy said, "And it seems to be working well."

"Good. Keep applying it." He placed his

instruments back in his bag. "I want you to stay in bed another day or so."

"I don't like lying around."

"Young lady, from what Rhine told me, you're lucky you're not lying in a grave. Take my advice, okay? The more you rest, the faster you'll be back on your feet."

"Yes, sir."

"And I must warn you, don't let these hellions influence you. They cause enough trouble for two towns."

Vera laughed.

Sylvia didn't.

Dr. Randolph held Sylvia's gaze. Eddy saw a softness in the contact overlaid with something she couldn't define—regret? She wondered how long she'd have to be in residence before she could ask Vera about them. Not that she planned on staying in Virginia City. California was still her final goal.

"You take care of yourself, now," he said to her. "If you need me, Sylvie and Vera know where to find me. Good day, Miss Eddy, and welcome to Virginia City."

"Thanks."

He gave her a nod and departed.

Vera broke the thick silence following his departure. "You know, Sylvia, you two aren't getting any younger."

"Don't meddle, Vera."

"You're just being stubborn."

"Did I ask for your opinion?"

"No. Just thought I'd give it anyway." Vera turned to Eddy. "Keep healing. I'll see you soon." And with that, she left.

"I'll take that tray now, Eddy." There was a sadness in Sylvia's eyes.

"Yes, ma'am."

"Rest up. I'll come back and check on you later."

When Carson Fontaine married Sally Ann, the newlywed couple celebrated the occasion with a grand tour of Europe. Rhine's enslaved mother Azelia was brought along to attend to Sally's needs, and apparently Carson's, too, because nine months after the return to Georgia, both Azelia and Sally gave birth to sons less than two weeks apart. Both grew tall, lean, and devilishly handsome, and favored each other enough to have been mistaken as twins more than a few times. The only physical feature that set them apart were their eyes. Rhine's were green like their father's. Andrew had Sally Ann's brown. It was their stations in life that set them apart the most though. When they turned eight years old they were no longer allowed to share carefree days hunting frogs and turtles, climbing trees and splashing in nearby creeks. Drew began training with Carson to run the plantation he stood to inherit upon

Carson's death, and Rhine began life as his brother's personal slave and valet. There were shirts to iron, beds to make, boots to polish, and baths to draw. After Drew deserted during their first battle of the war, he went west, and Rhine joined the Union army. They lost track of each other, only to be reunited in Kansas City after the South's surrender, and now the half brothers sat in a fancy San Francisco restaurant, eating and sipping champagne while reminiscing over old times.

Pouring more champagne into his flute, Andrew asked, "I wonder whatever happened to Melissa Drummond?"

Rhine smiled. "No idea, but that was quite a night she treated us to."

Andrew raised his goblet in mock salute. "To the many bawdy nights gifted us by Georgia's randy southern belles."

And he was so right. The brothers spent the years leading up to the war bedding belles and in some cases their mothers, too. "Do you think Carson knew about our wayward ways?"

Andrew shrugged. "He was so busy cuckolding his friends I don't think he cared what we were up to. Poor Mother."

"Have you gone back to see her?"

"Why? She hated me as much as she hated you and Sable. It infuriated her that I refused to treat you like a slave."

And Drew hadn't, whenever he could manage it. From insisting that Rhine be allowed to sleep in a proper bed instead of on the floor of his room, to refusing to take his lessons unless Rhine was allowed to join him, to never laying a whip on Rhine's back.

"But she hated my mother most of all," Rhine pointed out. Fueled by jealousy, Sally Ann would've had Azelia whipped from sunup to sundown had she not been afraid of Carson's wrath.

"Yes, she did." As if needing to move the conversation away from those painful times, Drew changed the subject. "So are you still planning on marrying that little bauble you introduced me to the last time I visited?"

Rhine cut into his steak, and although his misgivings about Natalie rose, he said, "Yes, but as I said at the time, it's not a love match. Her parents are fairly influential Republicans and their support will be needed if I decide to pursue a career in politics when I'm done on the city council." Rhine had one year remaining in his three year term.

"Why you'd want to poke around in the cesspool known as politics is beyond me. Find you someone to love and live out your old age in contentment as I plan to do."

"I need to help, Drew."

Andrew paused and said seriously, "There are

other men helping in their own way. Leave it to them. I don't want you lynched or beaten to death. Even White men are being killed by the supremacists now."

"I know, and I appreciate your concern, but a stand has to be made to protect the gains made since the war. If I can put myself in a position of power to do so, why shouldn't I?"

"Because not even you can stop the backsliding Republicans. Every day they're moving farther away from what they once stood for. Your people have taken to calling them Lily White Republicans."

"I know, and it's very apt."

After using the Black vote to swing political power their way and elect Grant to the presidency, more and more Republicans were now focused on gaining White voters in order to hold onto that power. Many were turning a blind eye to the rampaging supremacist groups like the Klan and the Order of the White Camellias even as their members were killing Colored men on their way to cast votes for candidates running on the Republican slate. It was maddening, but Rhine felt uniquely qualified to be a voice for those who did care, because of his passion, education, and ability to pass for White. He may have turned his back on being Black, but not on his race. Politics aside, he asked something that had been plaguing him. "Have you heard from

Mavis?" Mavis was Drew's sister and Rhine's half sister.

"No. I hired the Pinkertons. If anyone can find her, they can. Hopefully she's still among the living." Just as Drew and Rhine were connected by their close birth dates, so were their sisters. Mavis and the enslaved Sable had been born six minutes apart.

"Any word on Sable?" Drew asked.

"No, I'm still placing yearly notices in all the big papers, hoping she'll see it, but so far nothing. If we are fortunate enough to be reunited, I'm not sure how Natalie will react, but I miss her dearly. I may have to go the Pinkerton route as well."

"Rhine, I know you're rowing your own boat, but is Natalie really the woman you want to bind your life to?"

Drew had been married for three years to the daughter of one of his clients. Her name was Freda, and they had a two-year-old son named for Drew. The way she and Drew lit up a room in each other's presence testified to their strong loving bond. A part of Rhine envied that closeness, but having never known love, he was certain he could live his life very well without it. He cared for Natalie, but as he'd stated, the marriage would be one of convenience, nothing more. Eddy's face played across his mind but he instantly pushed the image away. "I'll be fine." He looked past the doubt in his brother's eyes and his own inner doubts and steered the conversation to a subject they both enjoyed: money, stocks, and profit.

Later that night, while lying in the bed in Drew and Freda's guest room, Rhine thought about Drew's advice on both politics and life. Rhine was certain he could make a difference, but did he really need to do it on such a grand stage? He'd thought about running for Congress but in truth wasn't sure whether to actually pursue a political career. He was already on the city council, where he and a few other like-minded Republicans were doing their best to keep the Colored community's rights from being trampled. He was also helping in small, quieter ways by making loans and investing in businesses the White bankers refused to service. Knowing he had the ability to pass for White was one of the reasons he'd crossed over, that and that he hated being treated like less than a man simply because of the circumstances of his birth. By walking among those who deemed themselves better because of the circumstances of their birth, he could secretly laugh at their blind ignorance of who he really was and use his presence as a way of fighting back. It came at a price though: hearing the cruel and tasteless jokes told by bigots at gatherings, and being looked at oddly for pointing out how tasteless they were; knowing that even though his Union Saloon opened its doors to the weddings and celebrations thrown by the Colored community, he couldn't participate fully because he was no longer a member of the race. By passing, he'd gained a lot in terms of wealth and prestige, but he'd lost a lot as well.

And now, Eddy. For the first time since leaving Virginia City he allowed himself to think about her fully. He was drawn not only to her beauty but to her strength and determination to carve out a better life. He thought back on the story she'd told about how hard life had been after the death of her parents and he was moved all over again. Was it any wonder that he'd become so affected by her in such a short span of time? Were he his true self, he'd waste no time pursuing her, but he wasn't, and therein lay the problem. The man he was pretending to be had nothing honorable to offer. When he left her at Sylvia's that evening, he'd tried to convince himself that putting her out of his mind would be easy, but so far his mind was refusing to play along.

It took two more days of bed rest for Eddy to get back on her feet, but if Mrs. Stewart had had her way, the stay would've lasted longer. While waiting to be officially released, Eddy endured more burned food and continued to use the aloe concoction on her hands and face. Although she was unfamiliar with the plant and its benefits, she was glad for Mrs. Stewart's expertise because it was helping her skin heal and dulling the pain of the burns.

However, having worked from sunup to sundown most of her adult life, lazing around in bed was not only still frustrating, it also gave birth to a strong sense of guilt. Each time Mrs. Stewart brought in a tray of food, Eddy wondered if she was eating the kind woman out of house and home.

On the third day, when Mrs. Stewart entered the room carrying the breakfast tray, Eddy was on her feet and dressed.

"What are you doing up?"

"I'm ready to begin earning my keep. What chores need doing?"

"Eddy, I—"

"Please, I'm done lying in bed, and I'm strong enough to help out, so I start today."

"Not used to following orders, are you?" Mrs. Stewart asked, sounding amused.

"No, ma'am."

"Then the two of us are going to get along just fine. I don't follow orders well either."

Eddy eyed the burnt breakfast on the tray.

Mrs. Stewart saw the look. "You're welcome to make your own breakfast if you like."

"I'll do it tomorrow. I don't want to waste food."

"Honey, I've been wasting food since you arrived. Go fix you something to eat. There's plenty."

Eddy took the tray from her hand. "Tomorrow."

The action caused Mrs. Stewart to view her silently before replying knowingly. "Yes. We're going to get along real well."

Eddy forced herself not to mind that the bacon, eggs, and toast were again all burned. Washing the charred tastes down with a cup of coffee, she picked up the tray and left the room.

Even though it her first full day on her feet and she felt well, she knew better than to overdo it, so she descended the stairs slowly to the main floor. At the bottom of the staircase was a large room that held a number of small tables with two chairs each. She wondered if it was the common room where the boarders took their meals.

She found Mrs. Stewart in the big kitchen attached to the back of the house that Rhine had carried her through on the night she arrived. Rather than wonder if he'd returned from San Francisco, she took a look around. There was a large modern stove, a sink, lengths of countertops, and a slew of cabinets. The kitchen walls were screened to let in the outside air. "So, what would you like for me to do, Mrs. Stewart?"

"First, I'd like for you to call me Sylvia or Sylvie. Mrs. Stewart is reserved for boarders and the like."

"Yes, ma'am."

"Now, let's talk duties and wages. Have a seat." She gestured at the table in the center of the room and Eddy complied. "So, how well do you cook?"

"Rather well, I'm told. My mother made her living as a cook to wealthy families in Denver and I grew up helping her. I'm experienced with steaks, quail, trout, and everything in between. I've cooked for individuals, families, and large to-dos like banquets and weddings. I do well with cakes, tarts, pickling, marmalades, jellies, and pies."

"Breads?"

Eddy nodded.

"Excellent. You'll be preparing breakfast and dinner for the boarders daily. I open the dining room to the public three days a week: Tuesdays, Thursdays, and Sundays, with Sunday being the busiest day. Can you handle all that?"

"Yes. How many boarders, and how many people come on Sundays?"

"I have three boarders, and usually ten to fifteen people on Sunday. Too many?"

"Not at all." In fact, Eddy couldn't believe how small a cooking job this would be. During her years at the hotel, she and the staff fed at least fifty people daily.

They talked wages next, and when told how much her weekly pay would be, she asked, "What other chores will you be wanting me to do?"

"None. Just cooking."

The proposed amount was twice what she was paid as a cook before being demoted to scrubbing floors. "No floors or wash?"

"No, I have other people to do those."

Eddy wasn't sure how to respond.

Mrs. Stewart explained, "If you're as good a cook as you say you are, I don't want you hired away by someone who'll promise to pay you more. There's a lot of money here in Virginia City, and the wealthy have the means to pay for the best."

"I see." She wondered if Sylvia Stewart was one of those wealthy residents.

"So, since you haven't seen the city, let me give you a tour. You need to meet some of the farmers and storekeepers you'll be dealing with and learn your way around. Later you can meet the boarders. Gabe Horne works in the mines, Whitman Brown works at one of the banks and is also a Baptist preacher. August Williams is a dishwasher at one of the hotels."

"There's a hotel here?"

"Yes, which is why I'm paying you so well. I don't want you deserting me."

"Don't worry. While I'm here, I'm all yours. I owe you a lot for taking me in and offering me work." Then she thought of something she needed to make clear. "I left Denver to go to California, and soon as I save up enough money, I'll be moving on."

"Understood."

"Thank you very much for the job."

"And thank you for arriving right on time. Let's take that tour."

While Sylvia drove the small buckboard pulled by an old mare named Dilly, Eddy took in Virginia City. According to Sylvia, the initial silver strike in 1859 turned penniless miners into millionaires who built mansions, imported fancy furniture and smoked even fancier cigars. With all that money they also built churches, business establishments, and the International House hotel that Sylvia told her had one hundred rooms and an elevator. There were gaslights lining the streets and sewer lines beneath the city, thus making it more cosmopolitan than she'd imagined. Many of the buildings were made of brick and had fancy glass windows. There were a large number of saloons, and it seemed as if the owners were in some kind of competition to see who had the fanciest doors. Most were very ornate and sported not only glazed glass windows but intricate gold leaf lettering and etched carvings.

As they drove past Piper's Opera House, Sylvia said, "It's known for its high-toned entertainment, but for all of Virginia City calling itself a Republican town, we're not welcomed."

Seeing the place made her think of her last evening with Rhine. "Is there much bigotry here?"

"Some of it's subtle and some of it isn't. For example, I told you about Piper's not welcoming us."

"Yes, you did."

"None of the Whites here will patronize Rhine

Fontaine's Union Saloon because it caters to the Colored community. On the other hand, the local schools aren't segregated."

"That's something," Eddy remarked, and wondered how Fontaine felt about not being patronized by his own kind.

Eddy was told that there were nearly 25,000 residents in the gaslit city, but the Colored community numbered less than a hundred.

"And most of them are men. You can count the number of ladies here on less than both hands. Good thing you're not staying, otherwise you'd be beating the men off with your frying pan."

Eddy smiled at the picture that created in her mind.

"There's a large group of Chinese though. They settled in after helping build the railroads. Lots of Paiute Indians, Irish, Cornish, and Englishmen live here, too."

As the tour continued, Sylvia pointed out Vera's dress shop. "She's the best seamstress in town."

The place was on Main Street, and two beautifully gowned dress forms were displayed in the big glass windows. Eddy met the fishmonger, a Colored man from Louisiana named Amos Granger and Mr. Carter, one of the local barbers who shared his business with hairdresser Janet Foster. Sylvia then stopped so Eddy could meet Mr. Rossetti, who owned and operated one of the town's general stores and markets. As they drove along, Eddy saw chickens walking along some of the main streets.

"We have farms interspersed with the buildings," Sylvia offered in explanation. "But many of the wild chickens once belonged to Lady Ruby before they escaped and struck out on their own."

"Who's Lady Ruby?"

"A madam. Owns one of the bordellos—Lady Ruby's Silver Palace. Has a number of coops behind the place and her chickens lay some of the best eggs around. It's where I get my eggs."

Eddy had never heard of an egg-selling madam.

"She's from the West Indies and is quite a character. The Stanford twins over at the orphanage freed some of the chickens. Those little boys are something."

"There's an orphanage?"

"Yes. Run by a former nun named Mary. We'll go by there later in the week so you can meet her. Wonderful lady. Many in the community do our best to help her out whenever we can because she takes in Colored children."

Eddy looked forward to making her acquaintance.

During the entire tour, the earthshaking noise of the mine machinery filled her ears, and Eddy was still convinced she'd never get used to it.

As they drove on she spotted fashionably dressed women carrying parasols and men in suits and bowler hats moving singularly and in pairs on the crowded city walks. She wondered what kind of lives they led and what it was like to live in the desert city. The air was certainly warmer than in Denver. It would probably take her as long to get accustomed to the heat as it would to the constant drone of the mining machinery. As Sylvie turned a corner, they came up on a construction site. Men of all races were laying brick, toting lumber, and wielding hammers. "What are they building?"

"A new bank, from what I've been hearing. Ah, there's Ezekiel Reynolds." She pulled back on the reins. "He's someone I want you to meet."

A Colored man looked up from his sawing and upon seeing them showed a smile that lit up his handsome brown face. He called out, "Hey there, Miss Sylvie."

"Hi, Zeke."

"Who's that pretty lady with you?"

"My new cook. Come, let me introduce you."

The man said something to one of the Chinese workers, wiped his hands on a rag and walked over.

While he turned his smile on Eddy, Sylvie said, "Zeke, Miss Eddy Carmichael. Eddy, Ezekiel Reynolds. He's one of our Republican leaders. Works tirelessly on our behalf."

Eddy nodded a greeting. "Pleased to meet you."

"Same here."

"Eddy's from Denver."

"Denver's loss is our gain. Welcome to Virginia City."

"Thank you."

"You planning on putting down roots?"

"No. I'm going on to California, hopefully before winter."

"Pity. Pretty woman like you would give us poor men someone to look forward to seeing every day."

He was a charmer.

"How'd the Reno meeting go?" Sylvie asked him.

He sighed. "Not well. Doc and I will talk about it at the next Lincoln Club meeting. Some of what's happening in the South is starting to draw concern."

Sylvie explained. "The Lincoln Club is our Republicans committee. They keep us abreast of what's happening with the race both here and across the country."

Eddy was pleased to hear that. It spoke to the progressiveness of the community. There'd been a similar group in Denver.

"Zeke, we won't hold you any longer. I just wanted Eddy to meet you."

"I'm glad you did. You should bring her to the baseball game. Be a nice way to introduce her around."

"That's a wonderful idea."

"Do you enjoy baseball?" he asked Eddy.

"I do. My father played on a team when I was growing up."

That seemed to please him. "We play the White Republicans once a year to raise funds for the cause. Proud to say, we've beaten them three years running and I don't see that changing this year."

Even as Zeke held her eyes, Eddy wondered if Rhine played for the other side.

Sylvie brought the short interlude to a close. "We'll see you there."

He nodded and said to Eddy, "Nice meeting you, Miss Eddy. Looking forward to seeing you at the game."

"Same here."

He walked back to the site, and as Sylvie got Dilly moving again, Eddy glanced over and found Zeke Reynolds still watching her. He nodded. She nodded in reply and was shyly pleased by his obvious interest.

"He's a nice man," Sylvie pointed out. "Owns a carpentry business and is very much in demand in the area. He's the cousin of our boarder August. Zeke's also unmarried."

"You aren't going to be playing matchmaker, are you?"

"Who me?" she asked innocently. "Of course not. I was just letting you know about him."

Eddy chuckled. "I see."

Chapter Seven

THE NEXT DAY, as Eddy walked through the streets on her way to do business with Amos Granger the fishmonger, she felt like a bird freed from its cage. The morning air was already stifling, but she didn't let it foul her mood. She was no longer confined to bed and there was a pep in her step because of it. Sylvia tried to convince to her to drive for the errand, but Eddy had walked everywhere in Denver and she wanted to see the city. Besides, the shop wasn't that far away. Most of the Whites she passed looked through her. Accustomed to being invisible to them, she didn't let that impact her mood either. The Colored people she passed eyed her curiously and she assumed it was because she was a new face. They nodded politely, however, and she responded in kind.

Entering the fishmonger's establishment, she met the steady eyes of the very large Amos Granger. Were he made of bricks, he could've passed as a building on the street. "Good afternoon, Mr. Granger."

He nodded. She could tell by the way he was studying her that he was trying to place her face, and then he said. "You were the little lady with Sylvia yesterday."

"Yes, sir. I'm Eddy Carmichael, Sylvia Stewart's new cook."

"Howdy-do, Miss Carmichael. What can I do for you?"

"I'm interested in buying some of your fish."

"Bass or trout?"

"Whatever you have the most of."

"Bass." He walked over to a large wooden barrel and removed the top. Reaching in, he extracted one from the ice inside.

Eddy took it from his hand and gave the frigid fish a good sniff. He eyed her silently, and she wondered if she'd offended him. If she wanted to do business with him in the future it wouldn't do to start off on the wrong foot. "No offense, sir, but I wanted to make sure they were fresh."

"None taken. It lets me know you know what you're doing. How many do you want?"

Not real certain just how much the boarders would eat, she decided to err on the side of more than not enough. If she purchased too much, she could always make soup or chowder, although the thought of serving either in this heat made her perspire even more.

"You want me to gut and scale them?"

"No. I can do it myself."

"You sure?"

"Positive. I've been doing both most of my life."

He seemed pleased by that and put her fish in a brown bag along with a small bit of ice. "Anything else?" he asked, handing Eddy her purchase.

"Yes. Sylvia's is open to the public on Thursdays and I'd like to do a weekly fish fry. Would you have enough to supply me each week?"

He paused for a moment. "I do, but I'd have to short some of my other customers and that's not really good for business."

"I see." Eddy really wanted to do the fish fry because she knew it would be a profitable venture. She eyed the fishmonger. He looked like a man who enjoyed eating. "I understand about your other customers, but suppose, just suppose in addition to paying you for the catch, I throw in your favorite dessert. Say, twice a month. Would that be enough compensation, Mr. Granger?"

When a smile lit up his face, she knew she had a deal.

Rhine's first order of business upon returning to Virginia City from his three days visit to San Francisco was to attend the scheduled city council meeting. It was billed as an agenda meeting and therefore closed to the public. He was tired after the traveling and would've preferred resting up, but council business could be volatile at times, as different factions volleyed to put their own stamp on the city, so he had to show. Upon entering the room at the town hall he was greeted by Natalie's father.

"Welcome back, Rhine. How was the big city?"

Rhine took a seat at the table. "Thanks, Lyman. Just fine."

"Does Nat know you're back?"

"Not yet, but we're having dinner later. I'll see her then."

Lyman nodded approvingly and took his seat. The other six members, including council president Daniel Watson, greeted each other, and after a few minutes of chitchat the meeting was officially called to order. On the agenda under old business was the ongoing discussion about where to place the new cemetery. Even though mining had slowed a bit, no one wanted to place a cemetery on open land that might one day yield silver ore, so the decision was tabled once again. Other old business dealt with whether to sic the sheriff on the businesses behind on their taxes, and finding money in the budget to replace or repair a number of the nonworking gaslights along Main Street. They then moved on to new business, and Rhine didn't bother hiding his disgust with fellow councilman Clyde Swain's proposal to segregate the city's schools. Called Wally behind his back due to his corpulent body and the heavily waxed, turned up mustache that made him resemble a walrus, Swain was in Rhine's mind everything that was wrong with the present day Republican party.

"So, Swain," Rhine said, interrupting the man's bigoted soliloquy on the advantages of the plan.

"Are you proposing we build a separate school for the children you mean to displace?"

"Of course not."

"Then where are they to get their education?"

He shrugged as if not caring. "I'm sure their folks can come up with something. It's unseemly for my children to have to sit in the classroom with them. Let them build a school of their own. It's being done in other places around the country."

Natalie's father Lyman tried reasoning. "Clyde, there are only three of their children in our schools."

"All in my daughter's classroom," he tossed back angrily. "How would you like it if it were Natalie?"

"She wouldn't care, nor would her mother or I."

Wendell Barnum, Swain's brother-in-law, spoke up. "Other states are keeping Coloreds out of their schools and I think we should follow suit."

"And I don't," Rhine countered.

"Neither do I," said Patrick McFarland. McFarland was a saloon owner, too, and although he didn't openly encourage Colored patronage he didn't openly bar them either. However, being Irish, he knew how it felt to have the boot of bigotry on his neck.

Swain huffed, "I say we vote."

The six men at the table turned to council president, Daniel Watson. Watson, a reasonable man, said, "You don't have the votes, Clyde. Let's move on."

"But!"

"Let's move on. I could maybe support a look at your proposal if there were hundreds of Colored children, but not for three."

Swain's face twisted with anger and he sat back forcefully against his chair.

The next order of business was of particular interest to both Rhine and McFarland. A newly formed group of women who'd organized to rid the city of vice wanted a permit to hold a march.

McFarland asked, "Do we have to grant them a permit?"

Watson said, "Since my wife is one of the organizers, yes."

Rhine was torn between amusement and ire. The last thing any of the saloon owners wanted was a gaggle of women kneeling in prayer in front of their establishments or taking up axes in their misguided efforts to "clean up" the city.

Watson said, "They'll be marching two weeks from today. I've told my wife—any damage to buildings will get them arrested."

Rhine was thankful for that at least. It was bad enough that some of the other business owners in the city wanted to raise the taxes on the vice establishments, as the saloons, bordellos, shooting galleries, and dice palaces had come to be called. So far the council had not seen fit to put the proposals to a vote, but now he was having to deal with a bunch do-gooder ladies as well. He wasn't pleased with this newest assault on his livelihood, and hoped Natalie wouldn't be among those marching.

With nothing else pressing on the agenda, the meeting adjourned a few minutes later. Rhine ignored Swain's angry glare, said good-bye to everyone else and left the room. Although he would be meeting Natalie for dinner, the urge to see how Eddy was faring was stronger, bedeviling him since getting off the train, so instead of driving to the Union like he was supposed to do, he turned the Rockaway towards Sylvia's boardinghouse.

Eddy was out in back of Sylvia's scaling the fish she planned to serve to the boarders for dinner when Rhine Fontaine's carriage pulled up. Every effort she'd made to keep him out of mind suddenly dissolved and she fought to keep her features schooled.

When he reached her, he inclined his head politely. "Miss Carmichael."

His green eyes were even more arresting than she remembered and her heart thumped madly. "Mr. Fontaine. How are you?" she asked lightly.

"I'm well. Thought I'd stop by and see how you were getting along."

"I'm fine. Up and around as you can see. How

was San Francisco?" To maintain the distance she needed from his tempting presence, she began filleting the fish she'd already scaled.

"Good. I spent time with my brother and his wife and saw to some business matters. Are you settling in?"

"I am."

"Sylvie treating you well?"

"Yes. She's a wonderful woman." Eddy hoped he'd only stopped by to make good on his pledge to check up on her and would leave directly. "How's Mr. Dade?" she asked.

"Ornery as ever. He sends his regards."

"Please give him mine."

"I will." He watched silently as she worked. "You wield a very wicked knife, Miss Carmichael."

She chuckled in spite of herself. "Years of practice. This will be my first time feeding Sylvie's boarders. Just hoping I don't burn anything."

"I doubt that will happen."

"When you cook, anything can happen." Getting accustomed to a new stove could be tricky, and she was very nervous about how the meal would turn out, but his presence had her even more at sixes and sevens. "I really need to get this fish done."

A small smile curved his lips. "Is this your polite way of telling me to be on my way?"

"Yes."

For a moment he didn't say anything, and a silence rose thick with all that had to remain unsaid. "You have a scale on your cheek," he told her.

When he reached for it, Eddy gently backed out of range and brushed it away with a blind hand. "I'm covered with them," she added with false amusement, in yet another attempt to keep the conversation light. In truth, as much as she wanted to feel his touch, she didn't want the memory of it added to the inner turmoil she was already battling because of him.

If he was offended, he didn't show it. "Have dinner with me."

Her heart was pounding so loudly she was certain he could hear it, but she kept her wits about her. She studied him with his fine good looks and even finer clothes. "Will your fiancée be joining us?" she asked pointedly.

His head dropped.

"I had no idea you were a dishonorable man, Mr. Fontaine."

"I'm not." He added, "At least not usually."

"Then you should go home."

A long moment passed. "Eddy, I—"

"I have work to do, Rhine," she said quietly.

He looked off into the distance for a moment, then turned back and nodded tersely. "My apologies."

She watched him walk back to his carriage and

drive away. Confident she'd done the right thing, she returned to the fish.

As Rhine drove off to meet Natalie for dinner, he tried to put his finger on how he felt in the wake of Eddy's response to his invitation. *Humbled.* He'd never had a woman back away from his touch before, but then he'd never met a woman like Eddy Carmichael before. Considering how fragile and near death she'd been when he and Jim came across her in the desert, seeing her fully recovered was immensely pleasing. However, she was like a fish knife through the chest of a man's ego. She apparently didn't care that he was wealthy, charming, or that women had found him irresistible since birth. He had a fiancée, and although they hadn't talked about it directly, he knew he was the wrong race. Rhine considered himself to be a man of honor, and as one already engaged he was supposed to be leaving her alone, but something inside still refused to listen.

"So, when does the saloon go on sale?"

Rhine paused over his glass of wine and studied Natalie's hopeful eyes. He set the glass down. "Are you ready to order?" They were eating at McGuire's, one of the fanciest and most exclusive places in town. The place was crowded but he had no appetite.

She smiled at him over her menu. "Rhine, I

know that's why you went to San Francisco, so stop teasing me. When?"

He had one woman in his life that he couldn't have, and a woman he did have that he'd begun to question his future with. "Have you decided what you want to eat, Natalie?"

"Oh all right, pull my leg a bit longer."

The waiter came over. Natalie ordered the lamb and Rhine chose a steak. When the waiter thanked them and left to take their requests to the kitchen, Natalie said, "Since you're so intent upon making me wait for my surprise, I'd like you to accompany me to Vera's dress shop so I can pick out my wedding costume."

"When?"

"Sometime soon. Whenever your schedule allows."

He nodded. "I'll let you know."

"Before the end of the month, though, Rhine."

"Understood." He picked up his wineglass and wished for something much stronger.

"You're awfully solemn," she said. "I know you were keen on keeping the saloon, but selling it is for the best. You'll see."

He wanted to yell at her, but having never yelled at a woman in his life, ever, he signaled for more wine.

As he drove her home after the meal, she linked her arm with his and leaned close. "Thank you."

"You're welcome. McGuire's always has fine food."

"They do, but I'm saying thank you for selling the saloon."

He chuckled bitterly. "I'm not selling the saloon, Natalie."

She smiled. "Stop teasing."

He pulled back on the reins and halted the carriage. "Listen to me now. I didn't go to San Francisco to sell the Union. I'm not going to sell the Union."

She looked startled. "You're serious."

"Just as I've always been."

"But I want you to."

"I understand that, but I don't want to. If I sell my source of income, who's going to pay for all the hats and gowns you care so much about?"

"Papa says you're one of the richest men in the state. You have stocks and property."

"And once I go through all that providing for you, then what?"

"A man is supposed to defer to his wife," she said accusingly. "And make her happy."

"Then maybe you need to marry someone else, Natalie."

"I'm the last of my friends to become engaged, the gossips will have a field day if I call it off. Take me home please."

He set the carriage in motion. They rode the rest of the way in silence.

When they reached her house, he handed her down. "Natalie, I will marry you, care for you, and provide for you, but I will not sell my business for you."

"Let me know when you have time to accompany me to Vera's." And she walked off and left him standing by the carriage.

He waited until she was inside before driving away. He needed a drink.

Sylvia was right about there not being any food left over after dinner. Miner Gabe Horne was short and stocky. He appeared to be only a few years older than Eddy but seemed so shy he wouldn't hold her gaze more than a second or two. He ate silently but upon leaving said, "Nice to meet you, Miss Eddy. Good food. Next time, cook more, please."

The other boarder, young August Reynolds, the hotel dishwasher, was a tall, lean beanpole of a man who after eating his fill of the fish, vegetables, and biscuits, said to her, "Miss Eddy, not even the International Hotel serves food this good. Once word gets around, they're going to want to hire you."

"I'm only working for Miss Sylvia."

"Good to know because I'll enjoy coming home each evening to the way you cook."

Eddy liked the two men. However, the third boarder, Whitman Brown, was another story. He came in after the other two had gone up to their rooms. He was bright-skinned and annoying. "I'm a pretty important man around here," he announced when she placed his plate on the table in front of him. "I handle all the Colored accounts at one of the banks."

"That's nice."

"I'm also the Baptist preacher here."

"Miss Sylvie told me."

"Are you a churchgoing woman?"

"No." And after meeting him, even if she had been, she wouldn't be attending any services he conducted. She didn't care for his pompous manner. Before she could politely excuse herself, he went on to tell her about being from Cleveland, attending Howard College, and having previously worked at the Freedman's bank. She decided it would be rude to ask if he was one of the men responsible for its inept operation.

"I need to get back to the kitchen," she said finally in the middle of him telling her again about his important duties at the bank.

Later that evening, as she sat on the back porch with Sylvia drinking lemonade, she asked, "Is Mr. Brown always such a blowhard?"

"Always. And he's convinced he's better than the rest of us poor Coloreds because of his bright skin. Says his mother won't allow him to propose to anyone darker than a brown paper bag, so he's still unmarried."

After listening to his inflated opinions of himself, she didn't find that surprising. The brown paper bag test was well-known. Eddy always saw it as both shameful and ridiculous. The bigotry practiced by those outside the race was harmful enough without bigotry being meted out by those within.

After Sylvie excused herself to go inside and write a letter to her brother back East, Eddy reviewed her evening. She was pleased that her food had been so well received and that she hadn't burned anything. It would take her a little while to learn all the ins and outs on the stove, but she knew becoming completely comfortable with it would only be a matter of time. Being healed up and back on her feet made her feel good as well. She felt as if she'd been bedridden for years.

Her thoughts then turned to Rhine Fontaine. His invitation to dinner had been surprising and, yes, insulting, if she were being truthful. Did he believe she thought so little of herself that she'd keep time with a man engaged to be married? She supposed with his looks and money some women might have jumped at the chance to take him up on the offer, but she was not one of them. Did he often dally with women outside his race? Was he one of those men who slaked their lust with women of color but treated their own women like fragile regal queens? Was that why he proposed what he had? Eddy doubted she'd ever get answers to the questions, but decided she was okay with the not knowing. Her new life didn't include him anyway.

Still in need of that drink, Rhine threaded his way through the Union's evening crowd. Behind the bar his young bartender, Kenton "Kent" Randolph, looked up from the drink he was pouring for his father, Dr. Oliver Randolph, and smiled. "Evenin', Rhine. Where've you been?" Kent asked.

Rhine could barely hear him over the noise.

"Took Natalie to dinner." And had his ego filleted by one Eddy Carmichael. Rhine went behind the bar and took down a bottle of bourbon. As he treated himself to a healthy portion, he glanced curiously between father and son. The Randolph men were so estranged these days, he was surprised they weren't shouting at each other, which was their usual means of conversing. "How are you, Doc?" Rhine asked.

"Doing just fine, Rhine. You boys ready to get whipped on Friday?"

The doctor was referring to the annual baseball game between the Colored Republicans and the Whites. His teasing added another barb to an already trying day. "How about letting us play with fifteen men?" Rhine asked.

Kenton laughed. "Your side could play with thirty and we'd still whip you."

Doc chuckled, raised his glass of gin, and drifted off into the crowd.

Rhine asked Kent, "You two make peace?"

Kent put the top back on his father's favorite gin. "Hell, no. He's a customer. I'm the barkeep. As long as he's not telling me how to handle my life, I don't have to tell him to mind his own business."

An amused Rhine thought that made sense. Kent was eighteen. His father wanted him to go back East to medical school so Kent could take over his clients once he retired. All Kent wanted was to be a rancher. They'd been arguing over the matter for the past six months. Rhine was friends with them both so he stayed out it. "I'm heading up to my office. Anything I need to know?"

"Edgar Carter wants to rent the place in a few weeks to celebrate him and his wife's thirty years of marriage. I told him I'd talk to you and let him know."

Edgar was the barber who cut Micah and Christian's hair. Rhine made a note to ride over to the orphanage to see how the twins had been behaving while he was away. "Does Edgar have a date in mind?" The Union Saloon also served as a social hall for the city's Colored community, being the only venue in Virginia City they were allowed to use for such celebratory purposes.

"I wrote it down. It's on your desk."

"Okay, as long as there's nothing else going on, I don't see why he can't."

"I told him that, too."

Rhine saluted him with his glass and headed to the kitchen.

Jim Dade looked up from the pots he was washing at the large sink. "How was dinner?"

"Long. Why did I propose to Natalie?"

Jim stopped, gave him a look, and went back to the pots. "I asked you that question six months ago."

Rhine sighed. "I'm hoping she breaks things off before I lose my mind and have to be sold to the circus."

Jim laughed softly.

"It's not funny."

"Sure it is. Sometimes you can be brilliant as\ the sun—like having us install the new gas-lighting—and other times you're dumber than the bacon in the cold box, like proposing to her."

Rhine saw no sense in arguing with the truth, so he took a draw from his glass instead. "And I saw Eddy today."

"How is our little lady?"

"Doing well. She sends her regards. I asked her to have dinner with me."

Jim spun. "What?"

Rhine tried to explain himself. "It wasn't something I planned to do. One minute I was talking to her and the next minute . . . God, Jim she's so beautiful. Tough as nails, too."

"So what did she say?" Jim asked pointedly.

"Asked me if I was inviting Natalie along with us."

Jim laughed so loud the walls rang. When he recovered he tossed out, "Cut you off at the knees, hey pretty boy?"

"Yes, and she didn't even need to use the fish knife she had in her hand."

"I knew I liked her." He then turned serious. "You know she's not for you."

"I do."

"Then let her be."

"I'm trying."

"Try harder. She's a nice girl, Rhine. Don't mess things up for her here."

Rhine sighed aloud in frustration and regret.

"Unless you're going to toss Natalie aside and tell Eddy who you really are."

Rhine saw the seriousness in his partner's gaze. Outside of his siblings, Jim was the only person who knew his true heritage.

When he didn't respond, Jim said, "Then go get drunk."

Rhine toasted him with the glass. "Thanks. I think I will."

Chapter Eight

SYLVIA'S DINING ROOM would be opening to the public that evening, so Eddy began preparations before dawn. There were cakes to make and chickens to pluck. She peeled potatoes and shucked corn and sat outside with a bowl in her lap and shelled peas. By the time she took the cornbread out of the oven just before the diners arrived, she was more tired than she'd imagined she'd be. Luckily, she didn't have to serve, too. Sylvia had hired help for that, a Paiute woman named Maria Valdez and her adolescent sons, Jonas and Wilson. The Indian family was both friendly and efficient.

The number of diners was small, but like the boarders, must have found the food very much to their liking because Maria kept coming into the kitchen for more servings. At one point Eddy told her, "This is the very last piece of cornbread, Maria."

"Mr. Granger the fishmonger isn't going to be happy, but I'll let him know."

Sylvia came in while Eddy was slicing the last cake. "Eddy, honey. The people want to meet you."

Eddy glanced down at the food-stained apron covering her skirt and blouse.

Sylvia wouldn't let her beg off. "Just come. It'll only be for a minute or two."

Giving her hands a quick rinse under the tap, Eddy stepped out into the dining room. Boisterous applause greeted her entrance, which filled her with both embarrassment and appreciation. Carpenter Zeke Reynolds was among them and she sent him a shy smile. Then one by one the diners introduced themselves, telling her how much they enjoyed the food and welcoming her to Virginia City. She already knew Mr. Granger and Zeke, but she didn't know the others and hoped she'd remember their names. She would, however, remember this special evening and how they made her feel. They promised to spread the word about her great cooking and that they'd be back on Sunday with friends.

As people paid their bills and departed, Eddy began clearing the tables. Zeke walked over to her. "I may have to marry you, little lady. Your food was outstanding."

Eddy laughed. "Is that the only qualification you're looking for in a wife, Mr. Reynolds?"

"Call me Zeke."

She nodded. "Okay, Zeke. Is it?"

"Hmm. Let's see, good cook, beautiful, well spoken, likes baseball."

Eddy chuckled. He was indeed a charmer. "I need to get back to work."

"I understand." But for a moment he simply

stood there, his interest in her on full display. "I'll see you at the big game."

"I'm looking forward to it."

Basking in her triumphant first outing and brimming with happiness over the nice encounter with Zeke, she joined Maria and her sons in the kitchen for the cleanup. When all the dishes and pots were put in their places, they went home. Maria did the housekeeping so she'd be back in the morning.

On the heels of their departure a smiling Sylvia breezed into the kitchen. "You made the house quite a bit of money this evening, Eddy Carmichael."

"Glad to hear it."

"And the food was delicious. My old cook was good but he can't hold a candle to you."

It had been a long time since Eddy had been praised for anything, and she hadn't realized how much she'd been craving a kind word until then. "I enjoyed myself."

"So did the men, especially Zeke. I saw him talking to you."

"He's nice."

"That he is. Did I mention he was unattached?"

Eddy laughed. "Yes, Sylvie, you did."

"I wasn't sure. Now, did you get a chance to eat?"

"Yes, ma'am, I did."

"Then go on up to your room and get some rest, you've earned it."

"I'm going to get the kitchen ready for breakfast in the morning and then go up."

"Okay. So pleased to have you here, honey."

"Thank you."

"After breakfast in the morning, I'm going to visit the orphanage to talk to Sister Mary about fund-raising. Would you like to come along?"

"I would."

Sylvia nodded and left Eddy alone. Still buoyed by her success, she stepped outside into the fresh air and drew in a deep breath. She'd start her preparations for breakfast in a moment. Off to the west the sun was slowly sliding towards the horizon, tinting the sky with the reds and grays of evening. After all she'd been through in the past few weeks, she finally felt like her world had settled. She had a nice place to live, a landlady she adored, and most importantly she was earning a wage with her cooking. Now all she had to do was save up enough to restart her journey to California. Meeting Zeke was also something positive. Even though she had no plans to stay in Virginia City, it might be nice to spend time with a gentleman whose interest was more easily encouraged than Rhine Fontaine's. The thought instantly brought the face of the handsome saloon owner to mind. Determined not to dwell on him, she went back inside and began the preparations for breakfast.

• • •

Friday morning, after breakfast with Jim, Rhine drove to the orphanage. He hadn't visited since returning from San Francisco and he wanted to see how his favorite set of twins were doing. As soon as he parked they tore down the front steps to greet him.

"Miss Mary has some crates at the freight office," Christian told him excitedly. "She said it's okay if we ride with you to go get them. Can we go?"

The earnest plea on his face made Rhine chuckle. "Why aren't you in school today?"

Micah explained. "Mr. Reinhart is sick so there's nobody to teach us."

Reinhart was the school's only teacher. "How about I go in and speak with Miss Mary first. I don't want to find out later that you're pulling my leg."

Micah looked surprised. "We wouldn't do that."

Rhine was fairly sure the boy was right, but who would've thought he and his brother would pay a visit to Lady Ruby's chicken coop in the middle of the night? "Are you off punishment now?" he asked as they accompanied him up the steps.

"Yes," Christian replied proudly. "We get dessert today."

"Congratulations."

"But Miss Willa Grace went to visit her sister, so we have to wait until she gets back."

Rhine found Mary in her large book-lined office and she corroborated the boys' story about the crates. "The orphanage has been adopted by a Methodist church in Sacramento and the crate contains donations of some kind. I'd really appreciate it if you'd pick it up and bring it back."

"Is it okay if the twins go, too?"

"Please. Mr. Reinhart's been ill since the day you left for San Francisco, and with Willa Grace away, I'm at my wit's end trying to keep up with them."

"No pranks?"

"None."

"That's good to hear."

"The day's still young, Mr. Fontaine. I'm taking them to see Vera at ten for fittings."

He laughed and left the office to collect the twins.

"When was the orphanage founded?" Eddy asked as Sylvia drove them through the streets to the orphanage.

"About three years ago." She went on to tell Eddy about Mary's battle with her Order.

"I like Mary already," Eddy said. "Standing up to bigotry is an admirable thing."

"Yes it is. It's my understanding that the Mother Superior was very surprised by her challenge though."

"I'm surprised, too. I always assumed nuns to be meek little things."

"Not the nuns that taught me back home in Baltimore."

"You were taught by nuns?"

"Yes, at St. Francis Academy. It was founded by a woman from Haiti named Mother Elizabeth Lange. She started the Oblate Sisters of Providence, the first order of Black Catholic nuns in the country."

"I've never heard of her."

"Many people haven't but she's dedicated her life to serving young people enslaved, free, immigrant, and poor. The sisters at St. Francis gave me an excellent education, so I help out at the orphanage in their honor."

As Eddy and Sylvia climbed the mansion's steps, Eddy was surprised at the size of the place.

"It used to belong to one of the mining kings," Sylvie explained.

The door chime was answered by a young girl Sylvie introduced to Eddy as Susannah Bird.

"Pleased to meet you, Susannah."

"Pleased to meet you as well, Miss Carmichael. I'll get Miss Mary."

When Mary arrived, she ushered them into her office. The reason for the visit was to discuss the orphanage's ongoing need for funds. Although there were only four children currently in residence, they had to be fed and clothed and the mansion had to be maintained. The women discussed selling dinners and having a charity baseball game.

After listening quietly for a few moments, Eddy asked, "Have you ever considered having a services auction?"

Mary and Sylvia turned, their faces curious. "Explain that, please," Mary asked.

"Let's say Miss Vera asks for bids on having a gown made. Zeke Reynolds might offer carpentry work. Maybe Mr. Granger could put up a mess of fish, or I could offer to make a fancy meal."

Sylvia's face brightened. "What a great idea. Edgar could offer haircuts. I could have people bid on a Sunday dinner—which you would cook of course, Eddy."

Eddy chuckled, "Of course."

Mary eyed Eddy appreciatively. "Have you worked on an event like this before?"

"No, but the hotel where I worked in Denver hosted something similar. The sponsoring group was raising money for a hospital."

Mary asked, "I think people here would enjoy this. Do you have time to be in charge?"

Eddy looked to her employer. After all, this might take time away from her job. Upon receiving an enthusiastic nod, the planning began.

Using a dolly he borrowed from the freight office, Rhine, accompanied by the twins, managed to haul the large crate up the mansion's steps to the front door. He didn't know what was inside, but it was extremely heavy and he hoped the contents were worth the effort. Mopping the perspiration from his brow, he waited for the door chime to be answered. Susannah appeared and backed up so he could maneuver the dolly inside. The twins followed.

"My goodness!" Mary exclaimed upon coming out of her office and seeing the huge wooden crate.

Rhine opened his mouth to respond but the words died in his throat when he saw Eddy standing there with Sylvie. Caught off guard yet pleasantly surprised, he fought to keep his tone neutral. "I didn't know you ladies were here. Good morning."

"Morning to you, too, Rhine," Sylvie said.

"Hello, Mr. Fontaine," Eddy responded.

"Miss Carmichael."

Vowing to be on his best behavior and not make a fool of himself like he had he last time they were together, he reluctantly but smoothly moved his attention from her and over to Mary and Sylvie inspecting the mail stamps on the crate.

Mary said, "I wonder what could be inside?"

Rhine turned to the twins. "Micah, would you and Christian go look through the toolbox Mr. Zeke uses when he's here and see if there's a crowbar inside?"

Eager to help, they took off at a run, only to have Rhine, Mary, and Sylvie call out in unison, "Walk!"

They slowed and Rhine savored Eddy's responding smile. Forcing himself to look away and concentrate on maneuvering the crate off the dolly, he wondered if this was her first visit. Sylvia was a staunch supporter of Mary's efforts. Had she convinced Eddy to become involved as well? He spent a great deal of time at the orphanage. If she planned to do the same, his efforts to ignore her allure were going to be even more difficult.

"Rhine," Sylvie said, "Eddy has come up with a fine plan for this year's fund-raiser."

"What is it?" he asked after thanking the twins with a nod and taking the crowbar in hand. While Sylvie explained, he began prying the crate open.

When she finished, he was impressed with the novel idea. "I agree that it's a fine plan, and if you need any help, Miss Carmichael, I'm at your service."

"Thank you. I'll keep that in mind."

They were interrupted by the ring of the door pull. Susannah, who'd been standing with Lin and watching him work on the crate, hurried to the door. She returned with Doc Randolph.

"Oh, good, Sylvie. You're here," the doctor said, sounding relieved. "Jed Pentwater said Amelia's baby's on the way and they need you."

"Okay."

"Do you have your bag?"

"No, Oliver. Midwives always leave their bags at home."

His jaw tensed and his eyes flashed.

"I don't care if you're offended. I'm offended that you asked such a silly question after knowing me all these years." She turned to Rhine. "Will you make sure Eddy gets back?"

"Of course." Seeing Eddy open her mouth to undoubtedly protest the arrangements, he smiled inwardly, but Sylvie was already on her way to the door with the grumbling Doc Randolph. Eddy shot him one of her now familiar exasperated glares. He dearly wanted to tell her just how much he enjoyed being on the receiving end of those glares of hers, but he was supposed to be behaving himself so he said nothing.

The crate held lots and lots of mismatched dishes and even more pots and pans—all packed in a mound of sawdust that spilled everywhere when Mary and Eddy began the unloading. In addition to the pots and pans and tableware, there was a lovely cut-glass punch bowl along with matching cups and dessert plates.

"This is beautiful," Mary said in an awed whisper. The twins were skating on the dust as if it were ice. Mary viewed them with an amused shake of her head, then checked the small timepiece pinned to her blouse. "The children and

I are due at Vera's shortly. The rest of this unpacking will have to wait until later."

"I can finish the unpacking if you don't mind me staying," Eddy said to her. "I just need to know where everything goes. I'll wash the things first before putting them away of course."

"I'm never one to look a gift horse in the mouth, so thank you for the kind offer. Rhine, are you free to stay and help her?"

"I am. If we finish before you return, I'll lock up as well."

The look Eddy shot him almost made him burst out laughing but he kept his features even.

"Thank you, Rhine," Mary said. "Eddy, it's been a pleasure meeting you and I'm looking forward to working with you on our auction. The kitchen cabinets are fairly bare so you should have no trouble finding places to put the dishes."

"Okay. It's been a pleasure meeting you as well. I'll see you soon."

Once Mary and the children were gone, silence settled over the interior. Eddy looked at Rhine. He looked at her and said, "The last time we were together I put you in an uncomfortable position by asking you to have dinner with me. I'd like to apologize and hope you'll forgive me."

Eddy had to admit she hadn't been happy with the inappropriate invitation, even if a part of her wished she'd been the type of woman who would've said yes. "Thank you for that." There was a sincerity in him that spoke to her. "Let's agree to forget about it and go forward."

"Thank you. I felt like an ass afterwards."

"Good."

He laughed, and then a seriousness came over him that seemed so intense she wondered what he would say next. "And if I had no fiancée? Or is that too inappropriate as well?"

"No. I've asked myself the same question."

"You have?"

"Yes. Rhine, we both know something's in the air between us, so we may as well be adults about it, but there are other barriers as well. Barriers some have lost their lives trying to get around."

"I know."

She chose her words carefully. "I value myself too highly to be any man's mistress, so marriage would have to be a given, and we would have to love each other so deeply that the barriers wouldn't matter, but your engagement makes this conversation moot so let's get to work on this crate, okay?"

He studied her for a few long moments and then nodded in agreement.

By noon they were done with the washing and the putting away of the donated items. The sawdust had been swept up and the now-empty crate taken outside. As promised, he drove her back to the boardinghouse, and when they reached it, she said, "Thanks for your help."

"My pleasure."

Even though they hadn't revisited their conversation, Eddy could feel it hanging between them like something alive. "Do you visit the orphanage often?"

"Usually two or three days a week. I have a soft spot for Mary and the twins."

"The twins look to be a handful."

"That they are. Sounds like you may be there quite a bit, too, what with the auction and all."

"I probably will. I'm looking forward to it though. You should think about what you might want to put up for bid."

"I'll do that."

She opened the door and he made move to come around and help her down, but she shook her head. "I appreciate the gesture but I can get down by myself."

He sighed and looked off into the distance. When he turned back to her, he said, "My being a gentleman around you isn't moot, Eddy."

"I appreciate that and I meant no offense. I'm just not accustomed to being fussed over."

"Understood." He paused for a moment and then said, "Thanks for your honesty back there—about us."

"You're welcome. It needed to be said, don't you think?"

"I do."

Eddy was sure her attraction to him wouldn't evaporate overnight but hoped their talk would help spur the process along. She ignored the parts of herself that clung to tiny shoots of hope. "If Sylvie gets back in time, we're supposed to be going to the big baseball game. Are you playing?"

"I am, but I wouldn't call it playing. What my team does best is called losing."

She laughed. "Maybe you'll get lucky this time around."

"Only if the other side doesn't show up."

She stepped down to the walk and closed the carriage door. "I'll see you there."

"Good-bye, Eddy."

" 'Bye, Rhine."

He drove away and a thoughtful Eddy went inside. She had no regrets about anything she'd said and felt better after having shed light on something they really needed to come to terms with.

Sylvie returned by early afternoon and Eddy was glad to see her.

"How'd the birth go? Everything okay?"

"Yes. This was the Pentwater's fourth child and the baby had already made its debut by the time I arrived. Mother and child are doing fine."

"Good."

"Everything turn out okay at the orphanage?"

"Yes, and Mr. Fontaine brought me back here. Do you still want to go to the baseball game?"

"Of course. Would you make us some sandwiches to take along?"

"I'd love to."

・ ・ ・

Later that evening, Sylvie and Eddy loaded their provisions in the wagon bed and set out for the game. Eddy was looking forward to the outing, and to seeing Zeke Reynolds again now that she'd settled things with Rhine. "Where is the game held?"

"In a field out by the cemetery."

"Is it usually well attended?"

"Oh, yes, the entire town comes out. It's quite an event. Of course our side always wins but it's still a lot of fun."

Sylvie was right about the number of people. The field where they parked was filled with buggies and carriages and wagons. There were people of all races and ages, walking and carrying quilts and baskets. Well-dressed White women wearing straw hats were escorted by men in suits and bowlers. Little children ran here and there, as did a few dogs. She spied Colored couples making their way, and like their White counterparts, the men were in suits and the women wore straw boaters, too. Eddy, who had no hat, hoped her plain blouse and skirt didn't make her appear too shabby, but she had no money for special clothes. She was still bent on California. Every extra penny went into her savings.

Sylvie carried the basket while Eddy grabbed the quilts, and they set out for the field. It was a short walk and once they arrived they went to their side. The White Republicans and their supporters were on the other. Sylvie seemed to know everyone and their progress was halted more than once by greetings and Sylvie introducing Eddy to people she wanted her to meet. The Black Republicans were on the field warming up. Jim Dade was at home plate hitting the ball into the outfield while his fellows scurried to catch it or chase it down. She was glad to see him. She spotted Zeke speaking with Sylvie's beanpole boarder, his cousin August, and Doc Randolph along the sideline. Seeing her, Zeke waved. Smiling and pleased by the recognition, she waved back. Eddy couldn't remember the last time she'd attended such an event. The air was full of excitement and she looked forward to the fun. Over on the other side, she spotted Rhine talking with a group of people. Beside him stood an extremely beautiful dark-haired, young woman. As if sensing Eddy, he turned and met her eyes across the divide. He sent her an almost imperceptible nod before going back to his friends.

"That's Rhine's fiancée he's standing with," Sylvie pointed out.

"She's very pretty."

"Only on the outside."

Surprised by that, Eddy turned her way and Sylvie added, "Natalie Greer is as spoiled as a pan of milk set out in the sun. I still can't believe she's his choice for a wife."

Eddy glanced over again, taking in the woman's fashionable attire. At least she now knew what the fiancée looked like. She found it hard to fathom Rhine being with someone like that, but then maybe he saw something in his fiancée others did not. As Zeke, Jim, and the Black Republicans took the field, she put all thoughts of Rhine and his fiancée aside and joined the applause.

The White Republicans were trounced. Their team, made up of businessmen and bankers, were less fit than the carpenters, bricklayers, and day laborers fielded by their opponents. As the winners celebrated the ten-to-nothing victory and shook hands with the losers, a grinning Doc Randolph raised a bronze bust of President Lincoln high overhead while his side of the field cheered loud enough to be heard back in Denver. "Why's he holding up that bust?" Eddy asked.

"That's the trophy," the applauding Sylvie explained. "The winning team gets to display it until next year's game. Doc says he's going to have Zeke build a permanent display for it in his home because the bust will never reside anywhere else."

As the gathering ended and people began heading home, something made Eddy glance up, and there stood Rhine among a group of people. It was her turn to offer the slight nod. He returned the greeting and Eddy hurried off to catch up with Sylvie.

Chapter Nine

OVER THE NEXT two weeks, Eddy settled into a routine. She got up at four o'clock every morning to prepare breakfast for her two favorite boarders, Gabe Horne and August Williams, and at eight silently served what was left to the oh so important Whitman Brown. True to their promises, the dining room patrons began spreading the word about her great cooking, and more and more people began showing up on Tuesdays, Thursdays, and Sundays. She was delighted with the positive response and how nice everyone was to her. Zeke was eating there on a regular basis as well, but he respectfully maintained his distance, as if he didn't want to disturb her while she was working, and as if he was trying to gather his courage to approach her about seeing her outside of the dining room. The orphanage fund-raiser plans were moving forward, they'd set the date for next month and the auction would be held at the mansion. She'd bumped into Rhine a few times at the orphanage and although they both recognized that what lay between them had not dissipated, they chose not to acknowledge it or speak about it and that suited Eddy just fine.

"A couple of the men have asked if you have a sweetheart," Sylvia said one evening. Vera was in the kitchen as well. The seamstress often ate her evening meal with Sylvia and Eddy.

Eddy, washing dishes, found that amusing. "I hope you told them no, and that I'm not going to be around Virginia City long enough to encourage one."

"Now, now. Don't be too hasty. Zeke's becoming a regular. You never know."

Vera said, "I've seen the way he looks at you, but we must get you better clothing, my dear. You've been wearing that same skirt since you arrived."

Not enjoying having her poverty pointed out, her chin rose. "It's the only one I have."

"Then we need to fix that."

"I don't have money to waste on frills."

"Who said anything about you paying, and having more than one skirt isn't considered frivolous. You're representing Sylvie in that dining room and you need to be better dressed."

Keeping a lid on her temper, Eddy looked over at Sylvie, who, glaring at her friend, said, "Forgive her, Eddy. Vera sometimes doesn't think before she speaks."

Instantly contrite, Vera dropped her head and sighed. "I'm sorry, Eddy. Sylvia's right. I just want you to have the respect you deserve. Everyone's talking about your great cooking."

"And that's all I need them to talk about." She dried the last dish and walked out of the kitchen door. She'd always had a temper, and rather than treat Vera to a piece of it she took a seat outside. She didn't need reminding about her meager wardrobe. Every morning when she got out of bed and had to don the same skirt and blouse she'd washed out the night before, she told herself it didn't matter, but it did. Before the death of her parents, her father had provided well for his family. There hadn't been money to waste on luxurious things, but she'd had nice gloves and shoes to wear on special occasions. There'd been books and oranges for Christmas. The only nice thing she still possessed was her mother's locket. Sylvia paid well, but Eddy still had to use some of it for her room and board, and as she'd noted before, every extra penny went into her California fund.

When she went back inside the kitchen, Sylvie and Vera were no longer there, so she began putting together the dry ingredients for the morning's biscuits.

"Eddy?"

She turned to see Vera in the doorway. "Yes?" Her voice was cool.

"I came in to offer my sincerest apologies for hurting your feelings. As Sylvie said, I don't think sometimes, but I truly would like for us to be friends. Can you forgive me?"

Although Eddy had a temper, she wasn't one to hold a grudge, and Vera did appear sincere. "You're forgiven."

"Thank you. I would like to propose something, and I want you to hear me out."

Eddy waited.

"When I visited San Francisco a few weeks back there was a seamstress shop that provided little tea cakes and candies to its customers while they waited for their fittings. Although I am the leading seamstress in Virginia City, I'd like to up the ante a bit, just to keep the competition on their heels. Would you have the time to make me tea cakes maybe once or twice a week? I'd pay you of course, but I'd also like to pay you by making you a few skirts and blouses."

Eddy scanned her face. It was very apparent that Vera was trying to broach that last part as delicately as possible. Eddy had her pride, but she wasn't a fool. She was as tired of wearing her well-worn skirt and blouse as Vera was of seeing her in them, so she smiled. "I'd love to. How many cakes do you think you'll be needing?"

Rhine spent his evening at the city council meeting. This one was open to the public and it had been a boisterous one. The proposal to implement the vice tax came up for a vote. Natalie's father Lyman cast the deciding tie-breaking vote that sent the proposal down to defeat, thus giving victory to men like Rhine, McFadden, and the other saloon owners. A round of shouting, threats, and fist shaking from the measure's supporters followed, but it didn't change anything. After the meeting adjourned, Rhine was glad to return to the noisy but less angry confines of his saloon.

Kent nodded a greeting as Rhine approached. "How'd the meeting go?"

"We're still in business, that's all I can say. What are we serving tonight?"

"Lamb. Jim's in the kitchen. Wants to talk to you."

The hungry Rhine nodded and headed for the kitchen. He found Jim inside peeling and slicing potatoes for the Saratoga chips the customers were so fond of.

"Evening, Jim. Kent said you wanted to talk to me?"

"Yes. We have to change the Thursday menu."

"Why?"

"Fishmonger Granger's promised his entire Thursday catch to little Miss Eddy, so no more fish fry for us on that night."

Rhine was confused. "What? Why?"

"Because she's serving fish on Thursdays now, too, and folks are buzzing about her food like bees on flowers."

Surprise replaced the confusion. "Is that the reason we've been low on attendance the last two weeks?"

"That would be my guess."

So the beauty was not only haunting the edges of his mind, she was costing him customers.

Jim added, "Not sure if there's a way to change Granger's mind, but in the meantime I'll switch to quail or chicken for Thursdays, unless the farmers have promised her all those, too."

"Let's hope not. Anything else?"

"No. That's it."

"Okay. Is there something I can eat?"

Jim dished him up a plate of lamb, potatoes, and carrots from the pots on the stove and Rhine took it up to his office.

While eating, he pulled out his ledgers. Poring over the numbers of the past two weeks, he saw that the Union's profits were down about three percent. It wasn't a number that would make him close the doors but it was enough to make him wonder just what Eddy was cooking over at Sylvia's. He'd seen her a few times at the orphanage, and when he did, he was respectful and did his best not to dwell on her admission that she'd asked herself what might happen between them had he not been engaged. She surprised him with how blunt and direct she'd been that day, but then again, she'd been surprising him since the day she woke up in his bed and stubbornly tried to make it to the washroom under her own power, even though the desert had left her with none. It wouldn't be long before the men were lining up to eat at Sylvia's just to catch a glimpse of her, if they weren't already, and he was honest enough to admit that bothered him far more than the cut in his profit, because the attraction between them still lingered. He felt it and sensed she did, too, but it had to remain unrealized because he'd already chosen Natalie. He'd had dinner with her and her parents before the city council meeting and promised to escort her to Vera Ford's seamstress shop in the morning to view pictures of wedding costumes. He wasn't looking forward to it but she was his fiancée and it was what she wanted, so he'd go along and smile. It made no sense to be pining for Eddy because, as she said, the subject was moot. He just wished he knew how to make the pining stop.

The following morning, as Eddy stood in one of the nicely decorated back rooms of Vera's shop with her arms outstretched, she felt like a scarecrow as Vera's assistant, an Irishwoman named Shanna McKay, used her tapes to take Eddy's measurements. First had come ankles to waist, then waist to shoulders, followed by across her back, shoulders, and bosom. Once that was accomplished, soft cotton fabric was laid against her chest and she was told, "Just trying to get a look at what blouse material we want to use."

"Something sturdier than this. It needs to hold up to my day."

Shanna replaced it with another sample. "If you had your way, you'd be wearing denim from head to toe. Don't you want to look nice?"

"I'm a cook, Shanna. Nothing looks nice adorned with food stains."

"Miss Vera said she wants you to look like a lady of means."

"Well since I'm not, I'd prefer something practical."

Vera entered on the heels of that. "Is she giving you a hard time, Shanna?"

"Not really."

"Which means of course she is."

Eddy smiled. "I need practical wear, Miss Vera. Gravy stains are hard to wash out."

"Understood, dear, so let's do practical and pretty. You might want to go walking with Zeke or another gentleman at some point, and you'll be glad to have something nice."

Eddy concurred but in reality thought she'd do more walking back and forth to the market than anywhere else. She was glad when Shanna finally put away the tapes and then heard, "Come back tomorrow, Eddy. I should have the fabrics cut out and we can do some fittings. We don't want her looking like she's wearing a potato sack, do we Miss Vera?"

"Certainly not."

Eddy sighed. "I'll come by after breakfast."

"Good. Now let me get back to my other

customers, who are, by the way, Rhine Fontaine and his fiancée Natalie Greer."

"Ah." Eddy didn't want to see him with his fiancée, but since there was no way around it, she left the fitting room and walked out into the shop's main room. Her plan was to acknowledge them and quickly be on her way, but fate had other plans.

"Miss Carmichael?"

Eddy looked up into those emerald green eyes and silently chastised herself for still finding them and him so mesmerizing. "Mr. Fontaine."

"It's a pleasure to see you again."

Eddy offered an almost imperceptible nod. She'd seen him at the orphanage a few days ago.

"Miss Carmichael, my fiancée Miss Greer."

"Pleased to meet you," Eddy said.

The woman smiled falsely but gave no verbal reply. Vera's face took on a distinct coolness in response to the obvious slight, but Eddy let the rudeness roll off her back. Women like Greer thought it beneath them to exchange pleasantries with women like her, and it wasn't as if it was the first time Eddy had encountered the attitude.

Fontaine appeared perturbed as well before turning his attention back to Eddy. "Your cooking skills are causing such a stir my customers are deserting me."

"Just earning my wage, Mr. Fontaine."

His eyes never leaving Eddy's, he told his fiancée, "Miss Carmichael is the woman Jim and

I rescued in the desert. She's also spearheading this year's fund-raiser for Mary's orphanage."

Greer offered nothing in response.

Needing to distance herself from all that he was and the tiny shoots of hope that refused to die, Eddy said, "I have to get back to Miss Sylvia's and start dinner. I can't steal more of your customers if there's nothing for them to eat."

He chuckled, and his smile made the shoots inch higher. To save herself, she turned to the fiancée and employing the good manners the woman obviously lacked, said, "A pleasure meeting you, Miss Greer."

The blue eyes flashed dismissively, and Vera's jaw tightened in reaction.

Head held high, Eddy walked to the door. "Good-bye, Miss Vera, and thank you."

"You're welcome, honey."

"Miss Carmichael?" Fontaine called gently.

Eddy turned back.

"My apologies."

Eddy realized he was apologizing for his fiancée's lack of grace, and she found that so endearing there were no words. A quick glance at Miss Greer showed her red-faced. Whether it was from anger or embarrassment, Eddy didn't know or care. "Thank you," she replied softly.

"You're welcome."

With that, she pulled open the door and stepped out into the sunshine.

• • •

On the drive back to the Greer home, Natalie said, "Thank you for embarrassing me."

"I was about to tell you the same thing."

"I shouldn't have to converse with a woman like her."

"Is that why you were so rude?" A big part of Natalie's problem was that her parents had never pointed out unbecoming behavior, so if they were to be married, it was left to him. "I'm a Republican and after we marry, more than likely we'll be entertaining people of color in our home. You'll be expected to be polite. Do you think you can do that?"

"Why, you're genuinely upset with me," she said, sounding surprised. "She's just a Colored cook, Rhine. I don't have to converse with Coloreds or servants."

"She's a human being, Natalie—just like we are."

She blew out a breath. "Oh all right. I doubt I'll ever see her again, but if I do, I'll try and remember that."

"Thank you."

"Although I still don't see why," she pouted, and hooked her arm into his as he held the reins. "It's not like she means anything to either of us."

Rhine was silent for the rest of the drive.

Rhine had agreed to have lunch with her and her mother. Out of disapproval with her rudeness, he would have preferred to drop her at the door and go on about his day, but when they reached her home, he stopped the buggy, came around and handed her down. "Are you still upset?" she asked, looking into his eyes.

"No."

"Your eyes say something different."

"Let's go in. We don't want to keep your mother waiting."

Inside the spacious mansion, they handed their hats and gloves to the Chinese houseman and Natalie led Rhine into the dining room where her mother Beatrice sat waiting.

He walked over and kissed her cheek. "Good afternoon, Mrs. Greer."

"Hello, Rhine. You survived the dress shop, I see."

"I did," he said distantly. After helping Natalie with her chair he took a seat.

Natalie said, "He's upset."

Beatrice, dressed in the finery befitting her station, looked between the two. "What happened?"

Natalie blew out a breath. "I didn't speak to a little Colored cook at the dress shop, and he says I embarrassed him."

Conversation stopped as the Chinese maid brought in their soup. Rhine nodded his thanks to the woman, and after she exited, he explained, "I reminded Natalie that once we marry we'll be opening our home to people like

Miss Carmichael and that rudeness didn't become her."

"He's right of course, Natalie."

Natalie started in on her soup. "Having them in our home will be something I can't avoid, but I don't see why I have to acknowledge them publicly."

Rhine tried to mask his annoyance but apparently failed.

"I'm simply being honest," she said in defense. "I understand that you have a misguided fascination with them, and I'm willing to overlook it, but you should be just as tolerant of my *lack* of fascination."

Rhine reminded himself that she was only twenty years old and that she'd led a sheltered, privileged life. That she didn't seem to be bothered by her lack of charity didn't sit well, however.

Her mother said, "Natalie, your father and I were staunch abolitionists, as were your grandparents. They even entertained the great Frederick Douglass himself, so I'm not sure where this stance of yours is rooted."

"It's rooted in my ability to form my own opinions, Mother."

Beatrice must've seen the flash of disdain in Rhine's eyes and added hastily, "An opinion I'm sure you'll amend once you think long and hard about it."

"We'll see, but in the meantime this entire

tempest in a teacup has given me a headache. I'm going to up my room and lie down." She pushed back from the table and stood. "Rhine darling, I'll see you later."

He stood politely and watched her go.

When he retook his seat, Beatrice said, "I wouldn't put much stock in this so called opinion of hers, Rhine. She has abolitionism in her blood. She'll come to her senses."

Because of her beauty, he thought she might be the wife for him and the mother of any children he might sire. Admittedly, his own shallowness caused him to use that as a standard and overlook Natalie's lack of interest in anything but herself. She was stunning to look at—what more did he need? Now, he knew better and had no one to blame but himself. She didn't read the newspapers, had no knowledge of national or world affairs, and after witnessing today's rude behavior and listening to her attempt to justify it, he had more trouble seeing himself married to her. "Natalie and I may not be evenly yoked, Mrs. Greer."

"Oh don't be silly. As I said, she'll come to her senses. I'll have her father speak to her. By tomorrow this little matter will be water over the dam. You'll see."

"I'm not so sure. She's been pressuring me to sell the saloon."

"Honestly, I can see why she's uncomfortable

with your ownership, and it might help if you reconsidered her reasons. People have been whispering about your place since the day the doors opened. No wife wants to be the subject of gossips."

Rhine offered a bitter chuckle. "Then maybe I should cry off, because I'm not selling the Union."

She stiffened in reaction.

Rhine stood and inclined his head. "Thank you for the meal, Mrs. Greer. Now, if you'll excuse me." He made his exit.

"Rhine!"

He didn't look back.

On the drive to the saloon an irritated Rhine thought about the many reasons he refused to sell the Union. First and foremost it was his, and gossiping aside, only he had the right to decide whether to place it on the block. Secondly, having been a slave who'd never owned so much as the clothes on his back, reaping the benefits of a profitable business whose deed bore his name meant a great deal. It also meant a great deal to his patrons, not only socially but economically. Three years ago, when Cecil Roland came to town and couldn't find anyone who'd lease him space to open his blacksmith shop, Rhine offered up one of the properties he owned, just as he'd done for two of the town's barbers and a laundress. The investments turned out to be good ones, as all four businesses were thriving. As owner of the Union, he helped purchase Bibles for the Baptist church —even though he had a keen dislike for the pompous Whitman Brown—and helped pay for the train ticket needed by Zeke Reynolds to accompany Doc Randolph to one of the civil rights conventions held last year. With all that in mind, selling the Union might make Natalie and the gossip harpies happy but it would have a very negative impact on the Colored community, and Rhine refused to be party to that.

Turning his carriage onto the main street, he decided to stop in and see the old fishmonger, Amos Granger. The Thursday night fish fry was one of the Union Saloon's most profitable events. Rhine hoped to convince the man to modify his decision to sell their usual supply to Miss Eddy Carmichael.

When Rhine walked in, Granger looked up from the fish he was gutting. "I suppose you're here about your fish."

"I am."

"Not changing my mind, Rhine. To have that pretty little thing come into my shop, I'd sell her my entire catch seven days a week. Be glad she only asked for one day."

Rhine's amusement made him smile. "She is quite lovely, isn't she."

"Makes an old man like me wish I wasn't. Real fine cook, too."

"So I hear. She's taking my customers."

"The way that girl cooks, you'll be lucky to have any customers at all if she stays around."

Rhine had been wondering if she was still planning on striking out for California. Not wanting Granger or anyone else knowing she'd spent those first few days at the Union, he said, "Sylvie told me she was on her way to California when the man who was driving her across the desert robbed her and put her off the wagon."

"That's what I heard, too. If I ever come across him, I'll gut him just like a fish. You don't do a lady that way."

Rhine wanted to gut the unknown man as well.

"So, not changing my mind about the fish," Granger added. "You and Jim will just have to pick out another night for the fish fry."

"You're a cold man, Amos Granger."

"Turn yourself into a woman as beautiful as Miss Eddy and promise me my favorite dessert twice a month and I may reconsider."

Rhine laughed. "She bribed you?"

"Sure did, and I took it like a politician at the state capital."

"Fine. We'll pick another night."

Granger nodded and went back to his gutting. Rhine left the shop and climbed back into his carriage.

So little Miss Eddy had Granger in the palm of her hand, too. Who else would she be impacting? he wondered. Even though he knew setting out for California was her dream, it didn't mean he had to like the idea of her leaving. Their truce notwithstanding, he selfishly wanted her to remain in the city, if for no other reason than to be able to run into her every now and again on the streets or at events. He admired the way she'd handled Natalie's gracelessness at Vera's. Thinking back on the incident brought to mind the dilemma his fiancée posed. Until today he'd had no idea how intolerant she was. Bigoted, was more the word if he were being honest. Her behavior in the shop and her words at the table added up to someone he found not only surprising but distasteful. He'd already made the difficult decision to cross the color line. Would he be able to stomach marriage to a woman who had nothing but disdain for the blood running through his veins, too? And what if they had children? Would they grow up mirroring that same intolerance? And because he knew the answer to that question, he couldn't marry her. Not and live with himself.

That evening, he paid a call on the Greer family and found them at dinner. He met Natalie's smiling eyes only long enough to nod a cool greeting. "My apology for showing up unannounced and interrupting your dinner, but Lyman, I'd like to speak with you privately if I may."

Lyman paused and shared a quick silent look

with his wife before placing his linen napkin beside his plate. "Certainly. Let's go into my study."

Once inside, Lyman closed the door and gestured Rhine to a chair. "What is this about?" he asked, taking a seat in the chair behind his desk.

"I've decided Natalie and I don't suit."

"Beatrice told me what happened, but rest assured, I've spoken with my daughter and she has seen the error of her ways."

"It's not that simple, Lyman, and we both know it."

"Surely you aren't going to break things off over one silly little incident?"

"You may consider it silly, but coupled with her insistence that I sell my business, I see nothing but tears and disagreements ahead. I'd like to spare her that and allow her to seek a husband who won't subject her to gossip or make her a laughingstock, as she's termed it."

"Rhine, I think you're overreacting. Natalie would make a perfect wife."

"Not for me, nor would I make the perfect husband for her, Lyman."

"This doesn't sit well with me, and I insist that for my daughter's sake you reconsider this decision. I can make things very difficult for you going forward, politically. Remember, my vote was the one to break the tie. Only because of your connection to Natalie have I remained on your side."

Rhine offered a smile that didn't meet his eyes. "Is that a threat, Lyman? Are you forgetting who owns this house?"

Lyman went ashen.

Beatrice Greer had no idea how much her town councilman husband loved to gamble, or how lousy he was at that love. Two years ago, in a poker game in the Union's back room, Lyman had wagered the deed to their home in order to cover a bet his funds could not. Rhine now owned that deed.

Lyman was visibly shaken. "Of course not."

"It sounded as if you might have."

"Rhine, please. This will break Natalie's heart, and once word gets out—"

"She can save face by saying she threw me over. I've no problem with being thought the cad. She's also welcome to keep the ring if she cares to."

"And the deed?"

"I'll keep it in play for now, just in case you suffer another case of amnesia." Rhine had genuinely liked Lyman, but his threat now changed things.

"Will you at least have the decency not to court anyone else in the immediate future?"

"I've no plans to. I've no desire to cause your daughter any more hurt than is necessary."

"Then I suppose we are done here."

"Unless you think I should tell your daughter myself."

"No," he said tightly. "I'll break the news to her."

"As you wish." Rhine got to his feet. "It will be impossible for us to avoid each other socially, but I assure you I will be a gentleman should we meet."

Lyman offered no such pledge in return.

Rhine didn't mind. "I'll show myself out."

On the drive through the darkened streets back to his saloon, he admittedly felt a strong sense of relief. Breaking the engagement had been unpleasant but the right thing to do. Natalie would find another fiancé and he would go on with his life. If he had to remain unmarried for the rest of his life, so be it, but if he did marry, the least he could do was honor his mother's ultimate sacrifice by finding a woman who didn't hold her and the Old Queens he was descended from in contempt. In some ways such a pledge made little sense to a man who'd left his race, but to Rhine it made all the sense in the world.

Chapter Ten

THE FOLLOWING MORNING, after preparing breakfast for the two early rising boarders and sending them off with wishes for a good, and in miner Gabe Horne's instance, safe day, Eddy was in the kitchen putting together Whitman Brown's omelet. He liked onions with the eggs, so she was chopping one when he sauntered in.

"Good morning, Eddy."

She didn't look up. "Good morning."

He came over to the table. "You know, it's a shame your skin is so dark. You're well spoken, clean, mannerly. You'd make someone a perfect wife, but—"

She did look up then. "Do you always insult women with knives in their hands, Mr. Brown?"

Upon viewing the gleaming blade, his eyes widened. "Uh, um . . ."

She pointed said knife at the doorway. "Leave."

"I wasn't trying to insult you. I was just stating fact."

"Go!"

He beat a hasty retreat.

Wondering where he'd been when the Good Lord began handing out brains, she went back to what she'd been doing.

Once his breakfast was ready, she took the piled-high plate out to the dining room, placed it on the table in front of him, and without a word returned to the kitchen.

She was still grumbling to herself when Sylvia entered. Eddy asked her, "Why is Whitman Brown such an ass?"

Chuckling, Sylvia replied, "I believe his overly inflated head is responsible. Has he gotten your goat already this morning?"

Eddy related his backhanded compliment, to which Sylvia replied, "I do wish he'd find someplace else to board, but he always pays his rent on time, and because of your cooking the only way he'll probably leave will be when Mr. Pringle the undertaker hauls him away."

"Arsenic can help that along you know."

"True, but outside of killing my boarder, what are you planning for the day?"

"I have to go over to Vera's for my fittings," she groused. "I also promised her treats for her customers, so I made a batch of sweet wafers last night and put the dough in the cold box. Once I bake them, I'll fancy them up by rolling them around a fork while they're still warm."

"I've never seen that done before."

"I'll bring you a few once they're ready. What are your plans for the day?"

"Going to Janet's and get my hair done, then attend this afternoon's meeting of the Lincoln

Club over at Rhine's place. Would you care to come along?"

She remembered Sylvie talking about the club when she was first introduced to Zeke. Even though the meeting was being held at Fontaine's saloon, she was interested in what the group was doing on behalf of the race. She was also interested in finding out if Zeke had returned to the city. He'd left about a week ago to do some carpentry work up in Reno. "What time?"

"Around three."

"Count me in."

"Good."

Sylvia departed and Eddy took her wafer dough out of the cold box and began rolling it out. Next, she used her smallest biscuit cutter to produce little circles, rolled each circle paper thin and placed them one by one on the tin baking sheet. Once they went into the oven, she had to keep an eye on them so they wouldn't burn. When they were done, she removed them from the sheet and gently rolled each wafer around the handle of a fork. They ended up resembling straws and would be a perfect accompaniment to whatever beverage Miss Vera planned to serve, be it coffee, tea, or punch. As promised, she took a few into Sylvia's office, along with a cup of coffee.

Sylvia took a bite and her soft moan of delight made Eddy smile and ask, "Good, aren't they?"

"Oh my, these are heavenly. Can we add these to our Sunday offerings?"

"I don't see why not."

Eddy was glad she liked them. "I'm going to take the rest over to Miss Vera, and after my fittings, walk to the market. I need to speak to Mr. Rossetti about donating something for the auction, and he said he'd have some oranges in today. I'd like to buy as many as I can so I can make marmalade."

Sylvia paused and her face lit up. "Marmalade? Eddy Carmichael, you make marmalade?"

"Yes. My mother taught me."

"You know, I'm never letting you leave me. I don't care if you do have your heart set on California. You are staying here."

A laughing Eddy left her alone.

Vera loved the sweet little wafer straws, too, as did her assistant Shanna. In fact, they ate so many, Eddy cautioned, "Vera, you aren't going to have any left for your customers."

"I don't care. These are wonderful." And she dipped the end of another one into the tea in her fancy china cup.

The door to the store opened and they all paused as Natalie Greer entered. She was wearing a nice gray walking dress with a little matching hat and carrying a fancy parasol in the same shade. She gave Eddy a cold glare before turning her attention to Vera. "Vera, I've come to cancel the wedding costume I picked out yesterday."

"If you've changed your mind and want to look at other patterns, that's fine."

"I won't need a costume. I've decided Rhine and I don't suit. The engagement's off."

"I'm so sorry."

"Don't be. I'm not."

Eddy couldn't help but wonder why she'd tossed him over.

As if having read Eddy's mind, she volunteered, "I want him to sell his saloon, and since he refuses, I won't marry him."

"I see."

"I'll not be the subject of gossip."

Vera simply nodded.

"Hopefully, rescinding the order won't be an inconvenience."

"No, Miss Greer. My shop and I will be fine."

"Good. Thank you for your understanding." After glaring Eddy's way again, she and her dainty little hat and parasol swept out.

In the silence that followed, Vera cracked, "So, he finally came to his senses. It's about time."

Shanna quipped, "And every eligible young lady in the state is singing hallelujah!"

Eddy found it interesting that even though the Greer woman claimed to have initiated the breakup, Vera thought otherwise.

Vera helped herself to another wafer. "Okay, Eddy, let's get your fittings done."

Kent stuck his head in the doorway of Rhine's office. "Natalie's outside. Says she wants to speak with you."

Rhine, seated at his desk glanced up from the report he'd gotten from his brother Drew on the oil fields they were investing in.

"She doesn't look happy," Kent commented.

Rhine pushed his chair back and stood. "She has good reason. I broke off our engagement last night."

Kent's jaw dropped.

"I'll tell you the whole sad tale when I return."

Outside, Rhine found her seated in the family carriage with their Chinese driver. "Good morning, Natalie."

"I'm here to see if you've come to your senses. I can't believe you'd beg off over something so trivial."

And therein lay the problem, he thought to himself, but he didn't want to argue. "We don't suit, Natalie. I'm sorry the engagement didn't work out the way we'd planned."

"Then I'm returning your ring. I've no desire to keep it." And she handed him the small velvet box. "I went by Vera's dress shop and cancelled the wedding costume."

"Whatever's needed. As I told your father, you

may place the blame squarely on my shoulders."

"Don't worry, I will. That little Colored cook you were so quick to champion yesterday was at the dress shop. Maybe I'll spread the rumor that you're keeping company with her as my reason."

His jaw tightened and his voice took on an ominous tone. "Don't stir waters that might flow back to drown you, Natalie. Just find yourself another fiancé and go on with your life."

"I don't need your advice." She tapped the driver on his arm with her parasol and said imperiously, "Drive on."

As the carriage moved off, Rhine walked back inside. He'd never been a vindictive person, but if one drop of Natalie's venom splashed on Eddy Carmichael, she and her family would be living in a tent on the outskirts of town.

"Frankly, I never knew what you saw in her anyway," Kent confessed after hearing Rhine's story. "She and I grew up together and she's never been the nicest person."

"Beauty can blind you."

"But it shouldn't make you stupid. Glad you came to your senses. Now she can be some other man's problem."

Rhine smiled. "You really don't like her, do you?"

"Name me five people in town who do and I'll buy you a drink." Kent smiled. "Now that you're free, how about going over to San

Francisco with me sometime soon. I'll introduce you to a cat-house with the prettiest women you've ever seen."

Rhine found the claim amusing. "I'll leave the cathouse kittens to you." Kenton Randolph's unabashed love for the ladies was yet another point of contention in his ongoing disagreement with his father. Then again, rumor had it that the good doctor had broken his fair share of hearts in his younger days, too.

Kent asked, "Will you be around for the Lincoln Club meeting this afternoon?"

"I will, but only as host. I don't want my presence to get in the way of an open discussion." The rift between Black and White Republicans was real. The men in his wing of the party were being lambasted for their perceived indifference to the ongoing bloody assault upon the South's freedmen. At the club's last meeting, Rhine had been called upon to explain the reasons for the silence and lack of outrage, but in truth he hadn't been able to. The party's choosing political power over supporting the hard-earned rights of the formerly enslaved was indefensible, at least for him, so he'd play host and allow the meeting to progress without his participation.

"We value your support, Rhine."

"I know, but a one man band is just that. I have no influence over the party's national agenda and it sticks in my craw as much as it does the people here. Is Jim preparing the food?"

"Yes. Says he needs lemons so he'll have enough lemonade. I'm on my way to Rossetti's to get them and save him the trip."

"How about I go? I need the air." He wanted to walk off the lingering effects of Natalie's maddening visit.

"Suit yourself. I'll help get the chairs and table set up."

"How many lemons does he need?"

"Two dozen or so."

Rhine nodded.

Eddy was glad to finally escape all the accidental pinpricks that went with her hour long fittings. She liked the idea of having new clothing, but walking down to Mr. Rossetti's store she felt like a pin cushion. It was a nice day, however, and the warmth and sunshine felt wonderful. As she made her way down the walk, she garnered a few waves and nods from people she'd met through Sylvia, like the blacksmith, Cecil Roland, and the barber, Edgar Carter, who was sitting on the bench outside his shop. "Mornin' to you, Miss Eddy."

"Good morning, Mr. Carter. Are you still planning on donating those haircuts for the auction?"

"Sure am, and looking forward to some of your good cooking on Sunday."

"Looking forward to serving you."

She'd been talking up the auction during the dinners at the dining room and nearly everyone she'd approached eagerly agreed to either bid or donate something. Because no one in the community could be termed wealthy, she didn't expect to raise a lot of money, but every penny taken in would benefit Mary and the orphanage.

A few moments later she entered Mr. Rossetti's store. She knew from talking with him on a previous visit that the middle-aged Spaniard's roots in the city went back to the days before the town was established, and that his first store had been nothing more than a tent on the side of Mount Davidson. Two years after the big 1859 Comstock strike, he'd built a permanent store to serve the influx of people and the growing town.

"Ah, the lovely Senorita Carmichael. How are you on this fine morning?"

"I am well, sir. And you and your family?"

"We are doing very well."

Mr. Rossetti was short, with a bulbous nose, and had a bright engaging smile that could light up the night. She explained about the auction. "Can you donate something people can bid on?"

He thought for a moment. "What about a washing wringer?"

Eddy's jaw dropped. "Really?"

He led her over to the area of the store where he

kept washtubs, soaps, and other laundry items, and there was a wringer set atop a crate. It was designed to be attached by screws to the side of a washtub, and by turning the handle, wet wash was fed between two tubes covered with India rubber. It was by far the best item the auction would offer so far. "Are you sure, Mr. Rossetti?" The devices weren't terribly expensive but they weren't cheap either.

"Yes. Very. A few years ago Sister Mary took in a little Mexican girl when the other orphanage turned her away. That little girl is now my daughter, Felicidad. And like her name, she has brought my wife and I nothing but happiness."

The emotion in his voice touched Eddy's heart.

"I wish I had more to give than just a wringer."

Eddy was so moved by the story it took her a moment to find her voice. "Thank you for your generosity, sir."

"You're welcome. My wife and I pray for Sister Mary and the orphans every night. She is a saint in our eyes. Now, come. The oranges arrived yesterday."

He led her past the dry goods, miners' equipment, and three ice cream churns for sale, to another area of the large store that held his perishables like cabbage, celery, cucumbers, and corn. Most of the vegetables came from the local farmers but the fruit came via trains from California. Eddy saw the large display of oranges and smiled. "May I buy a dozen or so?"

"You may buy two dozen if you like, there are more than enough."

"Thank you, Mr. Rossetti."

"You're welcome. Let me get back to my other customers. I'll drive the wringer over to the orphanage tomorrow."

Eddy thanked him again and still brimming with happiness at his generosity, opened the cloth sack she'd brought along and spent some time finding just the right candidates to purchase for her marmalade. She needed them to be fresh, fragrant, and firm.

"Good morning, Miss Carmichael."

The familiar baritone voice of Rhine Fontaine caught her so by surprise, she dropped the two oranges in her hand and they rolled away. Chastising herself for being rattled, she waited while he bent and retrieved them. Wearing a knowing look, he held them out for her to take, which she did but was careful not to let her flesh brush his. "Good morning, Mr. Fontaine. How are you?"

"I'm well, and you?"

"I'm well, also." Ignoring his veiled amusement, she turned back to the crates of oranges.

He asked, "Are you planning on using those to lure away more of my customers?"

She smiled. "I'm making marmalade for Sylvia and the boarders."

"You make marmalade?" he asked with the same wondrous tone Sylvia had.

"I do. Usually from peaches, but when Mr. Rossetti told me he had oranges coming in, I wanted to treat Sylvia as my way of thanking her for being so kind." Eddy saw some of the other customers eyeing them. "I need to finish my shopping."

"And I get no reward for finding you in the desert?" he asked, seemingly deaf to her hint to end their conversation.

"You have my thanks of course." A few short feet away, Eddy saw the frown on the face of a woman ostensibly picking out strawberries. She was obviously eavesdropping. "People are watching us," she whispered. "Go away."

"We're just discussing oranges."

"Scat."

He smiled, picked up a few oranges, but stayed right where he was. "Natalie said you were in the dress shop this morning when she cancelled her wedding costume."

"Yes, she told Vera she'd tossed you over. Shouldn't you be home mourning or something?"

"You've met her. What do you think?"

"My opinion doesn't matter."

"Honestly, we weren't well suited from the

start. She wanted me to sell my saloon and I realized I wanted a woman with more depth."

Eddy looked up into his eyes and saw an intensity in them that made her swallow dryly.

"We really need to have dinner, Eddy. With candlelight, I'm thinking."

Fighting to keep herself on an even keel, she whispered sharply, "If I make you marmalade, too, will you leave me be?"

"Probably not, but I will take the marmalade. I thought we were supposed to be adults?"

She didn't like having her words come back to haunt her. "You're the devil."

"Am I tempting you?"

Her blood rushed with so much heat, she had to close her eyes to keep herself upright. He was way better at this back and forth than she'd ever be. He'd melted her from the knees down. "How can you be so endearing one moment and so incorrigible—" She hadn't meant to say that aloud.

He paused. "You find me endearing?"

"No."

He folded his arms. "Well now."

"Go away."

"I want to hear more about how endearing I am," he said quietly, moving to stand beside her. "I say we discuss me over dinner."

Shooting him a hot glare, she ignored the people staring and strode away to pay for her oranges.

Rhine watched her determined departure. *Endearing.* The attraction between them continued to spark like summer lightning, and if he weren't mistaken, things had just ramped up several more notches. In spite of not scatting when she'd asked, he did care how their encounter might be perceived. The last thing he wanted was for her to be tarred by gossips. So when he saw the tight disapproving face of Mrs. Elsa Parker, the wife of one of the city's bankers as she stood by the strawberries, he said to her, "Those berries are almost as lovely as you are, Mrs. Parker."

She tittered and colored up. "You are such a flirt, Mr. Fontaine."

"Only with ladies as beautiful as yourself." Knowing his attentions would override any untoward story she might've spread, he asked, "Can you help a poor man pick out some good lemons? My chef needs them but I'm ignorant on the matter."

"Oh, of course."

Through the store window he saw Eddy march by. Bantering with her only increased his desire for more. He planned to hold her to her offer of the marmalade, and sometime in the very near future show her just how endearing and incorrigible he could be.

Chapter Eleven

LATER THAT AFTERNOON Eddy accompanied Sylvia to the Union Saloon for the Lincoln Club meeting. As soon as they stepped inside, all Eddy could think about was Rhine: being sequestered upstairs in his bedroom, their encounter that morning over the oranges, and that she could no longer use Natalie Greer as the excuse for keeping her feelings about him at bay. There were quite a number of people already inside and she discreetly looked around for Rhine. Not seeing him, she relaxed and followed her landlady deeper into the room.

This was Eddy's first time in the saloon proper. The interior was long and narrow yet spacious enough to hold ten tables and chairs. There was a bar to the left and on it sat a bevy of covered dishes and pitchers of water and lemonade. She assumed Jim had provided the food and wanted to go into the kitchen and say hello to him but didn't want to chance running into Rhine.

Eddy recognized many of the people in the room, like Janet Foster, the hairdresser, and fishmonger Amos Granger. She also saw Whitman Brown seated at a table with Dr. Randolph, and immediately settled her attention elsewhere, but there were a handful of men she'd not yet met.

Sylvia's boarder and hotel dishwasher August Williams was there as well, sitting at a table with a young woman Eddy also hadn't met.

"Let's sit with August and his fiancée," Sylvia said. "Her name's Cherry. She's a maid at the same hotel and they're planning to marry later this summer."

Unaware that August had a fiancée, a surprised Eddy followed her over.

Once they sat down, August made the introductions. "Miss Eddy Carmichael, this is my fiancée, Cherry Young."

Cherry said, "Nice to meet you, Eddy. August speaks very highly of you." She had beautiful brown skin and was as plump as her fiancé August was thin.

"That's good to hear," Eddy replied with a smile. "Nice meeting you as well."

Then to her delight, Zeke walked up. "Hello, Eddy."

"Hi, Zeke. You're back from Reno."

"Yes, last night. Finished up the job late yesterday."

She was glad to see him and hoped being in his calm presence would counteract having been melted like butter on a hot stove by Rhine.

August added, "All he's been talking about since getting back was seeing you again."

Embarrassed, Eddy dropped her eyes.

Zeke nodded. "He's right. Missed you, and your fine cooking."

"I'm glad you're back."

"So am I."

"Would you ladies like something to drink?" he asked.

"Lemonade for me," Sylvia said as she waved to Janet the hairdresser.

"I'll have the same," Eddy told him.

"Me, too," Cherry said.

The cousins stood and set off for the bar.

While they were gone, some of the men drifted over to introduce themselves to Eddy. First came bricklayer David Quinn, whose light skin showed off his freckles. Next came Barrett Garnet, Mr. Rossetti's butcher, followed by farmer Oswald Henry, who wanted her to meet his three daughters. Eddy was unaccustomed to so much male atten-tion and had no idea how to respond other than politely. She thought back on Sylvia saying she'd have to beat the men off with a frying pan and smiled inwardly.

Once the men moved off, Cherry laughed, "You may need to start selling tickets, Eddy,"

Sylvia commented, "I warned her. And Eddy, you don't want to meet Oswald's girls. His wife recently passed away and he's looking for someone to marry who'll help raise those little terrors of his."

Zeke and August returned with their refreshments, and she found herself peeking over her glass at Ezekiel. It pleased her that he was doing the same.

Doc Randolph called the meeting to order. While Sylvia eyed him tersely, Eddy wondered again about their mysterious past. The doctor began with what he called the race's current events. "We're pleased that the ratification of the Fifteenth Amendment to the United States Constitution was officially certified on March thirtieth by Secretary of State Hamilton Fish."

Applause greeted that announcement, and Janet Foster called out, "They forgot about us women!"

When laughter broke out, she countered, "Do I look like I'm joking?"

Doc Randolph said, "One thing at a time, Miss Jan."

He got an eye roll from her for that but moved on. "Mr. Hiram Revels of Mississippi has been sworn in as the country's first senator of color."

More applause and whistles and cheers.

"Things are looking up," he said. "But if the Kluxers have their way, our people in the South will be back in chains."

You could hear a pin drop.

Eddy knew from the newspapers that although Congress passed the Enforcement Act, giving the government authority to send troops to protect freedmen rights, the Kluxers and their supporters were running loose like rabid dogs.

Doc went on to tell them that North Carolina was on the verge of ending Reconstruction because of political assassination and violence. "In Alamance County, Wyatt Outlaw, one of the Colored leaders, was lynched this past winter. The state's governor has come out against the Klan, but folks there are pretty sure he'll be impeached before autumn." He added that Tennessee and Georgia were being overrun by insurrectionists as well.

Eddy sighed. There'd been so much hope in the years immediately following the war. Fisk University and Morehouse College were founded, the Fourteenth Amendment was sent to the states for ratification, and Blacks in Washington, D.C., were given suffrage over the veto of President Andrew Johnson. But during that same time in Memphis, Tennessee, a mob of Whites that included policemen killed forty-six freedmen and two White supporters. In the melee, seventy people were wounded and ninety homes, twelve schools, and four churches were torched and burned. A month and a half later in New Orleans, another mob, this time led by the police, attacked a convention of Black and White Republicans, killing forty and wounding 150.

"What about Mr. Sumner's civil rights bill?" Amos Granger asked. "Any news on it?"

Doc cracked, "Other than the Lily Whites are running away from it like their mustaches are on fire? No, and there's no guarantee it will even come to the floor for a vote, let alone be made law."

Sumner, the senator from Massachusetts, had drafted the bill along with John Mercer Langston, the founder and dean of Howard University's law school. Its wording would guarantee all citizens, regardless of race, equal access to public accommodations like theatres and public schools, and allow men of the race to serve on juries.

The doctor said, "The part of the bill those refusing to support it dislike the most is allowing children of both races to sit in the same classrooms. Folks are pretty sure that clause will be stripped away somewhere down the road."

There were disappointed head shakes all over the room.

"Now, I want to turn this over to Zeke."

Doc sat and Zeke walked to the front. "I just returned from Reno. Went up to handle a job and to attend a meeting with a man named Henry Adams. Since the end of the war, he and a group of men have been traveling across the South, taking stock of conditions and writing down what they've been seeing, like the children being forced to sign papers that indenture them to planters for the rest of their lives, sharecroppers being cheated out of their wages and homes, schools burned, teachers killed or run off. The men meet yearly to discuss their travels and turn their diaries over to Adams. I found him to be very passionate about the race and freedom. He'll let me know when and where the next meeting will be."

From the back of the room, Jim Dade asked, "What's he going to do with the notes?"

"He's hoping to take them to Congress at some point so they can have a real look at our so called freedom. He says some of our people in the South are talking about making an exodus west to Kansas and Nebraska to escape the Kluxers and lynchings."

He let that sink in before continuing. "On a more positive note, four new Colored colleges opened their doors last year: Clark, Claflin, Dillard, and Tougaloo. They keep kicking us but we keep striving."

Applause greeted that. Adding hers, Eddy was glad she'd attended the meeting. It had been sad at points but also informative.

When the room finally quieted, Doc Randolph said, "I'm sending a petition around the room for the men to sign. It asks the state of Nevada to support Mr. Sumner's civil rights bill. There's no guarantee they'll entertain it but at least they'll know how we feel." He then looked around. "Does anyone else have something to add before we eat?"

Whitman Brown raised his hand.

"Yes, Mr. Brown?"

He stood. "I say we should throw our votes behind the Democrats."

Loud boos greeted his words.

He pressed on. "The Lily Whites take our votes for granted. Why not do something to make them sit up and take notice?" Eddy knew it was a move being pushed by some of the race's national leaders, but it was also fiercely opposed.

Zeke called out, "If you want to align yourself with those blood-spilling supremacists, have at it. I'm a Republican."

Cheers rose.

Irritation soured Whitman's face. "Well, I'm thinking of running for council and I'm going on the ballot as a Democrat."

Eddy noted the shocked faces and those who shook their heads in disgust.

He added, "If anyone wishes to work with me on my campaign, let me know." With that he sat down again.

Doc Randolph glanced around and asked, "Anyone else?"

Silence.

"Then this meeting of the Virginia City Lincoln Club is adjourned."

Eddy was impressed by Ezekiel Reynolds. Very impressed.

August asked Sylvie, "I wonder who put Brown up to this?"

She shrugged. "Someone looking to dilute our men's votes probably. Who knows, but once again Whitman proves he's an idiot. How about we forget about him and get something to eat?"

Everyone at their table agreed.

Zeke rejoined them and Eddy enjoyed his company and the food. There was fried chicken, potato salad, slaw, and a light as air angel food cake topped with sweet strawberries. She looked around for Jim Dade but didn't see him. "Sylvia, do you think it might be okay if I went to the kitchen to thank Mr. Dade for the wonderful food? I really would like his recipe for this angel food cake."

And from behind her, she heard, "Good afternoon, everyone."

It was Rhine. He was standing directly behind her high-backed chair with his hands placed casually on the top rung. She was as aware of his nearness as she was her own breathing.

Sylvia smiled. "Hello, Rhine. You missed the meeting."

"Intentionally. I'm done trying to defend my wing of the Republican party. I was flayed pretty badly at the last meeting here. How are you, Zeke?"

"Good."

"Miss Carmichael?"

"Mr. Fontaine."

"I enjoyed our conversation at the market this morning. I'm looking forward to the marmalade." His hands were still on her chair, and if she didn't know better she'd think he was staking his claim. Seeing Zeke silently taking in Fontaine's position-ing gave her the sense that he might be thinking the same. She wanted to sock Mr. Green Eyes squarely in the nose.

Sylvie didn't help matters by saying, "Is Jim in the kitchen? Eddy wants his recipe for this angel food cake."

"He is. I can show you to the kitchen if you'd like, Miss Carmichael."

She could hardly tell him she'd changed her mind. She saw Cherry looking between them as if trying to determine what might be at play here. "I'll be right back," she said to Zeke in particular. He responded with a cool nod.

Rhine helped her with her chair. She tried not to see the interested eyes of the people in the room tracking their departure but it was impos-sible.

Once they cleared the kitchen doors she spun around. "How dare you embarrass me this way."

He folded his arms. "Did you not wish to see the kitchen?"

"I wanted to. Alone. You stood over me like I was yours."

"I was just being a good host."

"You're being the devil again."

"Tempting you, am I?"

"Tempting me to take a skillet to your head," she fumed, trying to rein in her temper. Only then did she see Jim standing near the stove. "Excuse me for yelling," she said contritely. "I didn't see you."

"Carry on, please. Women don't usually take a skillet to his head and I'm anxious to witness it, even if you have been stealing our customers and made me alter my menu because Amos Granger is selling you his entire catch on Thursdays."

Momentarily stung by guilt, she said, "I had no idea you were the customer being shortchanged on the fish, but I'm not going to apologize for taking the customers."

Jim said, "Nor should you. I understand Amos's thinking though. He's always been susceptible to beautiful women."

His compliment left her embarrassed. "I just wanted to come in and say thank you for the food and see if you'd give me the recipe for the angel food cake. I make one but it's not even close to this light. I'd love to have you make one for the auction."

"I appreciate the praise. As I told you before, folks don't usually seek me out to say thanks. They simply eat and leave."

His attention centered fully on Eddy, Rhine countered, "And as I said, I tell you how great you are all the time."

Jim rolled his eyes. "You should probably step

away from him, Miss Eddy. Lightning may strike any minute, or would you rather I hand you a skillet?"

The reminder brought her back to her irritation with his business partner, but before she could light into Rhine again, he said, "My apology if I embarrassed you. As for you being mine. Having found you in the desert at death's door makes me feel proprietary."

Lord, she wished she knew how to make herself immune to him. "I appreciate your concern but it's unnecessary."

Ezekiel pushed through the doors, and Rhine asked coldly, "May I help you, Zeke?"

"I came to let Miss Carmichael know we're preparing to leave."

"Thank you, Zeke. I was just on my way back to join you." She gave Rhine her best glare.

He responded by saying, "Don't forget my marmalade."

"I'll send it via post. Nice seeing you again, Mr. Dade."

He was grinning. "Same here. I'll get that recipe to you and think about the donation idea."

"Thank you."

Ezekiel offered her his arm. As she accepted, she watched Rhine's green eyes darken. "Good day, Mr. Fontaine."

He inclined his head.

She and Zeke exited.

After their departure, Jim looked at the scowl on Rhine's face. "As I said, try harder."

No response.

"I'm serious, Rhine."

Knowing that Zeke Reynolds, a man Rhine very much respected, seemed taken with Eddy Carmichael, too, didn't help Rhine's mood, and he ran his hands down his face.

"Just let her be," Jim added sagely.

Rhine left the kitchen, but instead of returning to the main room, he took the back stairway up to his office. Upon seeing Eddy at the market this morning, all he'd wanted to do was whisk her away so they could be alone. And although he hadn't meant to embarrass her just now, he'd had an overriding urge to lay public claim to her as if he were a dragon and she his treasure. He just had to convince her.

Downstairs in the main room, the meeting was indeed breaking up. People were saying their good-byes and gathering their belongings. Eddy stopped a few to remind them about the auction and they all pledged their participation.

"Eddy," Sylvia said. "I promised Aretha Carter I'd stop by and help her with the plans for her and Edgar's anniversary dinner. Would you mind walking back alone?"

"No. Not at all."

August piped up. "Zeke and I are walking

Cherry home, Eddy. You're welcome to come along with us if want."

"I'd like that. Sylvia, I'll see you when you return."

The four set out. August and Cherry walked in front while Eddy and Zeke brought up the rear.

"Is Fontaine bothering you?" Zeke asked.

Eddy studied his serious features. "I don't think bothering is the right word."

"Then how would you phrase it?"

She heard the muted censure in his tone. Dealing with Rhine was enough to handle. She didn't need Zeke trying to lay claim to her, too. "Let's just say Mr. Fontaine seems interested in me."

"Is that interest returned?"

"No." Her response was both a lie and the truth.

"Good."

Nothing else was said on the matter.

Cherry roomed in a house a few blocks away from Sylvia's, and once they arrived, Eddy and Zeke bade the engaged couple good-bye and continued on.

"Have you lived in the city all your life?" she asked.

"No. Augie and I are originally from Maryland. Came out here five years ago hoping to make our fortune in the mines, but we're about ten years too late. So he went to work at the hotel and I fell back on the carpentry skills I learned from my father."

"Do you have your own shop?"

"Not yet, but I'm working towards that. And you? What are you working towards?"

"Saving up so I can open my own restaurant."

He stopped. "Really?"

"Yes. Do you find that odd?"

He assessed her silently for a moment. "I uess not, but I figured a woman as pretty as you would be looking for a husband to settle down with and raise some babies."

She laughed softly, "I'm more than just a pretty face, and a bit past the wanting a husband and babies stage. I figure if I'm very frugal I can save enough to be on my way to California by maybe this winter."

"So, you're one of those newfangled women?"

Eddy sensed his stock sinking within her. "Both my parents worked to provide for our family. Many of the women I know worked, so if that makes us all newfangled, I suppose we are."

"Didn't mean to offend you. It's just I'm the kind of man who feels a wife should be at home when her husband comes in at the end of the day, but a pretty lady can make a man reevaluate this thinking."

His stock rose again.

They'd reached Sylvia's. "Thanks so much for walking with me, Zeke. I enjoyed myself."

"So did I. Got something special to donate to your auction."

"And it is?"

"A secret."

"Oh come now. I need to know."

"Nope. Not telling you, but it's something a lot of people are going to bid on."

Eddy was intrigued. "I'll need you to drop it off at the orphanage beforehand though, so we can put it on display."

"I understand and I will."

Eddy saw his smile and wondered what his donation might possibly be.

"The Baptist church is having an ice cream social Sunday afternoon," he said. "I'd love to escort you."

"Sunday is my busiest day here. I can't get away. Maybe some other time."

He looked disappointed. "Okay, but I plan to call on you soon. Wanted you to get used to me being around first."

"I'd like that."

"Take care of yourself."

"I will." Eddy climbed the steps to the porch and went inside still wondering what his secret would turn out to be.

"So, how are you and Zeke getting along?" Sylvia asked after coming home and finding Eddy in the kitchen peeling the oranges she'd purchased that morning.

Sylvie took a seat at the table.

"He's a nice man. We haven't spent much time together but I enjoy his company. He asked me to the church ice cream social on Sunday but I had to decline."

"I'm sorry."

"No, it's quite all right. My duties here come first. That's why you pay me."

"And Rhine Fontaine?"

Eddy paused. "What about him?"

"It was hard not to notice him standing over you the way he did."

"True, and I took him to task about it. He seems intent upon—I'm not sure what." Eddy didn't want to confess how she and Rhine had been dancing around each other, for fear of how Sylvia might respond. "Is he known for dallying with women outside his race?"

"Not to my knowledge, which is why I found his actions so surprising."

"What can you tell me about him?"

"Other than the fact that he's rich as King Midas and is a kind man, not very much. He came to Virginia City a few years after the war. Not sure how he made his fortune though."

"You were here then, correct?" Eddy got out the grater and began working on the now peeled oranges.

"I was. My late husband Freddy and I arrived just after the first big Comstock strike in 'fifty-nine. Freddy worked in the mines and I did a bit of nursing and minded the tent that served as a boardinghouse."

"Mr. Rossetti said his first store was a tent, too."

"The entire city grew from tents—the banks, the stores, the saloons. After I lost Freddy in a mine accident, I took some of the money he'd left me and began buying property. I originally owned the Union Saloon. It was much smaller back then of course."

Eddy remembered Rhine mentioning that fact, but she was saddened to learn that Sylvia had lost her husband in the mines.

"Once the city began growing by leaps and bounds, I decided I didn't want to be a saloon owner dealing with drunk miners anymore and put the place up for sale in 'sixty-eight. Rhine bought it. Paid me in gold and stocks. Between Freddy's estate, Rhine's gold and the stocks, I'm pretty well set for a Colored woman."

Eddy wanted to ask about her and Doc Randolph but decided not to. In truth, she was more interested in Rhine. "So does he own other places?"

"Yes, he's funded many of the Colored businesses and owns a number of other properties, too, like Lady Ruby's Palace."

"He owns her whorehouse?"

"And the plot that will soon anchor the Baptist church. Right now the congregation meets on the open land while they raise the money for the church to be built. He's a good man. He's done more for our community and its people than all the other Whites here combined."

Eddy thought on that for a moment. "Is he well-liked by his own people?"

"He is, although they whisper about him because of his Union clientele, but they don't turn down the money he gives to their charities, and he's invited to all the fancy balls and social events. Even if they don't like who he associates with, they like his money and influence. Now that he and Natalie are no longer engaged, he's going to be overrun with invites from mothers with eligible daughters. He'll be quite a catch."

Eddy put the grated orange pulp into a pot, covered the fruit with sugar and set it on the flame on the stove. She told herself Rhine being sought after made her no never mind, but . . .

Sylvia searched Eddy's face. "Something you want to talk about, honey?"

"No, ma'am."

Sylvia studied her again and said gently, "If and when you do, I'm here."

Eddy nodded.

"Zeke's an outstanding man. A girl could do worse."

"I was very impressed by him today."

Sensing Eddy wanted her to change the subject, Sylvia asked, "Tell me about this marmalade. How's it made?"

"Once I finish peeling the oranges, I take out the seeds and grate the flesh. We add sugar, cook it for about twenty minutes, and let it sit overnight. It'll be ready to spread on your biscuits in the morning."

"I can't wait."

"I promised Fontaine a bit of it. I ran into him at Mr. Rossetti's this morning. When I told him I was making marmalade for you as my way of saying thanks for your many kindnesses, he decided he wanted a boon, too."

And then Sylvia said without prompting, "Try and keep Rhine at arm's length, Eddy. For all his stellar qualities, men like him very rarely offer marriage to women like us."

"I know."

"But he is gorgeous to look at."

Eddy had to agree. She'd already told herself that if she was going to keep company with a gentleman, she'd prefer it be someone like Zeke. Dealing with Rhine Fontaine was like juggling lightning.

Chapter Twelve

THE FOLLOWING MORNING Eddy dipped the tip of a spoon into the marmalade she'd made the evening before and took a small taste. It was so delicious she moaned.

"How is it?" Sylvia asked, coming into the kitchen.

Eddy handed her a clean spoon and the jar. "Taste for yourself."

Sylvia complied and swooned. "Oh my goodness. I'll need you to make vats of this."

Eddy laughed.

"Irene Lee sells this at her bakery and she asks two arms and a leg for it. Now, she'll never get another dime from me. Thank you, Eddy."

"My pleasure. I just took some biscuits out of the oven."

"Great."

While Sylvia helped herself, Eddy thought about the marmalade she'd promised Rhine. Part of her wanted to put his portion in a jar and indeed mail it, or have one of housekeeper Maria's sons take it to him, but that would be the coward's way out and she was definitely not that.

But she set thoughts of him aside when Vera walked in bearing gifts.

"Morning, ladies. Eddy, Shanna and I worked

all day yesterday on getting some of your clothing sewn, so here's the first batch. I brought you two blouses and two skirts."

Eddy looked at the lovely garments and for a moment didn't know what to say. The soft white cotton blouse and the navy blue skirt were practical enough for everyday wear, but the other blouse with its lacy pleats down the front and thin band of lace bordering the wrist and throat was for nicer occasions and absolutely beautiful. "Thank you so much, Vera."

"You're welcome. And so you'll know, my customers raved about the sweet wafers."

"You actually had enough left to give them some?"

"Sassy child," she said with mock admonishment. "Yes, I did, and I'll need more when you have the time. Many more."

"I'll make the time."

Sylvia said, "Vera, pull up a chair. If you thought those sweet wafers were over the moon, wait until you taste this marmalade of hers. I'd bathe in this if I could."

A laughing Eddy left them to their treat and took her new clothes up to her room.

Standing in front of her vanity's mirror, Eddy surveyed her reflection. With her hair pulled back and wearing her new attire, she now resembled the woman of means Vera had alluded to. It had been quite some time since she looked so nice, and it felt good. She removed her mother's locket from the small ring box that was its home. Inside the locket were two tiny photographs—one of her beautiful ebony-skinned mother and the other of her stern-faced father. She touched their faces lovingly. She missed them now as much as she did the day the local sheriff came to the house with the terrible news. Since then she'd struggled, but kept her head up and done her best to honor their memories. She placed the frayed blue ribbon around her neck and tied the ends. She'd have to ask Vera for a new length of ribbon, but wearing it again felt right.

When she reentered the kitchen, Sylvia and Vera beamed with approval.

"The men around here are really going to have fits now," Sylvia said, smiling. "You look brand new."

Vera added, "There's something about new clothes that makes a woman feel good both inside and out."

Eddy agreed.

Sylvia said, "Wait until Zeke sees you."

"You're matchmaking again, Sylvia."

From the smile on Vera's face, Eddy assumed Sylvia had told her all about her meeting Zeke, but Eddy had to admit she was interested in his reaction.

"I should have the rest of your clothes done by

this time next week," Vera told her. "Then I'd like to do some fittings for a few day dresses and maybe a fancy dress or two."

Eddy wasn't sure about the fancy dresses, but Vera would plow ahead with the project whether she approved or not, so she kept her doubts to herself.

Walking over to the cold box, she took out the second bowl of marmalade and spooned some into a teacup. After covering it with a small doily, she secured it with an elastic band and placed it in a basket. "Sylvia, I'm going to take this over to Rhine."

Seeing Vera's confusion, Eddy explained, "I promised him some of the marmalade to thank him for saving me in the desert."

Sylvia groused mockingly, "Why do I have to share mine when he has his own cook? I'm sure Jim Dade is perfectly able to make Rhine his own marmalade."

Vera waded in around a bite of a marmalade-laden biscuit, "I agree."

"Now, now ladies. Let's not be greedy and uncharitable. I'll make you more. Promise."

Sylvia folded her arms and huffed like a small child. "Okay. I'm holding you to that, Eddy."

Eddy truly enjoyed Sylvia and her antics. "I'll be back shortly. I'll stop by Lady Ruby's and get eggs while I'm out, too. And don't eat all the marmalade while I'm gone."

No promises were made.

Walking down the crowded street, it was her hope that Rhine Fontaine would accept his boon, say thanks, and let her go on her way, but she doubted the encounter would play out that way. Regardless of the shoots that remained hopeful, she planned to continue keeping him at arm's length, even as she wondered what it might be like to take him up on his offer for dinner. Candlelight, he said. Eddy had never dined with any man other than her father, but knew there was no comparison. Fontaine would be charmingly bold while she would be all thumbs and nervous as a ewe with a wolf. No, dinner with him wouldn't be a good idea even though they did need to have another adult-to-adult talk. Yes, there was an attraction to him that was real as the sun in the sky but she didn't love him and he didn't love her and that would have to be in the equation if they were actually to become a couple. She didn't want to be tossed aside as soon as he found a Natalie with more depth. As Sylvia so rightly pointed out, men like Rhine might offer a dalliance but they rarely offered marriage to women like herself.

Knowing that no respectable lady entered a saloon alone or by the front door, she went around to the back door that led to the kitchen and knocked. Jim Dade answered and greeted her with a smile, "Good morning, Miss Eddy. What can I do for you?"

"I have Rhine's marmalade. Is he here?"

"No. He's out collecting rent from his tenants."

Eddy was relieved, or at least that's what she told herself. "Will you make sure he gets this, please?" She took the teacup out of the basket and handed it to him.

He opened the top, grazed a finger over the sweet contents and tasted it. "This is excellent. Whether there'll be anything in the cup when he returns is another story. Can you show me how this is made?"

"I can, if only to keep Sylvia from sulking over having to share."

He chuckled. "We can't have Miss Sylvie sulking, now can we. Let me know when you have some time."

"I will. Thanks, Jim."

"You're welcome, lovely lady. I owe you an angel food cake recipe. Haven't forgotten."

"Good."

"How's the auction going?"

"Going well. I hope you'll take me up on donating the cake." The event was less than a week away.

"I think I will."

"I'll be bidding."

He nodded, and Eddy set out for Lady Ruby's Silver Palace to buy eggs.

It wasn't very far away. According to Sylvia, the place started life as a mansion built by one of the mine owners back in the sixties. When his stock sank and left him broke, he moved his family to San Francisco and abandoned the home. How Ruby came to be in possession, Eddy didn't know.

The interior was quiet. A few of the girls looked bleary-eyed as they ate breakfast and nodded a greeting. Every time she entered she thought about her sister Corinne and her nieces. Eddy had written her a few weeks ago to let her know where she was staying, even though Corinne probably didn't care.

On the far side of the room, a man with sandy-colored hair was seated with his face down on one of the tables. She assumed he was sleeping off last night's revelry.

Lady Ruby was behind the long wooden bar. Her shoulder length red wig was slightly askew and she was wearing a voluminous silver wrapper on her tall large-boned frame. She was also sporting enough silver jewelry on her wrists and fingers to be officially declared a mine.

"Good morning, Eddy," she said in her lilting West Indian accent.

"Good morning, Lady Ruby."

"You are entirely too gorgeous for this early in the morning. You here for eggs?"

"Yes, ma'am."

"I've been thinking about the auction. Are you sure I can't offer a night with one of my girls."

Eddy smiled. "Very sure." They'd had this conversation on one of Eddy's earlier visits. "I don't think it's appropriate."

"Well okay. I'll see if me and the girls can come up with something else."

"That would fine." But Eddy had no idea what that would be.

Behind Eddy a male voice said, "Well, well. Look who's here. You made it, I see."

Eddy swung around to the sound of the slurred but familiar voice and looked into the red eyes of the man she knew as Father Nash. Furious, she turned back to Ruby. She had absolutely nothing to say to him.

"You know him, Eddy?" Lady Ruby asked with surprise.

"Just enough to know he's a thief and a snake. I'll tell you the story some other time."

"You trying to ignore me, girl?" Nash snapped.

Eddy said to Ruby, "Let me get my eggs."

Behind her, she heard the scrape of a chair.

"Look at me when I'm talking to you." He was now crossing the room.

She still refused to turn around.

Lady Ruby said, "One of you girls go get Phillip. Hurry." She then snapped, "Mister, go back over there and sit down!"

Phillip was the house bouncer. Eddy saw one of the girls run from the room just as Nash latched onto her upper arm and spun around her to face him. "Did you hear me?"

"Let go!" She tried to jerk free but his hold was tight as a vise.

A different male voice boomed angrily, "Release her now! Or I'll kill you where you stand."

Rhine Fontaine stood across the room with ice in his eyes and a Colt in his hand leveled at Nash.

Nash's eyes bulged and he quickly backed away.

Rhine didn't lower the gun. "Miss Carmichael, are you okay?"

A seething Eddy rubbed at her throbbing arm. "Yes."

Nash raised his hands. "I'm sorry," he said, chuckling as if the encounter had been a joke. "I didn't know she was yours. Had her a few times when she and I crossed the desert. Was just trying to renew an old friendship. She as hot for you as she was for me?"

Eddy saw red. He'd robbed her, left her to die, and was now intimating that they'd been intimate? She was so furious she wanted to shoot him her-self, but not having that option, she grabbed a long-necked bottle off the bar's top and slammed it hard across his jaw. The bottle shattered. Had she been taller she'd have brought it down on his head.

Lady Ruby shouted, "Hey! Who's going to pay for that!"

It wouldn't be Nash because he was already out cold before he fell over the table and slumped slowly to the floor. Eddy reached into her pocket, withdrew some coins and slapped them on the bar. "For your whiskey."

The old madam smiled. "I like your style, Eddy Carmichael."

But the still furious Eddy was already on her way to the back door. As she passed the stunned Fontaine, she said, "Now, you may shoot him!"

Out back, Eddy went to the coops and gathered the eggs she needed. Placing them in the basket she was carrying, she turned to go home and there stood Rhine Fontaine.

"Thank you for intervening on my behalf. Again. Good day."

"Whoa," he said, taking her arm gently. "Hold on a minute, please."

She cast a critical eye down at his restraining hand and then up at him.

Showing just a hint of a smile, he released her. "Who is he?"

"The snake responsible for me almost dying in the desert."

"I didn't expect you to bash him with that bottle."

"Had I a gun I would've shot him for lying so

scandalously." Just thinking about it made her seethe all over again.

"Did you cut yourself?"

She looked down at her hands. "No."

"How much did he take from you?"

When she told him, anger flared in his eyes.

She added, "He left me penniless."

"How about I drive you back to Sylvia's. My carriage is close by."

"No thank you. I need to walk off this anger." And come to grips with the fact that she might wind up being jailed if Nash decided to file charges.

"Let me drive you, Eddy."

"I doubt the gossips will approve of me being seen in your carriage."

"You were assaulted, Eddy. The gossips aren't going to approve of that either."

"No, I'll walk."

He looked so frustrated she almost felt sorry for him. Almost.

"I'll come by Sylvia's this evening and check on you."

"Not necessary."

"Plan on me doing it anyway." There was concern in his vivid eyes. "You're a hard nut to crack, Eddy Carmichael," he said softly.

"I'm a woman of color, Mr. Fontaine. A hard shell is necessary."

And with that, she turned from him and walked away.

Watching her go, Rhine sighed with frustration. He'd come to the Palace to pick up Ruby's rent, only to walk in and find Eddy being manhandled. He'd almost put a bullet in Nash's head there and then. What she made him feel was far more than proprietary. His attraction to her was growing with each passing moment, threatening to unravel him and possibly the life he'd so carefully planned for himself. Somewhere his mother and the Old African Queens were looking on knowingly.

Needing to vent some of what he was feeling, he went back inside. Nash was just coming to. Rhine grabbed him up and slammed him into a wall. "Don't ever put your hands on a woman in my sight again." He slammed him again. "Do you hear me!"

Nash cried out.

"Give me your money."

"What!"

Rhine pulled his Colt and placed it against his temple. "Your money. She said you robbed her."

Nash's face widened with fear. "The bitch is lying!"

Rhine eased the hammer back. "I say she isn't. Give me your money!"

He quickly surrendered. "Okay!"

Rhine stepped back. Nash fumbled through his pockets and with a shaking hand offered up fifty dollars in bills and coins.

"Where's the rest?"

"A man's gotta live."

"By preying on women and leaving them to die in the desert!"

Nash wouldn't meet his eyes.

"I want you out of town right now."

"You can't make me leave. Why're you so worked up over a nigger woman anyway?"

The fist that exploded in Nash's face put him back on the floor. "Be out of Virginia City by sundown," Rhine said icily. "Or I'll hunt you down like a rabid dog."

Rhine collected his payment from the shocked Lady Ruby and exited the Silver Palace without further word.

On the ride back to the Union, his encounter with Nash made him glad he'd stepped away from his race. As a man of color he would never have been able to champion Eddy the way he had; not without threat of arrest or a noose.

That evening, Eddy was in the kitchen making the dough for the dinner rolls she'd be offering with Sunday's dinner. With the steadily increasing numbers of people showing up to eat, she hoped tripling the batch would allow each diner to have two rolls to accompany their meal of roast chicken and vegetables. She'd already cut up and seasoned the chicken pieces and they were resting in large roasters in the cold box. She still had a few cakes to ice, but overall her work was just about done for the day. Sylvia had gone over to Vera's for their weekly Saturday night card game. August was spending his evening with Cherry. Miner Gabe Horne was working the midnight shift, and she had no idea where the always boastful Whitman Brown was, nor did she care. All that mattered was she had the house to herself for the evening. Once she was done in the kitchen, her plan was to draw a bath, soak away the day's tension and the large bruise blooming on her forearm from Nash's unwanted attentions, and generally relax ahead of what would be a busy Sunday.

With the dough done, she divided it up, placed each soft mound in a bowl, and covered the bowls with clean, flour-dusted towels so the dough could rise undisturbed overnight.

Taking out more butter and sugar so she could make the icing for the cakes, a knock on the back door made her look up. It was dark so she had trouble seeing who was there. Wiping her hands on a towel, she walked over and saw Rhine standing under the light. She'd spent the balance of the day trying to convince herself that he'd not make good on his promise to stop by and see about her. With it being Saturday night, she was certain he'd be far too busy with his saloon. She was wrong. She drew in a deep calming breath. "Rhine."

"I came to check on you."

"Thank you. I'm fine."

"I just wanted to make sure."

As the night echoed around them, they studied each other through the screen. Common sense dictated she send him on his way, but instead she heard herself ask, "Would you like to come in?"

"I would."

By inviting him in, she was aware that she was opening herself up to whatever might come to pass, but she was determined to keep the walls she'd built around herself erect and intact. She stepped back so he could enter. His eyes brushed hers, and the air in the room seemed to warm and thicken. "Sit if you care to. I'm in the middle of icing cakes for tomorrow's dinner and I need to finish."

"Thank you. What kind?" he asked, taking a seat in one of the chairs.

She was determined to keep the atmosphere light. "Two gold. Two silver. We sell them by the slice."

As conscious of his presence as she was of her own breathing, she whipped the sugar and butter and added the sweet milk a bit at a time until the icing reached the proper consistency.

"Why'd you invite me in?"

The quiet tone of his voice stroked her like a hand, but she chuckled softly, "Because you obviously don't take no for an answer."

"There is that."

"Also, it's dark. You were discreet enough to come to the back door. I'm also here alone. Both of which will hopefully save me from the gossips." She began frosting the cakes, all the while telling herself she wasn't nervous.

"You do that well."

"Years of practice. As I may have told you before, my mother was a cook." As she moved on to the second cake, she saw him reach into his coat and extract some money. She froze. "And that is for?"

"I convinced Nash to return the money he stole from you and he gave me all he had."

She relaxed. "Oh."

"What's wrong?"

She shook her head. "Nothing. Thank you."

"Did you think I was trying to buy your services?"

She told the truth. "Yes."

"You're not a whore, Eddy."

"I know that but I wasn't sure you did."

He sat back. "Damn woman."

She shrugged. "Like you said: hard nut to crack. I've no experience with a man like you, Rhine, or truthfully, any man." She looked away. She was a novice at this and he needed to know that.

"Will you at least give me a chance to prove myself?"

"To what end? A few days ago you were engaged

to marry, and now you want me to believe you're genuinely interested in me as something other than a dalliance."

A smile played around his lips. "You don't plan to make this easy, do you?"

"Why should I?"

"As long as you don't take a bottle to my head, I think I can handle the challenge."

It was her turn to smile. "My mother said I get my temper from my grandmother. She was sold twelve times during slavery because she never met a slave owner she could abide. She was whipped a lot because of that." It suddenly occurred to Eddy that she was talking to a man who may or may not have been a slave owner. "Sorry. I probably shouldn't be discussing such a subject with you."

"No. It's okay. Your grandmother sounds like quite a woman. What else do you know about her?"

Eddy smoothed more icing over the cake with her wide-bladed knife. "She was supposedly an African queen."

He stiffened.

"You think that's absurd, don't you?"

"Not really," he said, eyeing her keenly. "Anything is possible I suppose. Does that mean I should bow to you each time we meet."

"Yes."

They shared a smile.

On a more serious note, she asked, "Do you

think I'll be arrested if Nash presses charges?"

"No."

"I hit a man not of my race over the head with a bottle. That's grounds for jail."

"You were defending yourself."

"In many places that doesn't matter."

"I was a witness, Eddy, and so was Lady Ruby. He deserved it. You won't be arrested. I promise."

"You have that much influence?"

"Frankly, yes, and besides he's left town."

"How do you know?"

"After I relieved him of the money, I suggested doing so might be in his best interest."

She paused. "You didn't threaten him, did you?"

"If you call putting a gun to his head and promising to track him down like a rabid dog threatening him, guilty as charged."

That left her speechless.

"So, I don't think he'll be pressing charges, and I'd already spoken to Sheriff Howard the day after we found you in the desert. Stopped by again today to give him Nash's description. He plans to wire other lawmen in the area just in case Nash surfaces again."

Eddy found it hard to believe how much he'd gone out of his way for her.

"Surprised?"

"Yes."

"Not all men who look like me are like Nash, Eddy. Some of us are honorable."

"Were you a slave owner?"

"No. Were you slave born?"

She shook her head and said, "No. My parents were freed by their owner in Kentucky right before they married."

"A love match?"

"Oh, absolutely. They loved each other immensely." What she didn't say was that they loved each other so much that when their bodies were found they were entwined beneath the wagon where'd they sought shelter from the storm—apparently in an effort to keep each other warm. "Did you love your fiancée?"

He shook his head. "It was more of a business arrangement, at least on my part."

She found that surprising, too, and wondered if Natalie shared that view. "If I ever marry—and I doubt I will at my age now—I want the kind of love my parents shared. Did your parents love each other?"

He whispered, "No."

Eddy studied him. The one word reply seemed to resonate with pain and sadness. Had either of his parents loved him? She'd felt the love of her parents every day of her life and in many ways still did. She wondered what his childhood had been like.

"Thank you for the marmalade."

She sensed he'd deliberately changed the subject. "You're welcome. I told Jim I'd teach him to make his own for you."

"I prefer yours."

"It's the same recipe," she said, looking up from frosting the top of the last cake.

"Doesn't matter."

"Why not?"

"Are you really that innocent?"

Eddy saw soft amusement overlaying the hunger in his eyes, and the bricks in her wall shook slightly. "Yes, and no, I suppose."

"With yours, I want to put it on your lips and spend the night tasting it."

Eddy swayed. Cracks crawled up her wall's foundation.

"And if that isn't clear enough, I want you, Eddy Carmichael, in a way that has nothing to do with race, but everything to do with me being a man and you being a beautiful woman."

Her hand shook so intensely she almost dropped the knife.

He stood and walked over to her side. Once there, he gently raised her chin. Time slowed. Needing to take a stand, even as his declaration rattled her to her core, she whispered, "I can't give you what you want."

"I know, little queen . . . so let me kiss you and I promise I'll go."

She knew she should tell him no, but curiosity,

yearning, and emotions that had no name conspired with those little shoots of hope to keep her from denying him and herself. He lowered his mouth to hers and the kiss was so masterful and overwhelming, the knife slid slowly from her fingers to the floor. As he eased her closer, the heat of his body and the way his lips fit so sensually against her own was new, wondrous, and oh so glorious. She thrilled to the soft seeking of his tongue, the faint scent of his cologne and the gentle yet possessive pressure of his arm against her back. Soon she was drowning in emotions so riotous and breathtaking, she forced herself to take a step back and out of the embrace in order not to offer him more.

Branding her with his eyes, he reached out and slowly traced her lips. "I want another, but I gave you my word that I would go."

Eddy was so enthralled, she had no words. What was it about this man that made her lose herself so completely and toss logic to the wind? Parts of her wanted him to stay, and for a woman who'd always known up from down and right from wrong, it was terrifying.

He stroked her cheek. "Good night, darlin'."

And then he was gone.

Later, after her bath, as Eddy lay in bed in the dark, she wondered if Sylvia knew of a nearby insane asylum she could check herself into. That she'd gone temporarily mad had to be the reason she'd let him kiss her, and heaven help her, want more. She touched her lips and the memory made them tingle. Did all men kiss with such intensity? Having no answer, she hoped now that he had kissed her, he would be content and move on. Truthfully, she found that not much to her liking because it would prove that he'd only been toying with her, just as she'd suspected, but the fiery encounter left her mind and senses so muddled she didn't know what she wanted—except more of his kisses, a shameless part of herself crowed. Uttering a loud groan, she punched her pillow, turned over and hoped the drumming sounds of the mine equipment would lull her to sleep before sunrise.

Chapter Thirteen

THE SUN WAS just coming up when Rhine finally entered his apartments above the saloon. Saturday night was always the Union's busiest, and after all the revelry and noise, he looked forward to some peace and quiet and grabbing a few hours of sleep. As he removed his tie and began undressing, his thoughts turned to Eddy. She'd been on his mind since leaving Sylvia's, but only now did he have the luxury of fully reviewing the encounter. She'd admitted to having no experience with men and he'd tasted that reticence in the kiss, but as the intensity took hold, he'd also tasted a hidden wellspring of passion any man would want to coax to the fore, and he was selfish enough to want to be that man. Her innocence made her ripe for seduction. All he need do was let passion overwhelm her and she'd be his, but he had more honor than that. He wanted the little queen to come to him of her own free will; wanted to hear her whisper his name as he slowly undressed her, tease her with his touch until she lay twisting in his bed and then feel her damp heat sheath him while they made love until they were both too sated to move. But the only proper way to turn fantasy into reality was to court her, and in light of the barriers that stood between them, he had no idea how to go about it. At least not presently.

Nude, he climbed into bed, and in the dark she continued to hold his thoughts. Hearing her say she was descended from a queen had stopped his breathing. With the blood of queens flowing through his own veins he'd appreciated the irony. Had the Old Queens placed her in his life as a cruel joke? Was he being tested to decide once and for all who he wanted to be? Or was she a temptation he was supposed to gird himself against? He'd never been this baffled by his feelings for Natalie. Never once had he gone to bed craving to see her as soon as the sun rose, but he felt that way about Eddy. She believed in love, something he knew nothing about because other than Andrew and his wife, he'd never witnessed it. Although his mother Azelia bore two children, she certainly hadn't loved or been loved by Carson Fontaine, and Carson's obsession with Azelia had fostered only bitterness and anger from his wife Sally Ann. There'd been no love there. Rhine assumed he'd been loved by his mother, but he couldn't swear by it. He'd been only a bit past five years old when she died, and sadly, he didn't remember her. Turning his thoughts away from that loss and the immensely painful knowledge of how and why she'd died, his mind shifted back to Eddy.

How could he ensure a future that included her?

There was the mistress route, but she'd never agree and he'd never ask. He supposed his only options were to either leave her be, which he'd already eschewed, or grab the bull by the horns and turn his life upside down. Truthfully it was probably the only way she'd accept him and his feelings. But that choice was a difficult one filled with immeasurable ramifications, including turning his back on nearly everything he'd built since coming west. That he'd even be contemplating such a drastic move was scary, but to not have her in his life was scarier. He had no clear vision of what he should do but he had to make a decision—soon.

"Eddy, there's a line of fifty people waiting outside!"

Eddy looked up into Sylvia's startled face and took a quick glance around the kitchen at the food she and Maria and her sons were preparing to plate. "We don't have enough to serve that many, Sylvia."

"I know, but what a wonderful dilemma to have."

Eddy wasn't so sure. She didn't like the idea of not being able to feed the people who'd come counting on a meal. "Do you have a plan?"

"Other than turning some folks away, no."

Eddy didn't like that either.

"If the Sunday numbers keep rising, we may need to hire more help and enlarge the dining room. In the meantime, I need to go back out and see how many more I can fit inside."

As she left the kitchen, Maria removed a large pan of done rolls from the oven. "People love your cooking, Eddy," Maria said.

"I'm glad, but I don't want any hard feelings from those who'll be turned away." That said, she went back to mashing potatoes.

Usually Eddy and Maria's tasks were putting the food on the plates while Maria's sons took the orders out to the diners, but due to the day's extra large crowd, the women had to do both. Eddy had been warned about the number of people, but when she stepped into the dining room carrying a plate in each hand the sheer volume shocked her. There were miners sitting on the floor along the walls. The room held fifteen people comfortably but Sylvia had somehow managed to shoehorn in so many more that there wasn't room left to turn around. The people lined up outside waiting to get in reached as far as the eye could see. Squeezed into the far side of the room was an old trestle table taken from the storage building out back. Where Sylvia had gotten the benches for it to provide the seating, Eddy didn't know, nor did she have time to dwell on it. There was too much to do. She and the Valdez family raced back and forth between the kitchen and the dining room setting down filled plates and removing the empty ones.

Luckily there were no menus, folks got whatever Eddy cooked, so they didn't have to waste time waiting for the diners to make up their mind. The offerings were chicken, mashed potatoes, sweetened carrots, and rolls. The only choice allowed was the cake. Silver or gold. When Eddy first began working for Sylvia, those who came to eat on Sundays would often linger over their meals and spend time chatting with diners at tables nearby, but not this day. Sylvia was moving about the room politely doing her best to encourage people to eat quickly so those waiting outside could take their place.

Dinner was served from two p.m. until four p.m., and by four-thirty when the last satisfied customers paid their bills and departed, a weary Eddy dropped into a kitchen chair. She was hot, sweaty, and her feet ached. Luckily, she'd had the foresight to put food aside for herself and the Valdez family, otherwise they would've gone hungry because there wasn't a scrap left.

Sylvia joined them while they ate. "We made another pile of money today. Eddy, you are a gold mine."

She smiled tiredly.

Sylvia turned to Maria and her sons. "And we couldn't have done this without you and your sons, Maria. Thank you."

She, too, offered a tired smile. "We need more help, Sylvie."

Sylvia nodded. "We do. I'll ask around town tomorrow. If you know anyone who might be interested, have them come see me."

"I will."

Once they finished eating, everyone pitched in to clean up and then the Valdez family went home.

"I think I'm going to draw a bath and relax for the rest of the evening," Eddy said. She really wanted to get off her feet.

"You've earned it," the pleased Sylvia said.

But before Eddy could leave the kitchen, there was a knock on the back door. Sylvia went to investigate. "Why, Zeke," she said, turning and smiling knowingly at Eddy. "What brings you here? As if I didn't know."

He entered the room, and the smile he turned on Eddy buoyed her a bit. She was glad to see him.

"I know you had to work today, Eddy, but I brought you some ice cream from the social. Probably all melted by now though."

"That was so sweet of you, Zeke." She took the small bowl from his hand. The ice cream had indeed melted but not all the way through. "Please, sit," she said. "Let me get a spoon."

Sylvia said, "I'll leave you two to your visiting."

Eddy dipped her spoon into the mostly melted ice cream. "This is very good. How was the social?"

"Not a lot of people. I hear most of them came

here after church. Mr. Brown wasn't too happy because it was supposed to be a fund-raiser. Can't raise money when no one comes."

"We did have a rather large crowd today. Maybe next time we can put a jar out and have people put in donations and turn the money over to the church."

"That's an excellent idea." He paused for a moment and asked sincerely, "How are you?"

"Tired, but it's the good kind. Everyone seemed to love the food."

"I do, too. As I said before, you're a fine cook, Eddy Carmichael."

She knew it made no sense, but she found herself comparing having him at the table with Rhine. Zeke's nearness didn't charge the air like a summer storm nor did she have trouble keeping herself or her breathing on an even keel. Would his kisses be even-keeled as well?

"Penny for your thoughts."

"I'm sorry. I was just thinking about how tasty this ice cream is. Thanks again for thinking of me."

"To tell you the truth, you've been on my mind a lot since we met."

"That's nice of you to say."

"I'd like to spend more time with you."

She was just about to respond when she looked up and saw Rhine standing in the doorway and she almost dropped the bowl.

"Sorry to interrupt," he said smoothly.

Eddy got the sense that he wasn't sorry about a thing. Zeke's eyes narrowed.

"May I help you, Mr. Fontaine?" she asked, and tried not to let seeing him take her back to being in his arms.

"I have a business proposal for you, but I can come back later."

"Tomorrow during the day would be preferable." Last night's encounter had been so searing, she didn't need a repeat performance roiling her senses again.

"As you wish. I'm also returning your cup." It was one she'd put the marmalade in. He walked over and placed it on the table beside her. "The marmalade was . . . memorable."

It was impossible not to remember his talk of putting the marmalade on her lips. His eyes said he remembered it as well. "I'm glad you enjoyed it," she managed to say over her pounding heart.

"I did. Anytime you have more to share, I'd be appreciative."

He was talking about kissing her again, and while a part of herself thrilled at the prospect, the sensible part reminded her that Zeke was a safer, more rational choice. "I'll keep that in mind."

"Good. I'll see you tomorrow. Again my apology for interrupting. Zeke." He inclined his head and left them alone.

"What kind of business proposal does he have in mind?" Zeke asked tightly.

"I've no idea." And she didn't.

"I do think he's interested in you, but then again, so am I."

Eddy had gone from having no beau to more male interest than she knew what to do with.

"As I was saying, I'd like to spend some time with you."

"I'd like that."

"There's a band concert Friday night I'd like to escort you to. It's sponsored by Fontaine's saloon though and he'll be there. Not sure how you feel about that."

"I'd enjoy going with you."

"Then it's a date. Thanks, Eddy."

"You're welcome. Thanks for the invitation."

"I know you had a long day. Let me get out of here so you can rest up."

She walked him to the door. He stood there a moment, and from his hesitant manner, she sensed he might be trying to decide whether to chance kissing her or not. He nodded a good-bye instead. "I'll see you at the auction."

"Have a good evening."

Once she was alone, she thought again how nice he seemed. No roiling for him. She liked his well-mannered attentions even as the sensual parts of herself awakened by Rhine's kiss eagerly looked forward to tomorrow.

Rhine sat brooding in his office. The saloon was closed on Sundays so the place was quiet. He'd not been expecting to find Eddy keeping company with Ezekiel Reynolds, and when told by Sylvia that she was, common sense said he should've just left the premises. But he was finding he had no sense, common or otherwise, where the little queen was concerned. He'd entered the kitchen just as Zeke confided his wanting to spend more time with her, and wanted to grab him by his collar and toss him outside. But he had no right. That truth only further raised his ire, and he realized he was jealous.

Jim Dade stuck his head in the door. "So did she agree?"

"I didn't get to speak with her. She was entertaining Zeke Reynolds and told me to come back tomorrow."

"Is that why you're looking so morose and he's downstairs looking so mad?"

"Who?"

"Zeke. He's downstairs. Wants to talk to you."

Rhine sighed audibly.

"This is better than one of those dime novels," Jim told him. "Should I send him up?"

"Yes, and then go away."

"I want to watch."

"Go to hell, Jim."

Chuckling, his partner disappeared.

When Zeke entered he didn't waste time with greetings. "So what are your intentions towards Miss Carmichael?"

Rhine took in the chilly eyes and stony manner. Although the two men were evenly matched in height, Zeke had a more powerful build. If he was bent on a fight, Rhine would have to shoot him in both knees first to throw the odds in his favor. "I want her to make the cakes for the Republican dinner at the end of the month." The annual social event was one Rhine had sponsored for the past few years. There was music, food, dancing, and no speeches.

"And outside of that?"

Rhine gestured him to a chair.

"I'll stand."

Rhine sat back and observed him for a moment. "Did she send you here?"

"No."

"Then why make this your business?"

"Because a man like you has no business around one of our women."

"From what you know of me, have I ever treated any woman of your race dishonorably?"

"No. Not that I know of."

"Then why would you think I'd treat Miss Carmichael any differently?"

"Let me ask you a question. Are you interested in her as more than a cook?"

"She's a beautiful woman."

"That's not an answer."

"Okay, I am interested, but I doubt she'll have me."

"You've discussed this with her?"

"What she and I have discussed is between us."

"Then as a man of honor, leave her alone."

Zeke wasn't the first person to tell him this and more than likely wouldn't be the last. "Anything else?"

"No."

"Thanks for the advice." Not the first time he'd said that either.

Rhine sensed Zeke wanted to say more, but whatever it was he bit it back, turned, and left.

Rhine blew out a breath and again wondered where his desire for Eddy Carmichael would lead.

Jim stuck his head in the door again. "It must be your day."

"Now what?"

"Natalie Greer's out front in her carriage. Wants to speak with you."

Wondering what in hell she wanted, he stood and went to find out.

Once again she was accompanied by her Chinese driver. "What can I do for you, Natalie?"

"I came to see if you've come to your senses."

"Concerning?"

"Marrying me. You've had ample time to think things over."

He studied the beautiful face that was just a veneer over her ugly thinking. "I haven't changed my mind."

"Then I'll be accepting Ethan Miller's proposal."

Ethan Miller was not the best choice for a husband. If he wasn't somewhere getting drunk, he was somewhere cheating at cards. "I hope you'll be happy."

"I'm sure we will. I'll send you an invitation to the wedding."

"Not necessary."

"This is your last chance, Rhine Fontaine."

"Understood. But I won't be changing my mind."

"Fine. Drive on!" she snapped at the driver.

He set the carriage in motion. Rhine walked back inside.

Eddy felt much better after her bath. She and Sylvia often sat outside at the end of the day to watch the sun set and the moon rise, so she joined her.

"Did you enjoy your visit with Zeke?"

"I did. He wants to escort me to a band performance Friday. I told him I'd go. Never had a beau before."

"About time then, don't you think?"

"I suppose, but I'm not staying here, remember."

"I do, but sometimes life intervenes and changes everything."

"That's sort of the way I felt when my parents

died." She'd lost them and then her sister Corinne. "Nothing was the same after that."

"Falling in love with Oliver Randolph changed my life."

Eddy was taken aback. "Then why are you two so at odds?"

"Noticed that, have you?"

"Yes, but I didn't want to be rude and ask."

Sylvia reached over and patted her on the knee. "You're a good girl. My husband Freddy was a wonderful man. Our marriage was arranged by our parents. He looked after me and treated me well but he wasn't affectionate. When Oliver began paying me attention, it was like finding water in the desert. He complimented me, told me how beautiful I was—even stole a few kisses. It was so heady I broke my marriage vows." She looked up at the stars coming out for a long moment and said softly, "And while Freddy was underground working in the mines to keep me fed and clothed, I was aboveground being unfaithful. In fact, Oliver and I were together the night Freddy died in the mine accident. Never forgave myself or Oliver."

"I'm sorry."

"No more than I."

"Do you still care for Dr. Randolph?"

"I tell myself I don't, but I do. I was hoping after he married his Felicity, my feelings would fade, but they didn't, and when she died in childbirth and he approached me again a few years later—I couldn't. The guilt was too strong. Still is."

Eddy found that very sad. She also had too little life experience to offer any advice, so she simply sat with Sylvia and watched the stars.

After a few minutes of silence she asked, "Do you know anything about this business proposal Mr. Fontaine has for me?"

"Yes. He wants you to make the cakes for the big ball he throws every year. Jim always needs help with the food preparations, and in the past my old chef would assist him."

"What kind of ball is it?"

"It's for the Republicans. Very very fancy."

"Black Republicans, too?"

"No."

"Should I accept?"

"I think you should. Rhine always pays well."

Eddy thought that over. "I told him to come back in the morning. We'll talk it over then."

"Is he still showing an interest in you?"

"Seemingly, but it isn't anything I can't handle." It was a lie, but she hesitated admitting the truth.

"Good. Keep him at bay. But doing the cakes may be advantageous. If his folks love your cakes the way our people love your food, you might be asked to do some baking for them."

"You wouldn't mind?"

"As long as it doesn't interfere with your duties here, feel free to make a little money for yourself."

"Okay. Thanks."

"I'm going in. I have to write to my brother and see how my mother's doing. She hasn't been well."

"Sorry to hear that."

"She's getting up in age and I worry about her."

"Does she live with your brother?"

"She does and he takes very good care of her. Are you coming in?"

"It's such a nice night, I think I'll sit for just a bit longer."

Sylvia gave her shoulders an affectionate squeeze. "I'm enjoying you being here, Eddy."

"And I'm enjoying being here as well."

Sylvia went in and Eddy sat. The breeze stirred the air enough that the sweltering heat had abated a great deal. In the background was the muted drumming of the mining pumps, and she thought about Sylvia's story of her husband and Dr. Randolph. What a sad tale. Life had certainly changed for Sylvia, just as it had for her. For now though, her life was good, and because it was, the call of California remained, but it wasn't as strong or consuming. She supposed if she had to stay in Virginia City she could, especially now that she'd met Ezekiel, but she hadn't given up on her dream to have her own place. That remained steady and firm. She refused to think about what staying might mean for her and Rhine though because she just didn't know.

Chapter Fourteen

RHINE WANTED TO go see Eddy as soon as the sun came up but he knew that was ridiculous. More than likely she had early morning duties to attend to and he wouldn't endear himself by showing up and interfering. Yet, the knowledge that he would get to see her at some point made the prospect exciting.

"So, what did Natalie want yesterday?" Jim asked as they ate breakfast.

"To give me one more chance to come to my senses, as she put it." Thinking about her was enough to ruin his day.

"She still thinks you're going to marry her?"

"Apparently. She'd come to give me one last chance to change my mind before she accepted Ethan Miller's proposal."

Jim choked on his swallow of coffee. "Ethan Miller?" he croaked once he recovered.

Rhine raised a forkful of eggs. "That's what she said."

"Now that's news for the gossips."

"Better her than me. I can't fathom her parents agreeing to such a disastrous union."

"Neither can I."

"She said she'd send me an invitation to the wedding. I declined."

"Let's just hope Ethan doesn't send invites to Lady Ruby and her girls."

Ethan was a regular at the whorehouse and didn't seem to care who knew. "That, I would pay to see."

They laughed.

Jim asked, "Are you going to see Miss Eddy today?"

"Yes. I'm hoping she'll agree to make the cakes and we can discuss the ins and outs."

"And use the opportunity to spend some time with her."

"That, too."

"As I said before, if you just told her the truth about yourself, things might be easier."

"Let's see how it goes first." He didn't want to admit that he'd been seriously considering the idea, consequences be damned.

"You'll be going to Doc Randolph to be sewed back together if Zeke has any say."

"Hoping it won't come to that."

"She is a fascinating woman though."

Rhine observed him above his raised coffee cup. "You're not thinking of throwing your hat in the ring, too, are you?"

Jim shrugged. "Think I'll wait until the rest of you kill each other off, then I'll have a clear shot." He popped a piece of bacon in his mouth.

Rhine chuckled and they returned to their meal.

Eddy spent her morning wondering what time Rhine might appear and rebuilding the walls against him. If she kept in mind that Zeke was a better choice, she'd be fine, or at least that's what she told herself.

And she was fine until he walked into the kitchen.

"Good morning, Eddy."

"Rhine." Why did he have to be more handsome every time she saw him? Why couldn't he be unshaven and attired in dirty ratty clothes, instead of a perfectly tailored white shirt and a well-fitting brown suit? Why did he have to be so tall and commanding? And why did he have to have such a knowing look in his green eyes, as if he knew what she was thinking? "Sylvia said you wanted me to make some cakes?"

"I do. May I sit?"

"Please."

They both took seats and her eyes lingered over the curve of his lips; lips that had left her so breathless and unnerved it had taken hours to get to sleep. Chastising herself, she hastily raised her gaze back to his face, and the now familiar ghost of a smile was waiting. "So, what would you like?" she asked, struggling to maintain her equilibrium. "In terms of cake," she added to keep him from offering an outrageous response.

"In terms of cakes, there's usually five or six

offerings at the event. How are you, little queen?"

The soft intonation of the question spread heat. "I'm fine but can we stick to cakes, please?"

"Then I shouldn't tell you I had to force myself not to come and see you as soon as the sun came up, or how you've been on my mind?"

"No. Cakes."

"How about wanting to kiss you again."

"You're determined to make this difficult."

"No, darlin', I'm determined to hold you in my arms again."

She was unraveling like an old rug. "Where should I bring the cakes and on what date?"

"The town hall. Last Friday night of the month."

Her hold on her defenses continued to flow through her grip like grains of sand.

"You're fighting fate, Eddy."

"Maybe, but I'm going to continue to do so with everything I have."

"Because?"

"Because if I don't you'll break my heart."

He stilled.

"When you're done with whatever this is we're doing, you'll move on to some woman far more suitable to carry your name and your children and I'll be left behind, so I'll keep you at bay for as long as I can."

"Eddy—"

She shook her head and said earnestly, "It's the truth, Rhine, and we both know it. So, let's get back to the cakes." Eddy thought it best that she keep reminding him where she stood. She also needed to keep reminding herself.

For a moment silence hung between them, and she thought he might try and convince her that she was wrong, but he didn't. Instead he said softly, "Okay, we'll deal with the business at hand."

"Thank you." In his eyes she saw what appeared to be regret? Sadness? She wasn't sure but her own emotions were caught somewhere between the two as well. If only he were someone else . . .

For the next thirty minutes they discussed what type of cakes he wanted, the time they were to be delivered, and how much he was willing to pay. Never once during the discussion did he flirt or call her little queen or let down the distant mask he now wore. They conducted a business transaction—nothing more.

Once the cake arrangements were finalized, he asked, "Would you be willing to assist Jim with other parts of the evening's meal? I'm certain he could use your help. You won't have to serve. I have other people hired for that. I'd pay you an additional fee of course and make arrangements for you to be taken home once you and Jim are done."

"How late will it be?"

"Probably past midnight."

Eddy thought about how the extra money would boost her savings. Additionally, she was always interested in becoming a better cook, and Jim might be able to teach her things she didn't know. "Yes. I'll accept."

"Good. Thank you. Do you have any questions?"

"No."

He stood, and for a moment they studied each other in the silent kitchen. Finally he said softly, "I'll see you at the auction Wednesday night. Good-bye, Eddy."

"Good-bye, Rhine."

As he walked out of the kitchen, she sensed he was walking out of her life. She was incredibly saddened by that, but telling the truth had been necessary not only for him but to herself.

The night of the auction arrived. Eddy, dressed in her fancy white blouse and new skirt, scanned the items on display in the orphanage's parlor. There were cakes and pies and certificates that could be redeemed for everything from haircuts by Mr. Carter to a dozen eggs from Lady Ruby. Mr. Rossetti had brought in the wringer, and Zeke's donation, hidden inside a wooden crate, remained a secret. He promised to arrive before the doors opened to reveal the contents and she couldn't wait to learn what it was. Her excitement turned to something else when Rhine walked into the parlor. "Evening, Eddy."

"Evening, Rhine." They hadn't seen each other since their conversation on Monday. He was splendidly dressed in a dark suit and snow white shirt.

"You look nice," he said.

"Thank you. You do, too."

"My tie's not crooked, is it?"

She found herself smiling at that memory. "No."

"Good."

Regardless of their talk, her feelings for him had not lessened. The familiar pull rose but she didn't allow herself to surrender to it.

He said, "I figured you'd need more seating so I've borrowed some chairs from the saloon. The twins are going to help me bring them in."

"Thanks."

He stood before her for a moment, giving her the sense that he had something he wanted to say, but he must have thought better of it. "I'll get the chairs." And left her standing alone.

Minutes later the twins, dressed in starched white shirts and what appeared to be their best trousers, brought in the chairs. They went about their task so seriously she wondered if they'd somehow been replaced by another set of boys. Her question was answered when Mary and Willa Grace entered the parlor.

"Are the twins behaving themselves?" Mary asked.

"So far, yes."

Willa Grace, who Eddy thought resembled a little brown sparrow, said, "I threatened them with no dessert until Christmas if they even think about being rambunctious this evening."

Eddy smiled.

Mary glanced around at the displayed items. "Are we ready to get under way?"

"Yes. Just as soon as everyone arrives."

"I dearly want to thank you for this, Eddy."

"You're welcome. Rounding up the items has been fun." Between the auction preparations and the diner, she'd really gotten to know the people of the community and now felt a part of it.

Once people began arriving, Eddy, Mary, and Willa Grace moved around the room thanking them for attending and for their support of the orphanage. Susannah was manning the punch bowl. Eddy had baked dozens of cookies last night and they were available to be enjoyed with the beverage.

As the crowd grew and the room filled with the sound of voices, Eddy spied Sylvia and Vera, Doc Randolph and Jim, and August and his lovely fiancée Cherry, among the throng. She was particularly pleased to see Mr. Rossetti with his wife. With them was a young girl Eddy assumed was their adopted daughter Felicidad, who immediately went over to Mary and gave her a strong hug. On the far side of the room, Eddy wasn't sure what Whitman Brown and madam Lady Ruby were discussing but they were engrossed in something that had them both smiling. Eddy decided she didn't want to know. Rhine, trailed by the twins, moved around the room chatting, too. Every now and then his eyes brushed hers but he kept his distance.

She realized she hadn't seen Zeke, and as if she'd conjured him up, he appeared at her side.

"Brought you some punch."

"Thank you," she said, taking the cup from his hand.

"Quite a crowd you have here, Eddy."

"It is impressive, isn't it?"

"Almost as impressive as the lady who put this together."

"You are such a charmer, Zeke Reynolds."

He sipped and grinned.

"So are you finally going to tell me what your mystery item is?" she asked.

"When it's time to bid, I'll announce it."

She really wanted him to reveal the contents beforehand so people could be prepared, but he seemed set on keeping it a secret so there was nothing she could do but swallow her slight pique and wait.

Barber Edgar Carter, sporting his freshly trimmed muttonchops and shiny bald head, would be the auctioneer. When Eddy and Mary determined it was time to get under way, he stepped to the table set up at the front of the room.

It was a fun evening. Bids flew fast and furious for the offered items: Jim Dade's angel food cake went to Mrs. Rossetti, Janet Foster's hairdressing service went to Lady Ruby, whose eggs were won by Jim Dade. Sylvia had put up a full course meal for bid. It hadn't come up yet but Eddy was anxious to see who'd win it. She glanced over at Rhine and found his eyes waiting. He gave her a nearly imperceptible salute with his punch cup and she smoothly looked away. In light of their conversation on Monday, she hoped he wouldn't make a bid on the dinner, but knew there was no guarantee.

Zeke's secret turned out to be a window, of all things. He explained, "The folks up in Reno who ordered it changed their minds." Windows were expensive, especially the size of the one he had up for bid. He promised to install it for whoever got the winning bid. Edgar opened the bidding, and after a few rounds of back and forth between Whitman Brown and Janet, Whitman won.

"Going to use it for the new church once we get it built," he announced, and the applause filled the room.

"Next up," Edgar said. "A bottle of champagne donated by the Union Saloon."

A buzz went up and Eddy stilled. Rhine hadn't said anything to her about what his contribution would be. She turned and gave him a quizzical look. He simply smiled and inclined his head.

Edgar said, "Now who wants to give the first bid?"

Eddy was astounded to hear Rhine's voice ring out.

Beside her, Zeke asked critically, "What's he up to now?"

Eddy had no idea.

Because Rhine had more money than anyone in the room, he of course proposed a bid no one could match, let alone best.

"Sold to Mr. Fontaine," Edgar declared.

While everyone watched with confusion and curiosity, Rhine walked to Edgar, took the bottle and then handed it back to him. "My gift to you and Aretha for your anniversary."

Edgar's eyes widened. Aretha's hand flew to her mouth, and with tears in her eyes she rushed to Rhine and gave him a hug and a peck on his cheek. Edgar shook his hand excitedly and the crowd applauded wildly.

It was one of the sweetest gestures Eddy had ever seen. "How thoughtful," she said.

"Yes it was," Zeke replied grudgingly.

She heard the edge in his voice but paid it no mind.

By the end of the hour most of the items were gone. Sylvia won Mr. Rossetti's wringer, and Eddy knew housekeeper Maria Valdez would be pleased when laundry day came around.

The last item on the docket was Sylvia's full course dinner. To Eddy's relief, Rhine didn't bid, but Amos Granger did, along with Whitman

Brown and Zeke, but it was Doc Randolph who won the day with a bid so high it rivaled Rhine's offer for the champagne.

Doc walked to the table and told the crowd, "I'm giving this money to Sister Mary and the children under one condition."

Everyone waited.

"Sylvia has to be my dinner partner."

Eddy's jaw dropped.

Sylvia looked stunned. Her support of the orphanage was well known, and Eddy hoped she wouldn't cost Mary the large sum of money by turning him down. She didn't. In a voice as chilly as her eyes, she replied, "You have a date."

Doc nodded approvingly and slapped the gold coins down on the table.

The evening began breaking up and people were saying their good-byes.

Zeke said, "Sorry I didn't get the bid for your dinner."

"So am I."

"Maybe we can have dinner together sometime soon. Not many places in town that'll serve us but we'll figure out something."

"That would be nice." Eddy looked away for a moment to wave at Vera, who was heading to the door.

He brought her attention back by asking, "Do we still have a date for the music concert on Friday?"

"Yes and I'm looking forward to it."

"Good. I'll see you then."

"Thanks again for contributing the window."

"You're welcome."

He departed, and Eddy wondered if he was really the man for her, and if so why didn't she feel the same challenging excitement that she felt with Rhine. Having no ready answer, she set the troubling question aside. For the next little while she made a point of speaking with everyone who remained, and they congratulated her on the successful auction. All the goodwill further solidified her feeling like a member of the community.

She'd just said good-bye to the Rossettis when Edgar Carter stopped her to ask, "How'd I do, Miss Eddy?"

"You were a grand auctioneer, Mr. Carter. Just grand. Thank you."

"I had a good time, and what do you think about that Rhine Fontaine? When he gave me this champagne, you could've knocked me over with a feather." He showed her the bottle in his hand.

"It was a generous gesture."

"You think so?" Rhine asked from behind her.

Smiling knowingly at his timing, she turned and looked up into his handsome face. "It was extremely generous."

"I'm glad you approved."

Ignorant of the undercurrents between them,

Edgar said, "Thanks again, Rhine. I want you to give the first toast. You are invited, you know."

"I do and I'd be honored."

"Good, then. Let me go and find my wife so we can start for home. I had a wonderful time, Miss Eddy."

He left them then, and as they stood together, she felt the familiar pull of Rhine's call.

"So, am I endearing again?" Rhine asked.

"I've always known you to be kind, Rhine." She hoped those moving about the room thought they were simply having an innocent conversation about the event and nothing more.

"I think I prefer endearing."

"You know we aren't supposed to be doing this anymore," she said. No matter how many times she put her foot down, the dance between them continued.

"I do. Can't seem to help myself. And what's your excuse?"

She laughed. "We're back to incorrigible."

"I'll answer to that."

The twins came over. "Excuse us. Mr. Rhine?" Christian said.

"What can I do for you gentlemen?"

"Can you come upstairs and listen to our prayers before we go to sleep?"

Micah chimed in, "Miss Mary said it was okay."

Eddy stilled. His ties to the boys went deeper than she knew.

"I'd love to."

Quietly moved by Rhine's commitment to them, she said to him softly, "Endearing, again."

He shot her a wink and he and the twins departed.

She spent another few minutes making sure the winners left with their goods in tow. Once the last person departed, a tired but happy Eddy walked into the kitchen to help with the cleanup and found Willa Grace washing dishes and Sylvia drying. Eddy grabbed a towel and Sylvia promptly plucked it from her hand. "You've done your share. Find a place to sit until I'm done here."

"But—"

"You were up most of the night baking cookies, you prepared breakfast for the boarders, and spent the rest of the time setting things up here. Go and catch your breath. We'll head home as soon as Willa Grace and I finish up."

Eddy realized this was a battle she was destined to lose. "Okay. I'll be on the back porch."

When she stepped out into the darkness, the moon was up and there stood Rhine, gazing out into the night with his back to her. He was so still and seemed so deep in thought she felt like an intruder. "I didn't mean to disturb you. I'll go back inside."

"You aren't disturbing me," he countered in a voice as quiet as the night's breeze. "How are things going inside?"

"They're cleaning up. Sylvie wouldn't let me

help. Says I've done enough for the day." She wondered why he was out there alone. "Are the twins in bed?"

"Yes, prayers said, and Mary and Willa Grace have survived to fight another day."

That made her smile. "Do you listen to their prayers often?"

"No. Tonight was the first time. I was honored to be asked."

"You care about them very much, don't you?"

"I do."

Silence crept between them. "Are you okay, Rhine?"

He looked back at her over his broad shoulder, and the moonlight showed his sadness before he turned away again. "Let's just say I'll survive, too."

"What's wrong?"

He didn't respond at first, and as the silence lengthened she thought he wouldn't. He finally said, "Mary may have found a home for the boys —a couple from Sacramento."

"That's wonderful."

"Yes, it is."

Yet there was something in his tone that seemed to match the sadness she'd glimpsed. She was confused by that at first until the pieces of the puzzle slowly fell into place. "You wanted to adopt them, didn't you?"

She saw him nod. "Yes. Mary even made some

preliminary inquiries on my behalf, but I'm unmarried and the state preferred they be placed with someone of their own race."

"I'm sorry."

"Don't be. It's for the best."

The urge to wrap her arms around him and place her head against his tense back and offer solace rose with such strength she had to fight it to remain where she stood. "Have the boys been told?"

"Not yet. She'll speak with them about it in the morning."

Eddy didn't know what else to say, but wanted to offer whatever she could to help him sort things through. "I've a shoulder to lend if you need one."

Sylvie called from inside, "Eddy, I'm ready."

Eddy felt torn.

He turned and met her eyes in the moonlit darkness. "Go on home, little queen. I'll be fine."

She nodded reluctantly and went inside.

On the drive back to the saloon Rhine wasn't fine by any definition of the word, but there was nothing he could do about it. Mary's news had left him reeling even though he knew the day would come, but he hadn't had enough games of marbles with the boys or flying kites or answering their endless questions, and selfishly he wanted more time. The young childless couple were members of the Sacramento church that had adopted the orphanage, and from what Mary learned from the wires she and the pastor had passed back and forth, they were fine upstanding people. They'd take the train down this week-end to visit, and if things went well, she would set the adoption process in motion. Even though he was glad they'd have a second chance, that chance wouldn't be with him, and because it wouldn't, sorrow rode him. Logically, he understood the state wanting them placed with people of their own race but his heart didn't believe that should be the only measuring stick. What about caring and commitment? Admittedly, he knew next to nothing about child-raising, but he and the twins could have learned along the way. Maybe sometime in the future similar situations would be measured differently, but today in 1870, he'd be losing his boys.

His thoughts moved to Eddy. When she stepped out onto the porch, he'd wanted to ease her into his arms and hold her close in the hope it might salve his broken heart. During slavery, he'd been expected to absorb the daily slights and ill treatment as if he were made of wood, and he supposed he'd carried the mask he'd learned to hide his emotions behind to this day. But knowing the boys would be leaving his life forever made the mask slip, and he had no one to help him dull the pain—no mother, wife, or lover. During his conversation with her on Monday morning, she'd spoken about being left behind with a broken heart when he moved on to someone more suitable. Now that Christian and Micah were leaving him behind, he truly understood her words. As he'd noted before, the decision to cross the color line had allowed him to reap many benefits, but it had cost him, too, and this time that decision would haunt him for the rest of his life.

Chapter Fifteen

ON FRIDAY EVENING Eddy got dressed and went downstairs to await Zeke's arrival. This would be her first time stepping out with a man, and she was both excited and nervous. She was wearing the lace-edged blouse Vera had made for her and was glad the seamstress had overridden her protests about not wanting something nice.

Zeke arrived a short time later dressed in a worn but clean brown suit. He looked very handsome and the flowers he handed her touched her heart. "Thank you." Having little to no experience with flowers, Eddy had no idea what kind they were, but they were lemon-colored, fragrant, and beautiful. "Let me find a vase."

After finding one in the kitchen and putting the flowers inside, she rejoined him.

"Ready?" he asked.

"Yes."

He offered his arm. "I don't have a buggy or wagon, so we'll have to walk."

She took his arm. "I don't mind." Truthfully, she didn't. A majority of the city's residents walked to their destinations. Only the wealthy were able to afford buggies and carriages.

As they set out, Eddy felt a bit self-conscious, especially when they passed people they both knew and were given smiles and nods. Being together this way was a public declaration linking her with the handsome carpenter. "So tell me about the concert?"

"The musicians are an all Colored band. Mostly horns and a drummer. They perform at the Union a few times a year."

"Will it be inside?"

"Yes."

She hadn't seen Rhine since the night he'd found out about the twins' possible adoption. She'd felt his grief and since then had been wondering how he was doing.

"Eddy?"

She startled. "I'm sorry. I was woolgathering. What did you say?"

"I asked if you liked music."

"I do, and you?"

"I do."

Embarrassed to have been thinking about Rhine when her attention should've been on Zeke, she was determined not to do it again.

But it was difficult at first. The moment she entered the crowded gaslit interior, her mind once again went back to being upstairs in the soft silence of his bedroom and how kind and caring he'd been. And then, seeing his ivory-skinned face and jet black hair behind the bar made her remember all she'd learned and felt about him since then.

"How about we sit over there?" Zeke asked.

"That's fine." Determined once again to keep her attention where it belonged, she let Zeke lead her to the table and help her with her seat.

He asked, "What would you like to drink?"

"Lemonade would be fine."

"Be right back."

Instead of the tables being spread randomly throughout, as they'd been at the Lincoln Club meeting, they were now lined up in rows like in a school. At the front of the room was a long, flat, slightly raised platform she assumed would be the stage for the musicians. Unfortunately though, she was close enough to the bar for it to be in her peripheral vision and she only needed a slight turn of her head to see it. And when she did, she was instantly snared by a pair of intense green eyes that threatened to tow her under, so she looked away.

Zeke returned with her glass of lemonade. "Thank you."

He sat. The place was filling up. People now familiar to Eddy nodded or came over to offer a personal greeting.

"So," Zeke said. "How did you meet Rhine Fontaine?"

The abrupt question caught her off guard and she wondered where this was going. "I was robbed while crossing the desert. I was near death when he and Mr. Dade found me and took me to Sylvie. They saved my life."

"I see."

"And you asked me that why?"

"Was just curious as to how long you've known him."

Eddy didn't reply.

"I'm sorry if I'm prying. A man just likes to know where he stands."

Any other questions he may have had were silenced by the musicians taking the stage. The three horn players, a piano player, and a drummer spent a few minutes tuning up. People who'd been chatting took their seats, as did people at the bar. She hazarded a glance in that direction. When Rhine's gaze brushed hers and held, she again wondered how he was. She finally turned back, only to find Zeke staring her squarely in the face. She startled. He gave Rhine a long steady look before settling his gaze on her again. Radiating displeasure, he turned away and Eddy sighed silently.

The musicians were talented. They played favorites like "Jimmy Crack Corn," "Jeanie with the Light Brown Hair," "Listen to the Mockingbird," and closed the concert with a rousing rendition of "The Battle Hymn of the Republic," but throughout, Zeke had very little to say and offered even less interaction. Eddy was saddened by the indifference, but took full responsibility.

When it was time to leave, his voice was cool. "Let's get you home."

"That isn't necessary. I can walk back alone."

"No."

Rather than argue she let him escort her out.

The air between them was as chilly as a Denver winter. He didn't offer his arm. Eddy saw no point in trying to draw him out, so she didn't.

After a few minutes of walking together silently, he finally looked her way and stopped. "Has he kissed you?" he asked quietly.

She didn't lie. "Yes."

Even though it was dark, she sensed his frustration, hurt, and disappointment. "I had hopes for us, Eddy."

"I know. I'm sorry." She wanted to explain to him how muddled her feelings were about Rhine, and how hard she'd been trying to keep him at bay, and that she knew she had no future with him, but she didn't know how to do it so Zeke would understand. Instead she said, "Let's just keep walking, okay?"

As they reached Sylvia's, he held her eyes silently for a time. "I'm not going to compete with a White man for you, Eddy. I'd just lose. He's got more money and can give you things I'll never be able to afford, but he isn't going to marry you. I hope you know that."

She didn't reply.

"Real sorry this didn't work out. Take care of yourself."

She whispered, "You, too."

And he walked away.

When Eddy entered the house, Sylvie came out of her office and asked cheerily, "How'd it go?" But she must've seen Eddy's sadness. "What happened?"

"I doubt I'll be seeing him again. I'm going up. We'll talk in the morning."

"Eddy?"

"Night, Sylvie."

Lying in bed, Eddy tried to convince herself that because she wouldn't be staying in Virginia City there was no reason to be sad about the mess she'd made of the evening, but it was a lie. She'd enjoyed Zeke's company and had had hopes for them as well. Now, all was lost, gone like autumn leaves in the wind, and there was no way to undo it.

The following morning she sat with Sylvie in the kitchen and told her about everything, including Rhine's kiss. "My life was so much easier when all I had to worry about was surviving."

"Men do tend to complicate things."

Eddy smiled ruefully. "Poor Zeke. I felt so guilty. And in the scheme of things, if I had to choose a beau he'd be a much better choice. He seems steady and even, whereas Rhine . . ." She looked at Sylvie, "How can I possibly want to be with someone I know is forbidden and will probably break my heart?"

"I don't know, honey."

Eddy didn't either.

Sylvie said sympathetically, "Maybe it will cool down over time."

"Or, I should have dinner with him and be done. Maybe that will be the cure I need."

"Do you believe that?"

"No," Eddy said. "But it sounds good."

Sylvie chuckled. "Sorry I'm not more helpful but I can't even figure out my own dilemma with Oliver, and that's been ongoing for over a decade."

Eddy was just glad to have someone to talk to. "Did he say when he wants his dinner?"

"No, but I almost fell over when he made that declaration."

"Maybe you two will work things out."

"We'll see."

There was silence for a moment before Sylvie turned to her and said, "I want you to consider something for me."

"I'll try."

"I'm thinking of closing the dining room."

Eddy froze. "Why?"

"Because your cooking's bringing in way too many people and it's putting a strain on the house and on me. I'm getting old."

"But—"

"Now wait. Let me finish."

Eddy nodded.

"What I'd like to do is open a larger place and have you run it as part owner."

Surprise widened Eddy's eyes.

"This is something I've been considering since that Sunday the diners descended upon us like locusts. There's profit to be made, honey, and you are the golden goose. We need to strike while the iron's hot."

A dozen questions sprang to mind so quickly she wasn't sure which one to ask first.

Sylvia must have seen the wonder in her eyes. "I take it you like the idea."

"Yes, but I don't have the funds to invest to be an owner."

"That's okay. I'll take care of the investors and give them a small share of the profits in exchange. All you need do is cook. I've watched you, Eddy. You're knowledgeable, efficient, and talented. Truth be told, it's also my selfish way of keeping you here."

Eddy smiled.

"I enjoy your company," Sylvia continued.

"I enjoy you as well."

"Good. Think about my proposal and we'll talk more soon." Sylvie stood. "I'm going over to Janet's to get my hair done, then out to Aretha's to help with her anniversary preparations. The party's next weekend. You're still going to make the cake, correct?"

"Correct." Eddy looked up at Sylvie. "Thank you." She'd gone from nearly dying in the desert to maybe having her dreams come true.

"You're welcome."

Sylvie went back inside and left Eddy alone to think over the earthshaking news.

My own place! Even the idea of being part owner left her giddy. Her original plan for California had been to work herself to the bone until she saved up enough money to buy a place and then start small. She'd resigned herself to the fact that it might take years to be a success, but now? Now she could realize her dream here in the place she'd come to think of as home. She liked the small community of people here and they liked her. She wanted to jump up, throw her hands in the air, and run around the yard like a happy child. Sylvia Stewart was a godsend, and if the new place actually came to fruition, Eddy vowed to never make her regret taking her on.

In the days that followed, Eddy continued her cooking, and whenever she and Sylvia got the chance, they talked and planned. How big would the diner be? How large a staff would be needed? Sylvie talked of apartments being built above the place, where Eddy would live, a notion that filled Eddy with even more glee. After living in tiny cramped boardinghouses most of her adult life, having her very own washroom was unimaginable. They also took a ride around the city and looked at available properties. One, they ruled out immediately due to its close proximity to Beech's Shooting Gallery. The gallery was a combination saloon and shooting gallery. Miners could drink and practice their shooting on targets nailed on the walls. According to Sylvie, such establishments had been around since Virginia City's birth. So far no one outside or inside had been killed, but everyone believed it would only be a matter of time, which was why the town council had been trying to outlaw the place for years. However, there was an open lot not too far from the boardinghouse that met their needs.

"Do you own it?" Eddy asked once she got down from the wagon and looked around. It was located near a large Catholic church on the edge of town.

"No, but I'm pretty sure this is one of Rhine's. In fact, he owns most of the places we've looked at. I doubt the bank will let me buy new land without making me dance a jig and pay an extraordinary interest rate, so going with a plot he already owns might spare me the headache."

"Will he be one of the investors?"

"Yes. No one else will back us the way he will."

"Have you spoken with him?"

"I have. He likes the idea, and because he'll be

my largest investor, he'll be on the deed as a part owner."

Eddy thought about how that might impact her future. Having him be a part owner meant the two of them would be dealing with each other often, and considering their volatile relationship, there was no telling what effect that would have on her new life in Virginia City.

As if reading her mind, Sylvia continued, "I will say this about him. I've never known him to let personal issues get in the way of business."

Eddy decided to trust Sylvia on that and not let herself be overwhelmed by worries of what ifs.

Sylvia said, "Now I don't want you to be alarmed, but Zeke Reynolds will be our architect and builder. I've asked him to do some drawings for us to look at and approve."

"Lord, Sylvie."

She smiled understandingly. "I know, honey, but he's the best man available and this, too, is only about business."

Eddy sighed. Zeke had stopped coming to the dining room, and his cousin August had been very cool and distant lately.

"You'll survive," Sylvie promised. "We women always do."

Sylvia left the kitchen to attend to her duties, and Eddy went to the sink to start washing the breakfast dishes. She'd come to a decision. She was done doing the two-step with Rhine. If he still wanted to have dinner with her, she would. As she'd told Sylvie, she hoped it would be the cure she needed to move on with her future, but more importantly, looking down the road of her life, she saw no opportunities for her to experience what it meant to be with a man who desired her. And he'd made it quite plain through both words and action that he did. She thought back on the fervent kiss they'd shared, the way he'd melted her at the market, the ways he'd been calling to her senses since the first time he carried her in his arms, and how vulnerable he'd appeared the night on the porch at the orphanage. Rhine was as layered as he was handsome. She'd been practical, level-headed Eddy Carmichael her entire life, and for once she wanted to be reckless, throw caution to the wind and let him gift her with memories she might not otherwise have. Did the idea scare her? In some ways it did, but she set them aside. For one night she wouldn't care about barriers, what was forbidden, or who he was, because heaven help her, she was in love with Rhine Fontaine.

At breakfast over at the Union Saloon, Rhine told Jim, "Sylvie wants to build a new diner on a plot I'm going to sell her, and in exchange I'll be an investor."

"So, when she woos away even more of our customers, where will that leave us besides headed straight to the poorhouse?"

Rhine smiled. "We'll be fine. The miners aren't going to abandon this place and we both know it. Eddy's cooking is drawing such crowds, Sylvie can't feed them all."

Jim looked up from his plate. "And is Eddy going to be the cook?"

"Yes. If the plan works, Sylvie will make money and I'll plow my take back into the Union so you and I can make more money."

"Makes sense." But he had a knowing look in his eye.

"This has nothing to do with Eddy."

"I'll believe it when roosters start laying eggs."

Rhine raised his cup of coffee. "Okay, I'll admit it'll be nice having her stay in town rather than moving to California." And making her a part of his life permanently, if things could be worked out.

Jim eyed him for a moment. "Having her around has been good for you."

"How so?"

"She's got you thinking about things you might not have considered otherwise."

"Such as?" he asked.

"Who you want to be when you grow up."

He was right. One of the reasons Rhine had crossed the color line was his envy of men of power, because as a slave he'd had none. Men like his father, Carson Fontaine, and the other slave owners had the ability to alter lives, the freedom to come and go as they pleased, and the wealth to command respect. Viewing their way of life from the outside, he'd wanted that, craved it even, and was determined to be thought of in those terms instead of the insulting and degrading Constitutional designation as three-fifths of a man. For the past five years he'd achieved that status. Now? He was rethinking who he wanted to be, and yes, Eddy was the primary reason. He glanced at his very wise partner and friend. "Eat, King Solomon."

Jim smiled and nodded. "Eating."

Later that evening Rhine drove over to Sylvie's with the legal papers needing her signature for the property sale, but he found only Eddy. She was in the kitchen.

"Sylvie and Doc Randolph left here about an hour ago," she informed him. "They've gone to help Mrs. Singleton. Her baby's on its way a month and a half early."

Rhine knew the Singleton family. "I hope the babe will be okay."

"I do, too." She was seasoning chicken parts and placing them in a large roaster. It wasn't an alluring task but he found her beautiful nonetheless. "Do you mind if we talk about the new diner for a few moments?"

She didn't look up from working. "No. Sit

if you want. What happened with the twins?" she asked, pausing to wait for his reply.

"Mary said the visit with the couple went well. She's going to start the adoption process."

"And how are you feeling?"

Appreciating her concern, he sat and shrugged. "I've resigned myself to the situation. As we discussed, this is what's best for them and I want them to be happy."

She nodded understandingly.

Not wanting to dwell on the heaviness still clouding his heart, he asked, "Any idea what kind of appliances you want for the diner? I'll be doing the purchasing so I need to know your preferences."

They began talking about stoves. She wanted a flat top that would allow her to cook with varying temperatures, and they discussed size and dimensions. They then moved onto cold boxes and china, flatware, pots and pans, and all the rest. He had to admit the longer he was with her the more he desired her, but he kept it in check so she wouldn't toss him out on his ear. "Did you enjoy the concert Friday night?"

"I did."

There was a tightness in her tone that gave him pause, so he asked, "Did Zeke do something to upset you?"

She replied quietly, "No. He was the perfect gentleman. I—I just won't be seeing him anymore."

"Why not?"

He watched her hesitate. When she finally looked him in the eyes she said simply, "Because of you."

"Me?"

"Yes, you. Zeke senses there's something going on between us and asked me flat out if you'd kissed me."

"And you told him the truth."

"Yes, because I didn't think lying was any way to start things between us."

He thought about the lie he'd been living, though he'd be changing that soon.

She continued, "And I'd hoped he'd appreciate my honesty."

"But he didn't."

"No."

"I'm sorry."

She didn't respond but he could tell she'd been hurt by the encounter. He wanted to take her in his arms and soothe her, but he knew better.

She continued, "And now I have you investing in the diner, and him drawing up the plans. What a mess."

He smiled.

"It isn't funny."

He agreed softly. "No, it isn't, darlin', but you just look so put out."

She shot him a glare.

"And I love it when you do that."

"What?"

"Glare at me. I remember the very first time. It was the night you tried to stand in that cocoon you made out of my blanket."

"You weren't very helpful."

"As if you wanted help. I'd yet to meet a more stubborn woman."

"Determined."

"Stubborn." And he was stubborn enough to want her in his arms and ultimately in his life. Knowing she'd probably chop him up and season him like the chicken she was still working on, he asked anyway. "Have dinner with me."

"Fine."

He almost fell off the chair. "You're saying yes?"

"Yes."

"Why?"

"Because I want to know what it means to be desired."

Eyeing her wondrously he paused. "Say that again."

"You heard me the first time. I want to know what it means to be desired."

He was admittedly speechless. Still filled with wonder, he scanned her slowly. The thought of fulfilling her wish made his groin tighten with appreciative anticipation.

She shot him a shy smile. "Am I too bold?"

"No. Not at all." Still studying her, he crossed his arms to keep himself seated because he wanted to pick her up, carry her home, and take his time showing her just what being desired meant.

"You look pleased," she said.

"I'm more than pleased."

"It'll only be one dinner though. One."

If he got her alone in his rooms again, she might not surface until Christmas, but he kept that to himself. "So when is this momentous occasion going to take place?"

"You choose."

"Now."

She laughed. "No."

"You told me to choose."

"I'm up to my elbows in chicken parts. Choose another day."

"What about tomorrow?"

"The diner's open tomorrow so can you wait until Friday evening?"

"I suppose."

"Don't pout," she said, walking to the sink to rinse her hands.

He chuckled and walked over to join her. "Is there anyone else here?"

She shook her head, picked up a nearby towel, and dried her hands. "Why?"

He leaned in and gently brushed his lips across hers. "Because I'm desiring you, and I want to give you a taste of how much . . ."

She trembled sweetly but didn't pull away. "Your incorrigible side is showing again."

He drew her close until her warmth was flush against him and his arm across her spine kept her there. She was tempting, soft and so sweet, he felt as if he'd died and gone to heaven. His lips whispered over her jaw, and the sound of her breathless response thrilled him. The first time he kissed her had left him wanting more, but this slow unhurried taste of desire made him want to undo the tiny buttons of her blouse and savor the heat he knew he'd find against her silken skin. He ran a possessive hand up her spine while he coaxed her mouth to open so he could slide his tongue boldly inside and mate with hers lazily, wantonly. She groaned with pleasure and he couldn't wait to treat her body to the same fiery dance. "I want to touch you, Eddy." Putting actions to his words, he moved his palm over the nipple of her breast. "Here." Unable to resist, he lowered his head and bit the nipple hidden beneath the fabric of her blouse, and she crooned raggedly. He gave the other nipple the same heated salutation, then recaptured her lips while his fingers played with the now hardened buds of her breasts. More than anything he wanted to undress her and fully explore her beauty, but he reminded himself that they were in Sylvie's kitchen. That joy would have to wait. "I should go before Sylvie comes home and finds you spread out on the table like dessert." He dipped his head low again for another taste of her breasts, and when he raised it her head was back, her eyes were closed, and her lips were parted passionately.

As if she'd only then processed his words, her eyes opened sluggishly. "On the table?"

He kissed her deeply. "Yes, on the table."

"Why would you kiss me on the table?" she whispered.

He smiled at the innocence the question held. "Because desire sometimes happens in the oddest places, little queen. You'll see." He traced her lips. "Did you enjoy yourself?"

"Yes."

"I did, too. I'm looking forward to our one evening." No way was it going to be a one-night interlude. If he had his way it was going to be the first in a lifetime of passion-filled nights.

The sound of the door closing in the front room made them both look up. Rhine gave her a quick kiss, then hastily returned to his seat at the table.

When Sylvie entered the kitchen, Rhine was studying the papers he'd brought for her to sign and Eddy was wiping down the counter with the dishrag.

He spoke first. "Good evening, Sylvie."

"Rhine."

Eddy asked, "How'd the birth go?"

"Fine. No complications."

Rhine knew that if he stood, Sylvie would see the proof of what they'd been doing, so he stayed seated. That small short taste of Eddy had left him hard with arousal, and Eddy looked like she'd been thoroughly kissed—and she had.

For a few long moments, Sylvie took them in silently—first Eddy and then him, saying finally, "I hope the two of you know what you're getting into."

Neither of them responded.

She asked him, "Are those the agreement papers I need to sign?"

"Yes."

"I'll look them over and get them back to you as soon as possible."

"Thanks."

Taking them in one last time, she walked out and left them alone.

In the silence that followed Rhine said, "All things considered, I think we handled that pretty well."

Eddy laughed.

They fed on each other visually in the quiet kitchen, and he wondered how much of a fight she'd put up when he asked her to marry him. "What time would you like dinner?"

She replied, "Six? Seven?"

"Let's make it six. If we start the evening early we'll have more time to enjoy each other's company. "I'll send Jim around to drive you to the saloon." He hated that they needed to be discreet, but it was necessary due to the times.

"That would be fine."

Rhine didn't want to leave her but knew he must. The proof of how much he wanted her had eased enough for him to stand. "I'm going to keep my distance and bid you good night from here because if I walk over there, I'll kiss you again." He loved seeing the lingering remnants of desire in her lips and eyes.

"That might be best."

Taking a moment to view her a few seconds longer, he inclined his head, shot her a smile before his departure. Outside, he climbed into his carriage. Driving toward the Union her words came back: *Why would you kiss me on the table?*

He chuckled all the way home.

"So you decided to have dinner with him?" Sylvie asked Eddy on Friday evening as Eddy stood at the kitchen door gazing out unseeingly at Mount Davidson.

"Yes."

"You look very nice."

"Thank you." She had on one of her nice Vera-made blouses and a lovely brown skirt.

"Are you sure this is what you want to do?"

Eddy looked back. "Yes." She thought back on her heated encounter with Rhine, and just the memory made her nipples tighten shamelessly.

"Then you'll get no lecture from me."

"Is there an insane asylum nearby?"

Sylvie smiled. "No honey, but you'll have to be very discreet—both of you will."

"We're only going to have dinner this one time."

"That's what I said about me and Oliver. Passion can change your life."

Eddy would be the first to admit that it already had. "Thank you for not judging."

"I'm the last person to be judging anyone."

Eddy was grateful for her counsel and understanding.

Jim arrived a few minutes later and handed her into Rhine's carriage before driving them away. Eddy didn't want to second-guess herself but she was terribly nervous and the silence in the carriage was awkward.

"I made you an angel food cake."

That cut some of the nervousness she felt. She smiled. "Thank you."

"Rhine's a good man, Eddy."

She nodded and wondered who she'd be after their evening together.

The drive was a short one. Jim halted the carriage at the saloon's back door then came around and helped her down.

"He's in the kitchen waiting for you."

She gave him a nod of thanks. As he drove away, she drew in a deep calming breath, turned the knob, and walked inside.

Chapter Sixteen

"GOOD EVENING, EDDY."

More nervous than she ever remembered being, Eddy pulled the door softly closed behind her. "Good evening, Rhine." Looking at him made all the memories of their last visit flood back. He'd left her breathless and eager for more. Now they were embarking on their first evening together and a different kind of nervousness took hold, one fueled by sensual anticipation.

"Are you as nervous as I am?"

She smiled. "Yes."

"Then come, let's go upstairs and see if we can't put each other at ease."

He gestured for her to go first. He brought up the rear and closed the door at the base of the stairs, effectively sealing them off from the noisy saloon and the world. The gaslight on the wall offered just enough illumination for them to see their way up. The last time she'd been on the stairs, she'd been carried down them in his arms.

When she reached the top she saw the closed door that led to his bedroom and more memories rose.

As if able to see into her mind, he said softly, "Welcome back."

He ushered her a short distance down the gaslit

hallway to the closed door of one of the spare rooms and opened it. "After you."

The interior was sparkling with candlelight. She looked up at him questioningly.

"You said I could have candles."

Smiling, she entered. That they weren't using his bedroom eased the riot of butterflies in her stomach and she relaxed a bit. The table was set for an elegant meal. Over the years, she'd set many a fancy table. Never once had any of them been set for her personal enjoyment, however, and she was so moved tears stung her eyes. The gleaming china and glassware, the way the candlelight played over the white damask table-cloth, the beauty of the roses elegantly displayed in a cut crystal vase, were her undoing. The table was set as if she truly was a queen. "This is lovely," she whispered around the lump in her throat.

"I hoped you'd be pleased."

She took it all in again. "I'm usually the one setting a table like this, not dining at it."

"Tonight is not the usual."

She supposed it wasn't. The Eddy of old could never have imagined herself in such a situation. Not here with a man like this.

"You're not allowed to think about anything except having dinner."

"You didn't tell me there would be rules."

"Just a few."

"Such as?"

"That you enjoy yourself this evening and allow me to please you with my wit and charm."

She chuckled. "Anything else?"

He reached out and used his thumb to slowly trace her lips. "Yes. You can think about me being endearing, incorrigible, and of course kissing you."

Her knees melted.

Putting action to words, he gave her a series of soft humid kisses that slowly melted the rest of her. "Endearing enough, Your Majesty?"

Eyes closed, her body filled with a sweet trembling, she whispered in a voice as hushed as the room, "Very much."

He stepped back and once again traced her lips. "Then I've passed the first test. Shall we dine?"

He helped her with her chair before settling into one on the opposite side of the table. The distance allowed Eddy to try and regain her wits.

Over a grand meal of roast beef and gravy, vegetables, and light-as-air biscuits, they were too busy eyeing each other to converse very much. Every time she looked up, his vivid eyes were waiting, filled with a power that warmed her blood and made the sensual anticipation rise higher.

After the meal, he brought her a piece of angel food cake on a small glass plate. "Would you like a bit of champagne?"

In for a penny, in for a pound, she thought to herself. "Just a little, please."

He walked over to the sideboard, opened the bottle and poured some of the golden liquid into a lovely crystal flute and set it beside her cake plate. After pouring himself a portion, he returned to the table.

"The way the candlelight is playing over you in that beautiful white blouse makes you look like an angel."

She'd never been paid such a compliment before.

"My thoughts are hardly angelic, however."

"You're being incorrigible again."

"A beautiful woman does that to a man. How many buttons are on your blouse?"

She looked down at them and then across the table at him. "Ten, maybe eleven."

"Would you undo the first four for me, please?"

Fork in hand, Eddy paused and studied him.

"This is about the desire you wanted to learn more about."

Realizing she'd set her own trap and hoping he didn't see the slight shake in her hands, she put the fork down. Singed by the heat in his eyes, she slowly honored his request, feeling her body bloom with each button she freed.

"Thank you," he whispered. "I'm going to place kisses there when you finish your cake."

Eddy dissolved. He was way too good at this.

She'd expected kisses, not this pure seduction.

Although she had enjoyed the angel food cake in the past, she barely tasted it because she was too busy thinking about his stated plans. In need of bolstering, she took a moment to sip her champagne. She then set aside the plate holding the remains of her cake.

"Done?"

She nodded.

He stood. "Bring your champagne."

On shaking legs, Eddy did as asked. He took her hand and led her the short distance to a wingback chair upholstered in a beautiful jewel-like dark blue.

He sat and coaxed her to sit on his lap. "Hand me your champagne."

Having never sat on a man's lap before in her life, she handed him her flute, and he set it next to his on a small table near the chair. Gathering her in, he eased her close to his chest. The heat of his body melded with hers, and the light scent of his spicy cologne wafted gently to her nose. "I've never sat on a man's lap before. Can you feel me shaking?"

"I can, so just relax. We have all evening." He kissed the top of her hair, and after a few moments of being held by him, her tension eased.

"Better?" he asked.

"Yes."

"Good," he whispered. "Now, about those kisses I promised."

As his mouth descended to hers, Eddy tried to remain in control and not be swept away as she had been a few days ago in the kitchen of the boardinghouse, but she was still as new to passion as she was to the sweep of his fiery hands and lips. His mouth left hers to blaze a trail over the skin exposed by her opened blouse, and her pleasure-filled moan rose in the silence of the otherwise silent room. The tip of his tongue slipped over the edge of her new lace-edged shift, grazing the tops of her breasts, and for a moment she inanely wondered if he thought less of her for not wearing a corset. When his thumbs teased her already berried nipples and he slid the garment aside just enough to take the bud into his mouth, she was glad she refused to wear the constricting garment. Apparently he was, too. Rising up, he held her eyes and husked out, "Undo more buttons for me."

Eddy felt hot, scandalous, but gave him the boon. He rewarded her by easing the soft cotton down to free her breasts. He feasted in earnest, and a smoldering took root between her thighs. He claimed her lips again, and as his tongue played invitingly with hers, his large hand slid up and down her skirt-shrouded thigh. When that same hand slipped beneath to explore her stocking-encased limb, soft gasps escaped from her lips.

She heard him say, "I want to touch you, Eddy." Her skirt was rucked up high past her garter, and his palm was mapping the bare skin above it.

He asked huskily, "Yes? No?"

Her world was so hazy and she was so caught up in the storm she had no idea what he was asking.

"Open your legs, darlin'. Let me feel your desire there, too."

Feeding on his voice, she complied, and his bold touch followed. She then knew what he'd been asking. Bewitching fingers circled, dallied. She arched and panted softly, "Rhine."

"You're so wet."

The storm gathering in her body grew stronger with each indrawn breath. "Rhine," she cried helplessly.

"Go ahead, darlin', let it come, baby. I have you."

Her legs widened, his wicked fingers continued to bestow their enthralling magic. Suddenly, the storm broke, crackling through her body like summer lightning, and she was flung to the stars, hoarsely screaming his name.

Eddy didn't know how much time had passed, but when she opened her eyes he was smiling down. Still breathless, she asked, "What in heaven's name was that?"

"An orgasm. When your body can't hold any more pleasure it explodes sort of like black powder. Did you enjoy it?"

Embarrassment heated her cheeks and she turned away.

He gently turned her chin so she was again looking into his eyes. "There's no shame in anything we do together," he informed her quietly. "Only pleasure. Please don't ever be ashamed of enjoying yourself."

She'd never felt anything like the orgasm before. Even now remnants lingered, slowly beating between her thighs in cadence with her heart and breath. "Do men have orgasms, too?"

"Yes, but doing it properly usually results in babies, and we don't want that right now."

"No, we don't." But she wondered what a child made by the two of them might look like. Turning her mind away from that, she noted how limp yet full she felt. The logical and levelheaded old Eddy was appalled at how free she'd been with him, while the newly awakened woman inside wondered how long she had to wait to experience it again.

He repositioned her skirt and righted her shift. She shrugged back into her blouse and redid most of the buttons. "Thank you for the lesson."

"You're welcome." He slid a worshipping finger down her cheek and he took on a serious air. "Marry me, Eddy."

Hearing that, she sighed. "You know I can't. Please don't spoil our evening."

"I'm not trying to, but I'm serious. Marry me."

She looked away for a long moment and wondered why he'd bring up such a subject after what they'd shared. Maybe she understood it but it changed nothing. Yes, she loved him, but that didn't change anything either. Turning back, she picked her words carefully. "You know what we'd be facing. It might look to be an easy road from where you sit, but it isn't. You're not Colored and I'm not White. Us being together is against the law almost everywhere."

"But I'm not White either."

She chuckled and shook her head. She thought back on all the good she was told he'd done on behalf of the city's Colored community. "Maybe not inside."

"Not outside either."

When he didn't say anything else it was as if he wanted the words to sink in. She met his steady gaze and the hair rose on the back of her neck. Gooseflesh prickled over her and she stared, agape.

"I'd like to tell you a story."

Filled with wonder, she thought it couldn't possibly be true. A hundred different questions ran riot through her brain.

"May I?"

Stunned by the implications, she nodded horse-like.

"I was born to an enslaved woman named Azelia. The man who sired me was her slave owner, Carson Fontaine . . ."

Enthralled, Eddy listened as he told her about his life as a captive, his sister Sable and half siblings, Andrew and Mavis. Her heart broke hearing that Azelia took her own life after the birth of his sister, to prevent Carson Fontaine from siring any more children with her. Hurt filled her to learn he'd been five years old on that awful day and had no memory of his mother. "Oh, Rhine. I'm so sorry."

"No more than I."

He related the first time he learned he could pass, the whipping he'd received as a result, what he'd done during the war, and his decision to come west. "I couldn't wait to leave the South behind. I'd lost touch with my siblings, and when I learned the railroads were interested in hiring veterans, I signed up."

And in St. Louis he was reunited with his brother Andrew. "I ran into him at one of the gambling dens. He was at a table and had won so much money in stocks and gold, the stack was nearly as tall as you."

Eddy smiled.

"He was elated to see me as I was him. After the game ended he scraped up his pile of winnings, we took a room at a nearby hotel and got very drunk."

Amused, she shook her head.

His voice turned wistful. "The next morning, he gave me half that stack of winnings."

"My goodness. Why?"

"Said I was owed it for the years I worked for nothing, and because brothers looked out for each other. Needless to say, I was done working for the railroad."

Eddy nodded understandingly.

"When we left St. Louis, I came to Virginia City, bought stock in the mines, made myself even more wealthy. He went on to San Francisco, invested his money, made himself even more wealthy, too, and now he's a banker."

"Andrew sounds like a very special man."

"He is. I can't wait for you to meet him."

"Does Jim know the truth?"

"Yes. I told him when we became partners. He's kept my secret all these years."

Eddy had another question. "Why didn't you change your name? Don't most people who pass do that?"

"I wanted Sable to be able to find me. If I changed it, she wouldn't be able to."

"You must love her a great deal to take such a risk. Someone from your past could've shown up here and exposed you."

"I know. I relied on my faith in the Old Queens to keep that from happening."

"Old Queens?"

"Like you, Your Majesty, I too am a descendant of African royalty."

She stared. "No!"

"Yes, but I'll save that tale for another time."

Eddy found his story riveting. "So why change your life now? You could lose a lot."

"I already have. I lost the twins. Mary said had I been Colored she could have maybe passed me off as a long lost relative. The state probably wouldn't have cared. But since I wasn't . . ." He then said softly, "I didn't want to lose you, too."

The tiny shoots of hope she'd been harboring inside suddenly grew tall and straight under the bright sunshine filling her heart.

"I do want us to marry, Eddy, but truthfully, it's unfair of me to expect an answer right now. I want you to think about it for a few days."

She agreed. "I'll also keep your secret."

"Thanks. I need to contact Andrew. A few years ago we hatched a plan just in case I had a change of heart. Either way, my business holdings and money won't be affected. It isn't against Nevada law for me to own land or a business. I'll break the news to the White Republicans at the upcoming ball. After that, socially, I'll be a pariah in their circles, and will most certainly be asked to resign from the town council, but that's a small price to pay."

Eddy could imagine how people like Natalie

Greer were going to react. "Some might want to harm you."

"I know. If I have to protect myself or those I love, I will. And if anything does happen to me, I expect you to seek out my brother. He'll know what to do. Promise me."

"I will, but let's hope it doesn't come to that." There was so much bad happening around the country now that the war was over. She didn't want any of it spilling onto him for reclaiming his heritage.

He eased her back into his arms and she snuggled close. "You've led quite a life so far, Rhine Fontaine."

"I'm hoping you'll be with me for the rest of it, Eddy Carmichael, but in the meantime, I need more kisses."

She laughed and rose. "I thought you'd never ask."

It was very late when he drove her home. When he pulled up behind the boardinghouse, sadness claimed her. She didn't want to leave him. "I had a wonderful time."

"I did, too."

She reached up and cupped his cheek before leaning in and kissing him good-bye. "I'll see you later at the anniversary party."

"Do you think we can sneak off and open a few buttons?"

Chuckling, she said, "Don't even think about it."

"I have, which is why I said that."

"Go home."

In the silence that followed, they each mined all they'd shared. His voice turned serious. "Thank you for a grand evening."

And it had been grand indeed. "Good night, Rhine."

When she reached the porch, she waved. Once she was inside he drove away, and the changed-forever Eddy Carmichael tiptoed through the darkness to her room. She fell back onto the bed and smiled. Marriage. To Rhine. She then turned serious. His revelation continued to resonate. Having never been enslaved, she could only imagine the pain-filled memories he carried inside. The next few weeks were going to be trying for him. Turning his world upside down and having to face those who'd undoubtedly denounce him and maybe even threaten his life would take an incredible amount of strength. That he was willing to do so in order for her to be his wife—she had no words to describe how special and loved it made her feel or how much she loved him in return. As long he didn't expect her to give up her dreams—and she knew he wouldn't—she saw no reason to say anything but yes.

Rhine was having an equal amount of trouble putting his feelings into words as he drove back to the saloon. Spending the evening with her had been more than he could've imagined. No matter what he had to face, he knew he'd made the right choice to reveal his true self. He loved Eddy Carmichael. He worried that she might be angry about being deceived, but she hadn't been and that made him love her even more. He'd give her some time to think over his proposal but in his heart he already knew she'd say yes, and there were no words to describe how that made him feel either.

It being a Friday night, the saloon was still open. When he entered via the back door, Jim was in the kitchen.

"Well?" Jim asked.

"I told her and asked her to marry me."

His partner smiled. "Good for you. How's it feel?"

"She hasn't agreed yet but she took the story well. She's worried about retaliation."

"I am, too. Some of these folks aren't going to like knowing you were hiding right under their noses."

Rhine agreed. "I'll break the news to them at the ball and they can all howl at me at once. I'll wire Drew later today so he'll be abreast of the situation and start buttoning things down." Then he and Eddy would no longer have to worry about being seen together. He could start taking her driving out into the desert. They could dine publicly. Although dining in secret did have its advantages. "Are we all set for food and beverages for Edgar and Aretha's anniversary party?"

"Yes."

"Okay, then I'm going up and change clothes. Be back down shortly. Thanks for being a good friend."

"You're welcome."

Upstairs in his bedroom, Rhine changed clothes. The saloon would be open another few hours, and he had to go back downstairs and play host. His thoughts drifted to Eddy. Who knew she'd be so uninhibited? He cast his mind back to the memory of her rising and falling to his touch and he was aroused all over again. They'd have to have a repeat performance soon. In the meantime, he'd wait for her to say yes. He also planned to share the truth about himself with Sylvie and Doc Randolph as soon as possible. Over the years both had been stalwart friends, and deserved to know before anyone else.

Ready to head back downstairs, he quietly thanked the Old Queens for putting Eddy in his life and hoped that Sable wouldn't be far behind.

Chapter Seventeen

THE FOLLOWING MORNING, in keeping with his plan, Rhine walked to the telegraph office and sent his brother Andrew a wire with the one word message: *Azelia*. It was the coded word they agreed to use if Rhine ever decided to step back over the color line. Once the operator confirmed that the message had been received on the other end, Rhine set off for the return trip to the saloon to help with the preparations for the day's festivities. People were on the walks going about their morning errands, and he nodded a greeting to those he knew. When he came upon council member Clyde "Wally" Swain and his thin-as-a-hickory-stick, wife, Ora, Rhine said, "Good morning."

Swain, still angry over the failure of his proposal to ban the children of color from the local schools, offered a terse, "Fontaine," and didn't break stride. Rhine smiled to himself. Once word got out about who he really was, he was sure Wally was going to be ecstatic over never having to publicly acknowledge him again.

That afternoon, everyone had a good time at Edgar and Aretha Carter's anniversary party. Rhine gave the first toast, wishing them continued marital bliss, and the attendees responded with supportive cheers. Eddy received compliments and thanks from the happy couple for her cake, and she and Rhine moved through the celebration trying to be discreet and not stare at each other from across the room. It was difficult when all she could think about was how dazzled she'd been by his kisses, and all he could think about was finding a secluded spot so he could treat her to another fiery orgasm.

After the affair ended, Eddy stayed behind to help Jim with the cleanup while Rhine invited Doc Randolph and Sylvie upstairs to his office.

"Have a seat, if you would, please."

As they complied, Sylvie appeared and sounded wary as she asked, "What's this about, Rhine?"

So he told them. And when he was done, a smiling Sylvie thrust her palm towards Doc and crowed, "Pay up. I was right."

Tight-lipped, Doc reached into his pocket and slapped a gold piece onto her outstretched palm, and it was Rhine's turn to be confused.

Sylvie explained, "When you first came to town and started doing good works for our community, I bet Doc you were passing."

Rhine laughed. "What?"

She nodded. "I have cousins who are as fair-skinned as you, so it wasn't a stretch for me."

Rhine didn't know what to think. "And you never said anything?"

"Wasn't my place. If you'd wanted folks to know the truth, you would've told them."

Thoroughly outdone, he looked between the two of them. "Anyone else in on the bet, or maybe knows?"

"No one else was in on the bet," Doc assured him. "But that you might be passing has been talked about, at least among our people. Nine times out of ten we can usually tell. The Whites of course have no idea. The only see what's in front of their faces."

Rhine knew that to be true, but the idea that Doc and Sylvia had made a bet so many years ago was both surprising and amusing. "Thanks for keeping it secret."

"Being Colored in this country is not easy," Doc said. "And I understand those who pass and never come back. We all have to make choices in life. Why tell us now though?"

"Because I'm in love with Eddy and I want to marry her."

Sylvia's jaw dropped. "Oh my. That's wonderful. We haven't had a wedding in quite some time."

Doc said to her, "If you're so fired up about a wedding, how about you stop being so stubborn and marry me?"

She froze. "What?"

He tossed back. "I know you're aging, Syl, but I didn't know you were going deaf, too."

She shot him a glare so reminiscent of Eddy's, Rhine choked back a laugh. Sensing a brewing battle, he stood. "I will leave you two to work this out. If you need to reserve the Union for the reception, let me know."

Sylvia said, "I'm not marrying him."

"Yeah you are."

They were still going back and forth when Rhine made his exit.

Downstairs, he found Eddy in the kitchen washing dishes, and she asked, "You told Sylvie and Doc about your decision?"

"Yes."

"How'd they react?"

When he told her story about the bet, she laughed. "Leave it to them to have already figured it out. How do you feel?"

"Okay." And he did. That they'd guessed but never openly discussed it publicly only cemented in his mind just how special the two were.

"Is she ready to go home? I'm almost done here."

"Not sure. She and Doc are in my office having a small argument."

"Lord. Over what?"

"Whether she's going to marry him or not."

She went still as a post. "Really?"

"I told them if they need to reserve the Union for the reception to let me know, and then I tiptoed out before the cannonballs started flying."

She chuckled.

Rhine asked, "Where's Jim?"

"Took the rubbish to the dump. Said to tell you he'd be back shortly."

"Then I might have time to undo a few buttons."

"No, Mr. Incorrigible."

"I probably don't have time to treat you to an orgasm, but then again you were quite quick last night."

"Is that a bad thing?" she asked, her face serious.

"No darlin'. Not at all. In fact it was beautiful. You'll have more stamina the more we play. Speaking of which, have you considered my proposal?"

"I have."

"And?"

"I have one question. Are you expecting me to give up my dreams?"

"Of course not. I don't want you to change anything about who you are—except maybe your name."

"Good, then my answer is yes. I would love to be your wife."

He smiled and a thought occurred to him. Grabbing her hand, he pulled her away from the sink. "Come with me."

"Where are we going?" she asked, trying to keep up with his faster pace.

He opened a door in the wall of the kitchen and hustled her inside. "Storage room."

He closed the door behind them, and she found herself being so thoroughly kissed, any protests she may have wanted to voice slowly dissolved into pleasure. In the shadowy room with the potatoes, onions, shelved soup pots, and crockery, her buttons were undone and he treated her to a series of touches and heated caresses that made her arch and croon. He paid slow tribute to her breasts until she melted like chocolate in the sun. He then raised her skirt and murmured through the line of kisses he was placing against his throat, "Hold your skirt aside for me . . ."

She took the yards of fabric in hand, and he plied her so shamelessly and wantonly it didn't take long for her to explode. "You're so good at this," she breathed, her eyes closed. "So good."

He kissed her and whispered, "Aren't you glad?"

"Very."

They took a minute to right her clothing and slipped back into the kitchen. Aching with need, Rhine prayed their wedding night would come soon, because if he didn't get some relief he was going to be reduced to crawling on his hands and knees in order to get around.

With no baseball games, fund-raisers, concerts, or anniversary parties to attend, Eddy settled back into a regular routine of cooking for the boarders and the large crowds frequenting the dining room. Rhine was on her mind most of the time, as were his kisses.

One afternoon while she was in the kitchen

frying chicken before the diners arrived, Sylvie entered accompanied by a man Eddy didn't know.

"Eddy, this is Sheriff Blaine Howard. Blaine, my cook, Eddy Carmichael."

He was a tall man with white-blond hair and gray eyes. His star was pinned to his chest. "Pleased to meet you, Miss Eddy."

"Same here," she replied, all the while wondering why he'd come.

Eyeing the platter filled with the fragrant, golden chicken pieces, he said, "Just stopped by to let you know the sheriff up in Reno has apprehended the man you knew as Father Nash."

Eddy went still. "That's wonderful news."

"Yes, it is." His eyes were riveted on the chicken she was removing from the oil. "His real name is Ned Weathers and he's wanted from Nevada to St. Louis and back for everything from assault and theft to embezzlement. He made the mistake of stealing from the sister of one of the Reno bankers, and the sheriff caught him before he could leave town."

Because of the laws, Eddy doubted she'd be asked to testify, but it didn't matter as long as Weathers was charged and sent to jail.

The sheriff added, "Sorry we weren't able to grab him after your run-in with him at Lady Ruby's. I think he hotfooted it out of town."

Because he made it sound as if he were unaware of Rhine's threats, she didn't bring it up.

"I appreciate that, but it's okay. He's been caught." She wondered about the boy though. "When I met Weathers initially, he had a little boy with him he called Benjy. Did the Reno sheriff say anything about him?"

"Yes, they found him at a campsite Weathers was using. The boy said Weathers is his father. The sheriff is trying to verify that."

Eddy was glad the boy had been found safe, but what kind of a man takes a child along while committing crimes? Saddened by that, she hoped some kind of arrangements were made to ensure the boy had a more secure life going forward. Seeing Howard still eyeing the platter of chicken, she asked, "Sheriff, would you care for a couple of pieces of chicken as my way of saying thanks for bringing me such good news?"

"I thought you'd never ask."

She took down a plate and placed two hot pieces on it.

He sat. He ate. He smiled. "Been hearing a lot about how good you can cook. Be nice if I could get this on a regular basis, but—"

Eddy understood. Times being what they were, the Whites didn't patronize Sylvia's, but she had an idea. "Suppose we wrap it up and have someone bring it to you? We'd have to charge you a bit extra of course." Out of the corner of her eye she saw Sylvie beaming.

"You'd do that?" he asked.

"Of course. Would that be a problem, Sylvie?"

"Not at all. Just say the word and we'll send it over and no one will be the wiser."

He finished his chicken. "Can I pay you for say three more pieces?"

A smiling Sylvie said, "You bet."

When he left, Sylvie said, "Eddy Carmichael, I think you just tapped us into a gold mine."

And Sylvie was right. Over the next few days, some of the White businessmen in town began approaching Sylvie about placing orders. She happily obliged and hired Maria's youngest son Martin to make the deliveries.

Rhine was on a business trip to Silver City, and Eddy hadn't seen him since the Carters' anniversary party. Just thinking about their fiery moments together made her sigh at the memory of his shamelessness and her own. His tutoring her in what it meant to be desired had her craving more and she missed him. She was in the kitchen peeling potatoes when she heard, "Good afternoon, Miss Carmichael." And there he stood, handsome as the day was long and wearing a smile that matched hers.

"Miss me?"

"No," she tossed back sassily. "I haven't thought about you once in the three days, five hours, and twenty-seven minutes you've been away."

"Too bad because I've spent every minute

thinking about how you'd look on my lap with your skirt raised and your buttons opened."

Her eyes widened and she hastily looked around to make sure they weren't being overheard. "You are so scandalous."

"Not nearly as much as I'll be the next time I get you alone."

Heat filled her and she had to admit she couldn't wait.

Smiling as if he knew what she was thinking, he said, "I just left Sylvie the papers for the property she's buying from me. Everything is signed and sealed. She can begin building whenever she's ready."

Eddy's heart swelled. Her dreams were one step closer to reality. She was also gaining an incredibly generous, incorrigible, and scandalous husband, too. She considered herself the happiest woman on earth.

"When do you want to get married?" he asked.

"Can we make it as soon as possible?"

"Now?"

She chuckled. "No."

"Tomorrow?"

"How about we wait until after the ball so all that turmoil will be behind us." The ball was only a few days away. "Are you worried?" she asked.

"I suppose, but I'm more looking forward to starting life with my sassy little wife, who I'd really like to kiss right now, but I passed Whitman

Brown coming in, and I don't want him to see us."

"No, we don't want that." But she was dying for a kiss.

He turned serious. "I plan to be a good husband to you, Eddy. I don't want you to ever regret saying yes."

"And I don't ever want you to regret stepping away from who you once were, so I'm going to be the best wife I can be to you."

The look they shared silently sealed their pledges.

"Sylvie doesn't have a storeroom, does she?"

Eddy laughed. "No."

"Pity. I'll have to figure out a way for us to be together without prying ears or eyes soon."

"I'd like that."

"Any further word on Sylvie and Doc getting married?"

"No," she replied. "And I'm afraid to ask."

He chuckled. "Understood."

She shared the news about Father Nash's apprehension.

"Good. Hope he gets sent to the penitentiary for a very long time."

"I do, too."

For a moment there was silence, and Eddy saw a longing in his eyes that matched hers.

"I should probably go," he said. "Otherwise I might drag you into my arms and give the gossips something to talk about."

She figured after the ball the gossips were going

to have a field day anyway, but she and Rhine would be able to go on. "Glad you're back."

"So am I. I'll see you soon." He mimed a kiss and walked out, leaving her alone.

Looking forward to the time when they could be together permanently, Eddy sighed and resumed peeling potatoes.

The next afternoon, although she was truly looking forward to her life with Rhine, she wasn't looking forward to the meeting she and Sylvie would be having with Zeke Randolph about the architectural plans.

When he arrived, his demeanor was so cold and detached he may as well have been made of ice. He laid out the drawings on the kitchen table and went over the layout of the building, the size of the rooms, and their orientation. Eddy thought the drawings were excellent and told him so.

"Thank you," he said tersely. "Barring any problems with the weather or supplier delays, we should be able to get it built in six weeks. Do you have any questions?"

They didn't.

He gathered up the drawings. "I'll see you ladies next time." And strode to the kitchen door and was gone.

Eddy looked to Sylvie, who simply shook her head in response.

"Maybe he'll find someone else."

"Let's hope so."

Eddy wondered how he'd react once the truth came out about Rhine, but she supposed it didn't matter.

Over at the saloon, Rhine and Jim stood by the windows to watch the crowd of biddies outside marching back and forth with their signs, singing hymns, and shouting slogans denouncing the establishment. He spotted Natalie and her friends, the mayor's wife and a slew of women he was unfamiliar with. They'd been out front for over an hour. "When do you think they'll move on?" he asked Jim testily. "It's not like we're the only saloon in town."

"Who knows, but Natalie could have something to do with it. She seems to be yelling the loudest and wearing the angriest face."

Rhine focused on her, positioned at the front of the crowd, and had to agree with his partner. She'd never shown the least bit of interest in anything political the entire time he'd known her but now appeared to be boisterously embracing the cause. Dressed in all gray, she was shaking a sign that read: VICE IS THE ROOT OF ALL EVILS!! He folded his arms in frustration because the group was also verbally castigating his customers in an effort to shame them into not entering the saloon. When Cyrus Benton, a big burly carpenter, walked up, the women began their vocal assault. Cyrus, known for his quick temper, snatched Natalie's sign from her hand, threw it into the next county, and continued on inside. Natalie stomped her foot with fury, her companions cried foul. After a few moments the singing and chanting resumed but they moved on to harass another establishment.

Jim cracked, "I think Cyrus deserves a drink on the house."

Rhine chuckled, "I agree."

The night of the ball, a formally attired Rhine surveyed the buffet tables. He was known for putting on a big spread at this event, and Jim and Eddy had outdone themselves with the variety of dishes and desserts offered. Good thing, too, he thought, since this would likely be the last ball he'd sponsor, at least for the Lily White arm of the party. The wait staff had arrived and were getting into their supplied uniforms. In a few minutes his guests would begin arriving as well. He'd let them enjoy the food and champagne first before making his announcement.

Eddy walked up and cast a critical eye over the offerings. "Anything you want changed?" she asked.

"No. It's perfect."

"Good."

"You look very nice," she said.

"My tie straight?"

She grinned. "Yes. If you need anything, let us know. Jim's slicing the roast now. He'll bring it out on the platter as soon as he's done."

The first of his guests, the mayor and his wife, entered the hall.

"I should get back to the kitchen so you can tend to your guests," she said to him. "I hope things will go well."

"So do I," he replied. He was looking forward to it being over though, so he could spend the rest of his days with her.

As she turned to retreat to the hall's kitchen, he called to her quietly, "Eddy?"

She stopped and looked back.

"I'll be driving you home. Think I'll treat you to a black powder explosion outside under the moonlight."

She laughed and walked off. He ran appreciative eyes over the sway of her skirt then focused himself on getting through the evening ahead. Once it was over, kissing Eddy under the moonlight would be his reward.

While the musicians played, Rhine spent the first hour greeting his guests and encouraging them to help themselves to the food and drink. Some of the wives in attendance had been members of the marchers outside his saloon and he wondered if they felt like hypocrites for enjoying his hospitality. He knew better than to ask, and besides, after he made his announcement, none of it would matter. He spotted Natalie and her parents entering and walked over to them. "Welcome."

Lyman's nod was chilly. "Rhine."

Rhine turned to his wife and Natalie. "Ladies."

Natalie forced a smile and handed her wrap to the attendant. She said nothing to Rhine.

As if to balance the family's response, Beatrice Greer said genuinely, "Hello, Rhine. Looks to be a wonderful affair, as always."

"Thank you, Beatrice, and you look lovely. Help yourselves to the buffet."

She smiled, and they moved off to mingle with the crowd.

He did the same, and as another forty minutes crept by he noticed that some of the couples were dancing. He checked his timepiece. The noise level of voices had risen significantly, an indication that many of the men were well on their way to being drunk. The wait staff behind the tables were still dishing out food. Rhine had had enough. He wanted to get this part of the evening over with. He walked over to the musicians and asked that they stop playing. When they did, he called out, "May I have your attention, please."

It took a moment or two for the room to quiet, and once it did, he continued. "I'd like to thank you all for your attendance. As you know, the money raised by ticket purchases will be given over to the party as it always has been." He glanced around at the familiar faces, drew in a breath and said, "But what you don't know is that the man you've known as Rhine Fontaine was born a slave on a plantation in Georgia."

As if he were telling a joke, some people laughed, but the serious set of his features apparently made them think differently and soon silence filled the room.

"Say that again."

"I was born a slave."

People began looking at each other confusedly and a buzz went through the crowd.

A male voice yelled out, "A slave? You're a nigger?"

Rhine's jaw tightened at the slur but he nodded.

The buzz grew louder and seemingly tenser.

Natalie came over to him and said angrily, "Stop lying!"

"I'm not lying, Natalie."

"You're White and everyone in this room knows it!"

"No, I'm not."

"Yes you are! Why are you doing this? Haven't you humiliated me enough?" She'd gone from angry to furious.

"This has nothing to do with you, Natalie."

Another incensed male voice rang out. "You played us for fools all these years? Damn you!"

"That wasn't my intent."

"You Black bastard!"

Natalie yelled, "Tell them this is just a joke!"

"It isn't."

"Yes it is! Don't you think I'd know the difference between a White man and a nigger! There's no way I'd be engaged to one or let one kiss me!"

"Well, you were."

"No, I was not! Why are you lying!"

He heard glass breaking as people dashed champagne flutes and plates to the floor as if the contents were suddenly contaminated or held a contagion. Outraged men yelled out their foul opinions of him before gathering their wives and hastening to the exit, while others hurried over to tell him to his face just what they thought of the deception. More than a few slurred him. Another few told him he'd better leave town. Natalie, her eyes wild, screamed hysterically, "Damn you! Tell the truth!" and began hitting at him until Beatrice and Lyman stepped up to quickly pull her away.

Over by the kitchen door, Eddy watched the disintegration of Rhine's ball with a heavy heart. Only a brave man would've willingly stepped into such a firestorm of irrational hate. One moment they'd been his friends and now they were red-faced with fury, their fists balled as if spoiling for a fight simply because he'd revealed his true heritage. She glanced up at Jim standing beside her. His jaw was tight, his eyes keen, as if he was ready to step into the fray should any violence occur. When the glass began breaking, she said, "I'll get a broom."

He nodded but kept his eyes focused on his partner and the furious men circled around him. The wait staff seemed frozen in place. "Start clearing the tables, please," she told them. "Then go on home." They'd already been paid so there was no reason for them to stay any longer than necessary. She and Jim would handle the cleanup.

By then most of the crowd had departed, so Eddy began sweeping up the glass- and food-littered floor. But when she heard, "You! Get my wrap!" she turned and looked into Natalie Greer's haughty face.

Eddy studied her calmly her for a second. "I'm sure the attendant can help you with that."

"I want you to get it!"

Eddy saw a man and woman approaching. She hadn't met the girl's parents but from the facial likeness she assumed that's who they were.

"Come, Natalie," the woman said.

"I'm waiting for her to get my wrap."

Eddy had seen her attack Rhine and the crazed performance that led up to it. Even now there was an unhinged look in her teary red eyes. "As I said, the attendant will get you your wrap."

"And as I said, you get it. I'm your better. Do what I say!"

"Natalie!" her mother gasped, sounding shocked.

Natalie ignored her and snarled at Eddy, "You're

the reason Rhine is lying, aren't you! What kind of voodoo did you put on him to make him deny his race!"

Her father took her by the arm. "Come, Natalie. Let's go home."

"I want an answer!"

But her parents were already dragging her to the door while she raged and screamed the entire way.

Eddy resumed sweeping.

On the ride home after the ball, Rhine said to Eddy, "That wasn't so bad. They only called me a dirty Black bastard a few times."

"And how dare you play us for a bunch of fools, twice," Eddy added. She knew he was hurting from having to endure what he had, and she hurt for him.

"Natalie put on a particularly ugly performance, however. She's convinced I'm lying about all this."

"I saw. I had a particularly nasty run-in with her when folks began making a beeline to the door."

Rhine looked away from the reins for a moment. "What happened?"

"She demanded I retrieve her wrap in a tone I didn't much care for, but I was polite. She accused me of putting a voodoo spell on you to make you denounce your race. Her parents finally dragged her off, but she acted almost unhinged, Rhine."

"Hopefully she'll calm down at some point, but

the evening's over—all of it's over, and I'm glad."

Eddy still worried about future repercussions and knew he did as well.

When they drove past the boardinghouse, she said, "Speaking of unhinged. You just drove past the house."

"I know. Not taking you home yet. You have a date with the moonlight, remember?"

Eddy laughed. And without being asked began to undo her buttons.

They were in the desert when he finally stopped the carriage. The moon, full in a cloudless sky, bathed the surroundings in soft cool light. The night was breezy.

He turned to her and said, "Now . . ."

Eddy's senses began to rise.

His finger gently traced a slow fiery line across the skin bared by the open halves of her blouse then over the rise of her breasts above her thin shift before he leaned down and licked the tip of his tongue against the trembling nook of her throat. "Your sweetness is so much stronger than their hate."

She dissolved. His hot mouth trailed lazily up to her lips, and as he coaxed her onto his lap the kiss deepened and she caught fire. The rest of the encounter was a blur of sensation fueled by pleasure from his hands and lips. He boldly bared her breasts to the moonlight and after treating them to a series of tantalizing tributes left them berried and damp. Her skirt was raised, her drawers removed, and she didn't care. Magnificent touches plied her core with a boldness that made her thighs part and her hips rise in ardent response. He played, dallied, and circled until she was wet with wanting and gasping his name.

"Are you ready to come?" he asked in a voice as dark and hot as the night.

Eddy didn't want to, even as the forceful orgasm began building she wanted the pleasuring to continue, but the only word she could form was, "Please . . ."

"On our wedding night, I'll please you with my tongue and kisses . . . here." The sultry promise and the brazen way he plied the tight bud at the gate of her soul sent her over the edge and she exploded with a long shuddering cry.

Watching her ride out her orgasm made Rhine want to settle himself between her lovely little thighs and have at her until neither one of them could breathe. The sight, coupled with the feel and tastes of her had him insane with desire. He was as hard as a railroad tie, but he wanted to wait for their wedding night before loving her completely, and he would even if it killed him.

Moments later when she was back inside herself, he smiled down and said, "Now, I can take you home."

Chapter Eighteen

AT BREAKFAST THE following morning Jim dropped a stack of newspapers on the table. "You made the papers."

As Jim sat, Rhine sighed and picked up one. The headline read: RHINE FONTAINE—A LIFE OF LIES. He forced himself to read the article and the accompanying editorial that denounced him for what the paper termed "a cruel and callous hoax" on the good citizens of Virginia City. The story also demanded his immediate resignation from both the town council and the Republican party. Rhine tossed the paper aside and went back to his bacon and eggs. He'd been expecting it. Even though he'd been duly elected to the council, it had been as a White man not as a man of color. Neither mixed bloods or full bloods of African descent were allowed at the table. He supposed he should be angry and in many ways he was, but to have Eddy in his life he chose to look past the petty hate and focus on the future with her instead. With his wealth behind him, he could still make the road a bit easier for his people and that knowledge eased the bitterness, too.

A few minutes later Lyman Greer walked into the saloon. Rhine and Jim shared a silent look.

Wondering what Natalie's father wanted, Rhine wiped his hands on his napkin and stood. "What can I do for you, Lyman? How's Natalie?"

"As well as can be expected considering the lies you fed us," he replied accusingly. "I'm here for the deed to my house."

"Do you have what you owe me in exchange?"

"No, and I don't plan to pay you. Not after what you told us last night."

"A debt is a debt, Lyman."

"Not when it's owed to one of you," he shot back disdainfully.

Rhine folded his arms and assessed the man who'd once touted his abolitionist roots so proudly. "Your note is now owned by my brother. I sold it to him a week ago in anticipation of what last night's confession might bring. As you know, he's a highly respected banker in San Francisco and counts some of the city's finest lawyers and judges among his clientele."

The ashen Lyman swallowed.

"And for the record, he's White just like you. I've been kind enough not to ask you for payments. My brother will not be. Expect a letter from him soon demanding you begin payments or he'll foreclose."

His eyes went wide.

Rhine asked, "Is there anything else?"

His fury was plain. "No."

"Good day then."

If looks could kill, Rhine would've been dead on the saloon floor. Instead, Lyman sneered, "Nigger bastard!" and stormed out.

Rhine looked over at Jim, who shook his head sadly and said, "I expected better from him."

Rhine had as well.

Jim added, "Let's hope he spreads the word. Save folks the pain of getting their feelings hurt."

Rhine had investments in many of the businesses around town, and now that Drew's name was also on those investments, they wouldn't be able to cheat him out of his profits or wiggle out of whatever he was owed simply because he was no longer White. Knowing how furious that would make those who'd shown their true feelings last night made Rhine's morning seem brighter.

Before Rhine could retake his seat, Sheriff Howard came through the door, and Rhine wondered, What now? "Morning, Blaine."

"Morning, Rhine. Jim. Let me start by saying, I'm just a peace officer. Got no quarrel with anybody not breaking the law—Colored or White."

"And so you're here because?"

"Because Mayor Dudley and the town council don't have the balls to give you this themselves so they sent me." He handed Rhine a sheet of paper. "They want you to sign it as part of your official resignation."

Rhine read the top line. *I, Rhine Fontaine, guilty*

of lying to the town council . . . He didn't bother reading the rest before handing the document back to the sheriff. "I'm not signing it. Saying I resign is all they need."

"Understood."

There was silence as the two men faced each other. Howard said finally, "I don't pretend to know why you did what you did last night but I get the feeling it took a lot of courage."

Rhine waited.

Howard continued, "I say that to say I still consider you a good man, Rhine. One of the most honorable men I know. There are others in town who feel the same. If any of the ball-less bigots threaten you or cause you any trouble, let me know and I'll do my best to make sure it doesn't happen again."

Rhine nodded. "Thank you, Blaine." He stuck out his hand.

"You're welcome. Once all this nonsense cools down I expect you to start up the poker games again."

Rhine offered a small smile. "You bet."

Howard touched his hat, and after balling up the paper and stuffing it into his pocket, made his exit.

Rhine turned to Jim. "Well." That, too, brightened his morning.

"I've always liked him. He's a good man, too."

Rhine agreed. It was heartening to hear that

there were those who stood apart from the people yelling slurs at him last night, even if they never stepped forward publicly to pledge their support. "You know one of the best things to come out of all this—besides marrying Eddy?"

"What?"

"I finally get to play on a winning baseball team."

Laughter filled the saloon.

Over at the boardinghouse Eddy shared breakfast with Sylvia and filled her in on the events at the ball. They'd seen the newspapers. "I'm surprised no fists were thrown," Eddy said to her. "There was an awful lot of anger in the room." She then related Natalie's furious reaction. "She refused to believe Rhine was telling the truth, and acted almost deranged at one point."

Sylvie sipped her coffee. "Learning she'd been engaged to man of color probably did send her around the bend a bit, but I'm sure she'll get over it. Personally, I want to throw Rhine a welcome home party."

Eddy chuckled. "A welcome home party?"

"Yes. In a way he's come home, and I'm hoping a celebration will balance all the nasty reactions he's gotten. He's done so much to support our community. It's our turn to support him."

"I think that's a wonderful idea. When do you want to have it?"

"Next Friday night—Fourth of July weekend. We'll have it here, both in the dining room and out back. That way he won't have to close down the saloon."

Eddy thought that was a grand plan. Even grander was now that the truth was out, she and Rhine would no longer have to hide their relationship. They could be seen together and not worry about negative gossip—although the gossiping about his heritage would continue for some time, it would eventually fade away. "Do you have a menu in mind?"

"I thought we'd roast a few pigs and make it a potluck. People can bring their best dishes. That way you won't be too tired out from cooking to enjoy yourself."

Eddy liked that idea, too, then something came to mind she'd been meaning to ask Sylvie about. "Why hasn't Whitman Brown been to breakfast for the last few days?"

Sylvie chuckled softly. "Rumor has it that he's been keeping time with Lady Ruby."

Eddy's jaw dropped. "You're pulling my leg."

"No, but apparently she's pulling his, if you get my drift."

Eddy thought back on seeing them huddled together at the auction. "But he's supposed to be a reverend."

"And she's old enough to be his aunt. Hope he's not planning to take her home to his illustrious mama. I don't think that long red wig will pass the brown paper bag test."

Eddy laughed.

Later that morning, Eddy had just finished washing the breakfast dishes when Rhine walked into the kitchen. Seeing him filled her with more joy than she thought her heart could possibly hold. "Good morning, Rhine."

"Morning, mine."

She laughed.

He asked, "What are your plans for the day?"

"Since it's my day off, I hoped to spend it with you." She was still simmering from last night's steamy encounter under the stars.

"That was my hope, too," he said. "First though, I want to ride over to Mary's and find out what happened with the twins. Would you like to come along?"

"I'd love to."

On the way, she had him drive by the plot where the new diner would be built. They stopped and got out. There were no workers about, but piles of wood and stacks of bricks waited at the ready.

Rhine asked, "How long did Zeke say it would take?"

"About six weeks. When he came by the boardinghouse to show us the drawings he was very distant, but I'm hoping he'll thaw when he hears about you."

"Even if he doesn't, as long as he does a good job that's all that matters."

"You sound like Sylvie."

There was traffic on the street and people on the walks. As he helped her back into the Rockaway, someone driving by shouted, "Nigger!"

Eddy stiffened.

But Rhine didn't give the person the satisfaction of even turning to see who the culprit might have been. "When you've been whipped on and off since the age of ten, a word stings less than a pinprick."

That said, he picked up the reins and drove off, leaving her to wonder how deep his pain went and if she would ever know.

At the orphanage, he handed her down and they went inside. The twins mobbed him excitedly while telling him about their new ma and pa.

"Do you like them?" he asked.

"Yes!"

Mary came out and looked on with a smile before saying, "Boys, let me talk to Mr. Rhine and Miss Eddy in my office for a moment."

Micah asked, "You won't leave without saying good-bye?"

Rhine said, "I won't. I promise."

They seemed satisfied and scampered off.

Inside Mary's office, Rhine and Eddy took seats and Mary said, "I saw this morning's papers. You're an incredibly brave man, Rhine."

"I want to marry Eddy so I did what was necessary." He glanced at Eddy.

Mary nodded. "Had I known the truth, we might have been able to come up with a different solution for the twins."

"Is everything squared away?"

"Yes. The Dresdens will come by train on Monday to take them to Sacramento. I'm sorry, Rhine."

"You have nothing to apologize for. They'll be getting a home and that's the most important thing."

Mary nodded her agreement. "I'd planned to send you a message this afternoon to let you know they'd be leaving, with hopes you'd stop in and say good-bye. You've been a godsend to them and to the orphanage."

"I plan to continue to help out."

"And I'll tell anyone who'll listen that you're one of the finest men I've ever been blessed to know." She looked at Eddy. "You're getting a good man."

"I know." Eddy couldn't have asked for a better man to spend the rest of her life with.

Mary asked him, "Do you want to come by on Monday and meet the Dresdens?"

"No. I'll make a clean break and say my good-byes while I'm here. I don't want to interfere."

"I understand. In spite of their pranks and boisterousness, I will miss them dearly."

"As will I."

Eddy heard the emotion in his voice. Parting with them would be difficult.

Mary stood. "Then let me get them."

The boys entered a few moments later. Eddy stood. "I'll let you have some privacy."

Alone with them now, Rhine said, "I'll miss you two."

"We'll miss you, too," Christian said. "Will you come and visit us?"

"How about I let you get settled in first."

"We're going to be real good," Micah said.

"No pranks?" Rhine asked.

They shook their heads.

"No lampblack or snakes?"

"No," they said in unison.

"And you'll be respectful and do what your new parents ask?"

"Yes."

He opened his arms.

Both boys stepped into the embrace and Rhine placed a solemn kiss on the top of each head. "I'm taking you at your word that you'll be good."

"We will," they whispered, and Christian added, "Thank you for teaching us to fly kites."

Voice thick with emotion, he replied, "You're welcome."

On the ride back to the boardinghouse, both Rhine and Eddy were silent. She looked his way.

She knew he was happy about the twins' new life but also knew it would take time for him to get over his loss.

He finally spoke. "We haven't discussed this, but do you want to have children?"

"I do. I'd put away that dream when I was back in Denver. Didn't ever think I'd marry, but thanks to you, I'm dusting it off and shaking it out. What about you?"

"I do."

"After seeing you with the boys, I believe you'll be a wonderful father."

"I'd like to think so even though I've never had anyone to emulate. Carson was my owner. Nothing more." He quieted for a moment as if thinking, then said to her, "Unless my sister has children, ours will be the first freeborn child in my family since my grandmother was brought here in chains. That will make him or her very special."

"I know. I was born free and my parents often told me how special that made me."

"And you are."

The love she saw in his eyes filled her heart. She hooked her arm into his and leaned close. "Then we should get married as soon as possible so we can start working on this special child of ours."

He placed a kiss on her forehead. "I love you, Eddy."

"I love you, too, Rhine. And by the way, Sylvie is throwing you a party to welcome you home."

He chuckled. "Might be the perfect opportunity to let everyone know we're getting married."

"I agree. Do you think your brother might want to stand up with you?"

"I do. I'll wire him soon as we decide on a date. What about your sister?"

Eddy shook her head. "No. I don't see her coming."

"Still no response to your letter?"

"No." And that made her sad because she'd love to see her nieces. She supposed she'd just have to keep hoping that Regan and Portia were okay.

"Well, let's go ahead and make plans," he said.

Eddy agreed and so they set a date for two weeks away.

On Sunday morning, Rhine discovered that vandals had thrown a foul mixture of black tar and paint over the front of the saloon and painted *Tar Baby* across the windows. Furious, he surveyed the damage.

"They must have come right after we closed up," Jim said. "That paint will never come off the windows."

They'd paid hundreds of dollars for the big windows lettered with fancy gold script, and now an equal amount of money would be needed to replace them. A furious Rhine seethed, "Cowards." They'd attacked him verbally and in print and now they'd honed in on his livelihood. What would be next? People driving by slowed to get a good look at the damage. One or two applauded, but upon receiving the hard glares from the owners they moved along.

"We're going to need Zeke's help to replace the windows," Jim said.

"I know." And Rhine wasn't looking forward to meeting with him. This would be their first interaction since the night of the music concert, and from what he'd learned from Eddy, Zeke still had a bone stuck in his craw. There were other carpenters in town, but considering how some of the Whites were responding to the change in Rhine's racial status there was no guarantee they'd take the job. If Zeke turned him down, too, the search would have to be expanded to Reno or Silver City.

He knocked on the door of Zeke's room a short while later. When it opened, Zeke eyed him warily. "What can I do for you, Rhine?"

"Need to hire you to replace the windows of the saloon. They were vandalized this morning."

Zeke smirked. "Folks not happy with you claiming to be Colored all of a sudden?"

Rhine hadn't come for a pissing match. "Will you take the job or not?"

347

"Let me look at it first and I'll let you know." He was quiet for a minute and then asked, "So are you really Colored?"

"I am."

"Why change races now? You had life by the tail. Wealth, respect, and all the privileges that go with it."

Rhine decided he might as well know. "So I can marry Eddy."

Zeke froze.

"To have her, it was an easy choice."

Zeke looked him up and down. Tight-lipped, he said, "I'll come by the saloon in a little while." He closed the door.

Word spread quickly about the vandalism, and while Rhine and Jim waited for Zeke to arrive, members of the community showed up with brushes and buckets. Thanks to a tip from Doc Randolph, they used rubbing alcohol to soften the tar. Turpentine was employed to clean off the splashes of paint, but it was hard, painstaking work.

Late that afternoon, with as much of the damage removed as could be done for the day, Rhine and Jim were thanking everyone for their help when Zeke finally walked up. He assessed the damage. "They got you pretty good."

Rhine didn't respond. Unlike Zeke, he found no humor in the cowardly act.

"I'll take the job. Going to cost you a pretty

penny though—especially if you want the glass fancied up like it was before."

"I do," Rhine said.

"Okay. I'll get the glass ordered and let you know when it comes in."

"Thank you."

And with that, Zeke turned and walked back the way he'd come.

Rhine watched him go and wondered if the carpenter planned to stay angry and distant forever. They'd hadn't been close friends but they had come together as members of the Republican party on behalf of the race and gotten along reasonably well. Until Eddy.

Jim asked, "Think he'll ever come around?"

Rhine shrugged. "I was wondering the same thing, but I'm not going to worry about it. Either he will or he won't." He surveyed the bricks. They were still stained but as not badly. "Let's leave this for now and start again tomorrow. How about we walk over to Sylvie's and see if there's any of Eddy's food left."

Jim grinned. "Now that sounds like a good idea."

When they arrived, the place was packed. Upon seeing them, Sylvie said, "I heard about the vandalism."

Rhine said, "We got most of it cleaned up. Zeke's going to replace the windows. We came to eat. Anything left?"

"For you two? Yes. Follow me."

It was Rhine's first time eating there and as Sylvie led them through the crowded room to their seats, he understood why she wanted to build a larger place. There wasn't even room to turn around. Every inch of the room held someone eating.

Jim remarked, "You'd think she was giving away gold."

At the sight of Rhine, many people stopped what they were doing. They, too, knew he'd never set foot in the place before—at least not as a customer—but knowing what they did about him now, they smiled and greeted him with friendly nods. Some even stood and shook his hand. For Rhine, the acceptance was the balm he needed to balance the last few trying days. Knowing he'd see Eddy made him feel even better.

The food was everything he'd been led to believe.

Jim said, "Damn, this is good."

A chuckling Rhine agreed but was too busy chewing to voice it. There was ham, scalloped potatoes, collards, and a corn bread so flavorful he swore he'd never eat anything but Eddy's version ever again. He now knew why their customers were deserting them. His future wife could cook!

After their meal, Jim walked back to the saloon and Rhine stayed around to wait for Eddy to get done with her duties. He was seated on the back steps when she finally stepped out to join him. She sat close and he draped an arm around her waist.

"I heard about the paint," she said.

He nodded. "It's being taken care of. I loved the food. I understand why my customers are deserting us."

She smiled. "Not going to apologize."

"Don't expect you to. I'm looking forward to my part of the profits once the new diner is built. How was your day?"

"Long, but Sundays always are. And my day was no way as challenging as yours must've been."

He told her about hiring Zeke. "He's still upset about us though."

"As long as he fixes your windows, that's all that matters."

He agreed. He looked over at the woman who held his heart and still found it hard to believe his good fortune. "If we're going to start a family, I should probably find us a house. Unless you want to raise our special child in my apartments above the saloon."

She chuckled. "No."

"I thought not. There are a few vacant places in town. Would you like to see them in the next few days?"

"I would." She quieted a moment then said, "I feel like I'm in a dream, Rhine. I went from an impoverished scrubwoman, to head cook, to your intended in what feels like the blink of an eye."

"You've had a difficult life, darlin'. It's about time things began looking up."

She kissed his cheek. "Thank you for loving me."

He smiled in reply. "You're most welcome. Give me a kiss."

She didn't have to be asked twice.

Chapter Nineteen

ON MONDAY MORNING one of the nastier news-papers called the vandalism at the Union "a well-deserved comeuppance," which only upped Rhine and Jim's ire, but there was little they could do. When the sheriff stopped by, they took comfort in his vow to investigate the matter, even though they held little hope that the perpetrators would be found.

Later that day a young male clerk at the bank Rhine had been patronizing since arriving in Virginia City showed which side of the race issue he was on when he told Rhine he hadn't the time to give Rhine a list of the transactions that had recently crossed his account. He suggested Rhine wait until Whitman Brown came to work the next day. Rhine was already in a foul mood, but rather than punch the snotty little man like he wanted to, he held onto his temper and asked, "Is Graham in his office?" Graham Peyton was the bank's president, a Republican, and one of the men who often frequented Rhine's poker games.

The clerk said with disdain, "*Mister* Peyton doesn't deal with you people. As I said, you'll have to wait until Whitman comes in. I'm sure he'll be able to help you tomorrow."

Rhine strode over to Peyton's closed door and knocked.

Behind him the clerk yelled, "Get away from that door!"

Rhine knocked again.

"Did you hear me?" he squealed, coming out from behind his cage.

The other customers looked on wide-eyed.

Graham appeared in the doorway. "Morning, Rhine."

The clerk pushed his way between them and said tightly, "I told him he needs to wait for Whitman to come in."

The gray-haired, elderly Graham peered over his spectacles at the clerk and then at Rhine before asking the clerk, "What are you blathering about?"

"Whitman deals with his kind, but he insists—"

Graham held up a hand. The clerk quieted but shot daggers at Rhine, who slowly folded his arms. Graham continued in a voice that held quiet fury, "As you already know, Mr. Fontaine is one of this bank's biggest and most loyal depositors. Shall I fire you to prove that point?"

The clerk paled and quickly shook his head.

"Then get your arse back to your station, but first, apologize!"

The clerk looked mutinous.

Rhine waited.

Graham eyed the younger man.

"My apology," he offered grudgingly.

Graham snapped, *"Mr. Fontaine."*

He echoed, "Mr. Fontaine."

Rhine nodded.

The clerk made a hasty retreat.

Graham said, "My apology, too. I didn't know he was a bigoted idiot. Come on in."

Rhine closed the door behind him and sat down in the plush office.

Peyton said, "My apologies again. I heard about the ball and read the trash in the papers. If I could apologize for that, too, I would. What brings you by?"

Rhine told him what he'd wanted from the clerk. Graham got up, went to talk to the same clerk, and returned. "It'll be here in a few minutes. Anything else?"

"Do you keep the Colored accounts separate from the Whites in your vaults?"

"Of course not. It's all green."

"Then why handle them as if they are?"

Graham studied him for a moment. "Makes me look like a bigoted idiot, too, I suppose."

Rhine waited.

The snippy clerk handed Rhine his tally, and as Rhine left he felt better. Not only had the clerk been put on notice for the future but he'd given Graham Peyton something to think about as well.

By midweek Eddy and Rhine had looked at the

available houses and settled on one not far from the orphanage. It was of medium size, had two floors, three good-sized bedrooms, and a nice large parlor. The kitchen left a lot to be desired but Rhine promised her he'd have it enlarged and that was all she needed to hear. She fell in love with the gingerbread trim and the large porches on the front and back. Rhine made arrangement for the purchase through Graham Peyton at the bank and it was theirs.

Also by midweek Sylvie had two less boarders. Miner Gabe Horne left Virginia City for the city of White Pine to work at a mine owned by three Colored men they'd named the Elevator after the San Francisco paper. Both Eddy and Sylvie were sad to see the quiet little man go. Augie Williams moved out too to take a room that opened up in the boardinghouse where his cousin Zeke lived. And although he'd been distant the past few weeks, Eddy would miss him as well. Whitman Brown, rumored to be still courting Lady Ruby, was more often gone than in residence but continued to pay his rent, which was all Sylvie cared about. She wasn't sure if she wanted to advertise the two now vacant rooms but decided to wait until after the party on Friday to make a decision.

Friday's party was a big success. Vera made a large banner out of blue cotton with stitched-on gold letters that spelled out Welcome Home

Rhine. It was hung over the door of the boarding-house. Rhine was pleased when he saw it and gave Vera a big hug. Most of the community turned out for the celebration, although Zeke, Augie, and his fiancée Cherry were notably absent. The rest of the city was celebrating the nation's Independence Day, but the people of color were not allowed to participate in the parade.

"We were barred last year as well," Sylvie informed Eddy. "But it's okay. We do our celebrating on August first anyway, just like the rest of the country's Colored communities."

There were trestle tables of food, horseshoe competitions, sack races, and egg tosses while the fragrant scent of roasting pigs filled the air. When it was time to eat, people set out blankets on the large open area behind Sylvie's place and sat and talked and ate. Rhine sat with Eddy, and after the main meal was done he helped her up and they stood together.

Rhine looked out over the gathering and in a loud voice asked, "Can I have your attention, please?"

It took a moment for folks to quiet down, but once they did, he said, "First of all. Thank you!"

Applause rang out.

"Had I known I'd be given a party, I might have crossed back over a long time ago."

That brought on laughter.

"Eddy and I have an announcement to make. We're going to get married."

Applause, whoops, and hollers of joy split the air.

Fishmonger Amos Granger yelled out, "Is she still going to cook for us?"

More laughter.

Eddy replied, "Yes, Mr. Granger."

"Good. My congratulations then," he called back.

Vera asked, "Have you set a date?"

"Two weeks from today."

"So soon?" she replied. "That's not enough time for me to make your dress."

"I don't need a dress, Vera."

"Of course you do." Vera then asked the crowd, "Don't you all think Eddy needs a dress?"

Everyone agreed with Vera, and Eddy hung her head and laughed. "Lord," she said to Rhine.

Vera said, "Be at the shop tomorrow morning sharp so we can get started."

"Yes, ma'am."

Amos called out, "So Doc. Are you and Sylvie going to follow these two down the aisle?"

Sylvie snapped, "Hush up, Amos. Be a cold day in hell before I marry again."

Doc stood up and declared, "Then put on your coat, Syl." He walked over to where she sat at one of the tables, took her hand, and got down on one knee. The gathering grew so quiet you could hear the soft breeze. "Sylvia Stewart. I have loved you for over twenty years. We don't have a lot of life left but I'd like to spend it with you. I know what stands between us is painful, and if I could go back in time and fix that I would, but since I can't, we need to go forward. Marry me, Syl. Let's not waste another ten years."

Everyone waited.

A tear coursed down Sylvie's cheek and she looked at the man Eddy knew she loved and reached out and cupped his cheek. She nodded, and whispered, "Okay, Oliver. Yes."

Cheers filled the yard and an ecstatic Vera yelled out, "Two wedding dresses!"

Later, as Rhine and Eddy sat on the porch in the dark and watched the city's fireworks light up the sky, Eddy asked Rhine, "Did you think she'd say yes?"

"No. Did you?"

"No. She surprised me as much as she did everyone else. But Doc's right. No sense in them wasting any more time."

Rhine pulled her closer. "That's why we're not delaying our wedding day. I'm ready to start my life with you."

"I'm ready for the wedding night."

Rhine laughed. "Always plainspoken, Eddy."

"Yes, sir. You wouldn't have me any other way."

He kissed her. "Not at all."

Eddy and Rhine spent the next couple of days

looking through catalogs for furnishings for their new home—they planned to move in after their wedding day. They had a slight argument over his free-spending ways. Eddy thought the bed he wanted was way too expensive.

"I'm not making love to you in a cheap bed, Your Majesty."

That shot down her protests and she laughed, "When you put it that way."

He kissed her. "Good."

Rhine promised her a trip to San Francisco to pick out what the catalogs didn't offer in the days ahead. Having never been to the city before, she looked forward to it and to meeting his brother Andrew and his wife. She also didn't fuss when he promised her a new wardrobe worthy of a queen because she was learning that he'd simply spend the money over her protests anyway.

Eddy kept her word to Vera and resumed her role of scarecrow pincushion so her dress could be made. She had to admit it was beautiful. She'd never owned a gown with a full sweeping skirt and a heart-shaped bodice. The silk fabric was as close a match to Rhine's blue armchair as Vera could find on such short notice and it, too, was beautiful, but Eddy had little patience for all the fussing that accompanied the process. She did have patience for the new diner though, and at least once a day Eddy walked down to check on the progress. Although Zeke remained distant and terse even in the face of knowing the truth about Rhine, watching the building slowly take shape filled her heart.

A week after the Fourth of July festivities, Eddy was at Mr. Rossetti's market and was greeted with a smile. "I hear you and Mr. Fontaine are getting married. Congratulations."

"Thank you. We'd love for you and your wife to come."

"We'd be honored. I have a surprise for you."

"What is it?"

"A large shipment of oranges have arrived."

An excited Eddy followed him to the crates where they sat like globes of orange sunshine. "Thank you, Mr. Rossetti."

"You're welcome."

She picked out enough to make marmalade for Sylvia and Vera and Jim and Rhine. She was reminded of Rhine's heated words about what he wanted to do with it, so she threw a few extra into her sack.

When she got back to the boardinghouse, she began grating them right away while Sylvie let her in on her and Doc's plan to be married in San Francisco next month. There was a knock on the back door and Sylvia walked over to see who it might be. When she got there, Eddy saw her freeze and then begin to take small steps backwards. Natalie Greer holding a Colt followed her in. Fear gripped Eddy, and her words to Rhine about the young woman being unhinged came back to haunt her.

Sylvie said quietly, "Natalie. What is this about?"

But Natalie ignored her and turned to Eddy. "You come with me or I'll shoot you right here."

Eddy and Sylvie shared a silent look. "Sure," Eddy said.

"Sit!" Natalie barked at Sylvia.

She did.

A few seconds later Eddy was escorted outside to the Greer carriage a step ahead of Natalie and her gun. Inside, sat the family's terrified looking Chinese driver.

"Get in the front with him. If you call out while we're moving or try and alert anyone, I'll shoot you in the back right through the seat," she promised.

"Where are we going?"

"To the place where Rhine found you, and this time you're going to die. Drive!" she snapped at the driver.

The sun was high and the day so reminiscent of the last time she'd been in the desert, Eddy's fear rose. She knew Sylvie would immediately go for help, and prayed that help would find her before Natalie killed her.

Eddy saw the driver's hands shaking as he held the reins. He said nothing, however, and following Natalie's orders drove out past the city limits.

They drove for what seemed like miles, and the farther they went the more Eddy tried to manage her fear.

"Okay. Stop."

They were out in the middle of nowhere.

Hands still shaking, the driver pulled back on the reins.

"This is all your fault," Natalie said.

Eddy didn't dare look around. "What is?"

"Rhine lying about who he is. I hear you're going to be married."

"Yes, we are."

"You're the only reason he denounced his race, but he can't marry you if you're dead."

Eddy tensed. She and the driver shared another look.

Natalie continued. "And once you are dead, he'll tell the truth about being White, and he and I can marry the way we were supposed to. Now get out and walk. This far away from town with no water in this heat, you'll last maybe an hour. Out!"

Eddy knew arguing with her that Rhine was indeed telling the truth would only push the woman further into whatever madness she was in the grips of, so she slowly climbed down. On the horizon she thought she saw movement, but decided it must be a mirage. Before she had time to study it again, she heard Natalie scream, "Where are you going?"

To Eddy's surprise, the driver had left the carriage, too.

He said to Natalie, "I'm not being a part of this."

When he reached Eddy, he said, "Come, we will walk together."

"Get back here!"

Eddy saw movement up ahead again. Men on horseback were riding their way! "Look!" she urged her companion. Not giving Natalie a second thought, they took off at a run.

Natalie raged, "Stop!"

Eddy prayed the woman didn't know the workings of the Colt from a colander and kept going. She waved her arms to get the attention of the riders. The gun was fired and two bullets tore through her back like bolts of lightning. Crying out in pain, she dropped to her knees.

Natalie fired again and again, this time at her driver, but Eddy couldn't tell if he was hit because she was already facedown in the rocky sand and her world went black.

By the time Rhine, Sheriff Howard, and the rest of the posse reached the scene, Eddy was lying so still, Rhine's heart stopped. Her back was covered with blood. He yelled, "What have you done, Natalie!" He didn't bother to listen to her explanation. He jumped from his horse and ran to Eddy's side. "Eddy!" Natalie's driver lay a few feet away.

Jim and Doc Randolph were soon beside him. "Eddy!"

Doc placed his ear against her chest. "She's breathing. Can't tell how bad she's hurt. Jim, there's some clean towels in my saddlebag. Get them. Let's see if we can at least put some pressure on the wounds so she doesn't bleed to death." He then glanced over at the equally still driver. "Let me see to him right quick."

Natalie said from the buggy, "She's probably dead, Rhine. Now you can tell the truth and we can get married."

Another buggy drove up. The driver was Lyman Greer. His daughter said, "Hello, Papa. Everything's okay now. She's dead and Rhine and I can have our wedding."

Lyman's eyes widened.

Doc Randolph stood up and shook his head sadly. "He's dead, Blaine."

Lyman stared at his smiling daughter. "My God, Natalie."

Sheriff Blaine said, "Mr. Greer, your daughter is under arrest."

"She's ill, Blaine. You can see that."

"Ill or not, she's under arrest."

She said, "No. I'll wait for Rhine. He'll drive me back. We have to go by Vera's and pick out my wedding costume."

"Hand me the gun, Miss Greer," Blaine said quietly.

"Is she dead?"

Tight-lipped, the sheriff lied, "Yes."

"Good." And she handed over the Colt.

Doc said, "Rhine, we need to get Eddy back to town."

Caught between fury and heartbreak, Rhine said, "Lyman, I'm taking your buggy. You drive your daughter back with Blaine."

He nodded hastily. "Sure, Rhine. Sure."

Rhine picked Eddy up gingerly and carried her to Lyman's buggy and laid her on the seat. Doc said, "Keep pressure on those towels."

"Rhine!" Natalie screeched. "Where are you going?"

Jim quickly tied his and Rhine's horses to the back of Lyman's buggy. He then got in, picked up the reins, and headed Rhine and Eddy back to town. Rhine prayed the entire way.

While Doc and Sylvie were up in Eddy's room performing surgery, Rhine sat in the kitchen with Jim, still caught between fury and heartbreak. Natalie was indeed ill but he never wanted to see her again for as long as he lived.

"Doc's good at his job. If anyone can pull her through it'll be him."

Rhine knew that, but the thought that she might be beyond Doc's skill terrified him.

A man wearing a train conductor's uniform entered the kitchen. Rhine and Jim went still.

"I'm sorry to interrupt but I knocked and nobody answered." There were two girls standing beside him. Their shabby dresses were stained and both girls appeared tired and wan. "I'm looking for an Eddy Carmichael. Does she live here?"

Rhine stood and studied the girls. "Yes, she does, but she's unavailable right this minute." The two favored Eddy so much the hairs on the back of his neck stood up, so he asked, "Regan and Portia?"

They nodded, albeit warily.

"How did you get here?"

The conductor explained, "Their mother mailed them here by the train."

Rhine was stuck dumb by that. "Your mother's not with you?"

Portia, the older of the two, shook her head and said, "No. She's at home."

"I'm Rhine Fontaine. Your aunt had an accident. She's upstairs in her room with the doctor."

The girls looked at each other, and the younger one, Regan, asked, "Can we see her?"

"Just as soon as the doctor's done."

Jim was staring as well.

Rhine turned to the conductor. "I'm Miss Carmichael's fiancé and this is my business partner Jim Dade. You can leave the girls here. How much do I owe you?"

He quoted the sum, and Rhine reached into his

pocket and paid him what was owed plus a sizable tip.

The conductor grinned. "Thanks. 'Bye, girls."

" 'Bye, Mr. Hurly. Thank you."

He nodded and made his exit.

Rhine was still trying to get over the shock of their sudden arrival and that they'd traveled from Denver alone. "Would you girls like something to eat?"

"No thank you. We just want to see Aunt Eddy."

"Will you at least have a seat?"

"No thank you."

Rhine and Jim shared a look.

"Would—"

"Just leave us alone, okay," Portia said.

Rhine raised an eyebrow. He wondered what kind of home they'd come from. He knew Eddy had been worried about them, but she hadn't shared any details about their lives. From the look of their dresses, their worn shoes, and how painfully thin they were, he guessed they didn't have a lot. "Would you be more comfortable if Jim and I sat outside?"

The young one, Regan, said, "Yes."

So Rhine and Jim got up and went outside and sat on the back steps.

Jim said, "This is going to be quite a story I'm willing to bet."

Rhine agreed.

• • •

Eddy swam up to consciousness only long enough to hear the murmur of voices and get the sense that she was in a familiar place. Beside the bed stood her nieces, Portia and Regan. *Why am I in Denver?* She had no answer though, so she slipped back into sleep.

The next time she awakened, she didn't know how much time had passed but her mind was clearer and she looked around. Once again beside the bed stood the girls. "What are you doing here?" she asked around her sand-dry throat. That she was surprised to see them was an understatement.

Both girls threw themselves on her and she gathered them in. White hot pain shot through her back but she fought it off to hold them.

"We thought you were going to die," Regan cried.

"I'm not going to die, or at least I hope not. How long have you been here?"

"Two days," Portia said. "Mama sent us. She wrote you a letter."

Eddy's back was on fire. She remembered being shot but nothing more. Seeing them was such a joy, but she was too sleepy at the moment to appreciate it or read Corinne's letter. "Are you staying here with me and Miss Sylvia?"

"Yes."

"Are you being good for her?"

"Yes."

"Okay. Good. Is Rhine here?"

From the doorway, he said, "Yes."

She smiled. She was glad to see him, too. As he came in, the girls backed away from the bed. Portia had a decidedly sour look on her face but Eddy lacked the energy to investigate the cause, though she did have the energy to bask in the love she saw in Rhine's eyes. He placed a kiss on her brow. "How are you feeling, Your Majesty?" he asked softly.

"Better but not all the way. Surprised to see the girls. I thought I was dreaming."

"No dream."

"So I see. How are you?"

"Doing better, too, now that you're out of the woods."

"Good."

Sylvia came in. "Okay, everybody out. She needs her rest."

Eddy smiled but was asleep before they left the room.

Chapter Twenty

IN THE DAYS that followed, Eddy grew stronger and stronger, and as a result was able to spend more time with her visitors. She hated being bedridden again but knew it was for the best. Fortunately, Jim prepared her meals. Doc didn't want her eating Sylvia's charred food, and Eddy was thankful. From Rhine, she learned what happened after she was shot by Natalie. Hearing that the driver lost his life left her saddened. "So is she still in jail?"

"No. Lyman called in some favors and a few days later got a judge to allow him to take her to a hospital in upstate New York for treatment. She'll be there for quite some time."

"Good." Eddy wondered what Natalie's fate might have been had she not been so privileged, but in the end it did not matter as long as she never had to cross paths with her again. "I'm sorry we have to put off the wedding."

"You can't enjoy the wedding night you're so looking forward to if you're still healing, so don't worry about it."

She smiled. "How are you and the girls getting along?"

"Regan will at least talk to me. Portia barely tolerates me."

Eddy was saddened by that as well. "Has to do with her home life. She probably thinks you're like the men who come and visit her mother."

"What do you mean?"

"My sister Corinne is a whore."

He stiffened.

"I'll talk to the girls and try and explain our relationship. The only men they've ever come in contact with are Corinne's customers, so give them some time. Before long they'll love you as much as I do. Promise."

He didn't look convinced, but Eddy was.

"How long are they staying with us?"

"I don't know. I haven't been able to stay awake long enough to talk to them for any length of time but I will today. They said Corinne sent a letter. Are they in the hall?"

"Yes. They spent the morning with Vera. She's in heaven getting them fitted for new clothes. I told her to spare no expense."

"Better them than me," Eddy cracked, and grinned.

He kissed her softly. "I'll send them in."

"Rhine?"

He turned.

"Thanks for saving me—again."

"You're welcome. I love you."

"I love you, too."

The girls came in and Eddy asked, "Did you have fun with Miss Vera?"

Regan nodded. "Our new dresses are so pretty."

Portia stood by the window and looked out.

"Portia? What about you?"

"Why doesn't Mama want us anymore?"

Eddy stilled. "What do you mean?"

Portia handed her a folded piece of paper. "It's what she said in the letter."

Eddy looked at the pain and anger in her nieces' eyes and unfolded the letter. It read: *I'm getting married. My new husband doesn't want the girls because they aren't his, so they're yours now.*

It was the coldest, most callous thing Eddy had ever read. The tears standing in Portia's eyes made Eddy open her arms. Portia came to her and wept like her heart was broken. "I'm so sorry, honey," Eddy whispered, holding her as tightly as her healing back allowed. "So so sorry."

The dry-eyed, ten-year-old Regan said, "Portia, don't cry. Mama doesn't want us, so we don't want her."

Surprised and dismayed, Eddy said, "Regan!"

"I don't care about her. I've always wanted to live with you, Aunt Eddy. Always."

Eddy sensed that her new role was going to be a complicated one but hoped with the help of Rhine and Sylvie and folks like Vera and the rest, things would work out in the end. She then explained to them about her relationship with Rhine. The girls had never been around a marriage and thus had no concept of what the word meant.

"So he's going to live with us?" Portia asked doubtfully, wiping her eyes.

Eddy corrected her, "You two are going to live with me and Rhine."

"How long will he stay with you?"

"Forever."

Regan looked puzzled, and Portia asked, "So you will only have relations with him?"

Eddy blinked and stammered, "Yes. Only with him. When you marry, you only have one man in your house and bed."

She saw Portia and Regan share a look. "So does he pay you to have relations with him?"

Eddy had no idea they knew so much but remembered Corinne had been prostituting herself their entire lives, so of course they'd pick up on how these things worked. She was appalled though. "No. He doesn't pay, and when you have a husband, he won't pay you either. You'll come together out of love."

They both looked skeptical.

"Rhine is kind and caring and all the things you'd want a man to be when you love someone. You'll love him, too."

"Will we have to have relations with him when we do?"

Appalled again, she fought to keep her voice calm, "No honey. Rhine's an honorable man, and honorable men don't have relations with children."

"Oh."

Eddy noted how relieved Portia looked.

Regan said, "Mama said she was going to sell Portia's cherry for money."

Eddy stared. She was so angry with her sister she wanted to walk to Denver and beat her to death. "Here you're both safe from anything like that. I promise. Okay? I'm not going to let anyone hurt you, and neither will Rhine."

She opened her arms and they leaned in. She held them tight and whispered emotionally, "I'm so glad you're here." And she was. With her and Rhine, they'd be loved, cherished, and provided for. With them, they'd have a future. One day she'd forgive her sister but it wouldn't be soon.

Two weeks later she and her nieces got dressed for the wedding. Portia and Regan had on their new gowns, Janet had done their hair, and they looked like two ebony-skinned princesses in their finery. Rhine's brother Andrew and his family had arrived a few days earlier, and any misgivings Eddy may have held about meeting Drew's wife Freda were instantly dispelled when Freda eagerly took Eddy's hands in hers and said, "I'm an only child and I've always wanted a sister. I'm so glad to meet you."

Their son Little Drew would be the ring bearer. The wedding was going to be held in Sylvia's backyard. Whitman Brown was supposed to perform the ceremony but his mother had arrived for a surprise visit the week before, and when he boastfully introduced Lady Ruby as his fiancée, the forty-year-old Whitman had been instructed to quit his job and pack his things. He and his outraged and outdone mother were on the train back to Cleveland the very next day.

Sheriff Howard would officiate instead. Eddy didn't care who said the words as long as she and Rhine were husband and wife at the end of the day.

The backyard was packed with the invited guests, and when Eddy, flanked by her nieces and matron of honor Sylvie, came down the steps to join her intended in the center of the yard, she could barely contain her happiness. There was no music but she didn't care. Both Rhine and Drew were dressed in black and white formal attire, and although Eddy still couldn't get over how much the two brothers favored each other, in her eyes Rhine was the handsomest man in the world.

Sheriff Howard began reading the words. When he got to the part that asked if anyone had issues with the bride and groom being married, a female voice in the crowd said, "Yes. I do!"

Both Rhine and Eddy turned in shock and a woman walked up. She was as fair-skinned and as green-eyed as Rhine, and beside her was a big dark-skinned man wearing a scowl.

Rhine's eyes widened. "Sable?"

"How dare you get married and not send me an invitation?" She turned to Eddy. "Hello. I'm Sable Fontaine LeVeq. This is my husband Raimond. Are you sure you want to marry him?"

Eddy chuckled. Sable took a moment to give the stunned Rhine a strong hug and gave Drew one, too.

Raimond said, "I see your bride's a woman of color, Sergeant Clark. Hope this means you're back on the right side of the road."

Rhine dropped his head and chuckled.

Sable elbowed her husband. "Hush."

Sergeant Clark? Eddy was confused.

Sable said to her, "Pay him no mind, honey. I'll explain later. Now that I've made my entrance, carry on, Sheriff."

And so he did.

Later during the reception, they learned that Rhine's newspaper ads had finally paid off. One of Raimond's brothers saw one in a Boston newspaper on a trip there a few weeks ago and wired Sable about the find. After making arrangements to leave their four children with Raimond's mother, they'd purchased train tickets in their home town of New Orleans and arrived in Virginia City just as the wedding was beginning. Eddy was pleased that Rhine and his sister were finally reunited, and she couldn't wait to spend more time with Sable and Raimond—after her wedding night.

And what a wedding night it was. They drove from Sylvia's to the Union and he carried her up the stairs to his room. As they crossed the threshold, all Eddy could think about was it being the place where her adventure with him began.

But she didn't get to think much longer because he treated her to a night of lovemaking filled with enough sensuous memories to last a lifetime. He made love to her in her gown and then without it. They made love in the blue armchair, and when he laid her nude body on the table and boldly spread her legs, she was treated to the most carnal feasting of all. "Much better than wedding cake," he whispered with a grin as she rode out her orgasm.

Later, a thoroughly sated Eddy looked over at her sleeping husband and acknowledged her blessings. Her diner was almost ready to open, her nieces would have a chance at a fresh new life with her and Rhine, and his worries had been eased about his sister's whereabouts. She had a new house awaiting her and a community and friends she adored. She snuggled down next to her now snoring husband. She looked forward to a future of good food, good girls, and lots of good black powder explosions. Smiling at that, she joined her husband in sleep.

Dear Readers,

When Rhine Fontaine first made his appearance in my fifth Avon novel, *Through the Storm*, in 1998, questions from the readers began almost immediately. Did he really pass? What happened to him? Did he and Sable ever cross paths again? Then came the requests that he have his own story. As the years passed the clamoring became so intense that I lovingly dubbed those readers my Rhine Whiners. Rhine has always been in the back of my mind, but his story never solidified until recently when I ran across an article about an ongoing archaeological dig in Virginia City, Nevada. To the surprise of the archaeologists, among the 4,000 items found at one particular site was a hot sauce bottle and a brass trombone mouthpiece. Because of the hot sauce bottle they wondered if the site was somehow tied to African Americans. It was. What they'd located was the Boston Saloon, an upscale tavern owned and operated from 1866–1875 by William A. G. Brown, an African-American. Further digging unearthed ornate liqueur glasses and crystal stemmed goblets, clay pipes, a bottle of Gordon's dry gin imported from London, mineral water from Germany, and the bones of expensive cuts of meat, like leg of lamb. In 1866, the Virginia

City newspaper, the *Territorial Express*, described the Boston Saloon as "the popular resort for many of the colored population." Kelly Dixon, an archaeologist who started the dig in 2000 and serves as administrator of the Comstock Archaeology Center says, ". . . the mere existence of an African American saloon . . . alters our sense of the so called Wild West."

As I read more about the dig's findings and about William Brown from various other sources, I knew I wanted to write about this unique place and that Rhine would be the owner. As for Eddy, I found an account of a man having seen a Black woman marching across the desert with a cook stove on her head. I was unable to find any other information about her but the description was so intriguing I decided to give her a story, and thus Eddy was born. I do hope you enjoyed *Forbidden*, and that it was worth the almost ten-year wait. I also hope you enjoyed the quick peek at Sable and Raimond LeVeq, something else my readers asked for upon learning I was finally doing Rhine's story.

In writing *Forbidden* I also unearthed a trove of information about Virginia City and the Comstock Lode. Most interesting to me was that there was so much money coming out of the Comstock mines that in its prime Virginia City was the richest city in the U.S. and that its wealth helped finance the Union side of the Civil War.

Here are a few of the sources I used to bring *Forbidden* to life.

Newspaper Articles:

Scott Sonner. "Old Hot Sauce Bottle Offers Peek into Virginia City Past." *Arizona Daily Sun.* June 27, 2002.

Scott Sonner. "Archaeologists at Nevada Mining Town Find Riches at Black Saloon." *Lubbock-Avalanche Journal.* December 26, 2003.

Books:

Dixon, Kelly J. *Boomtown Saloons: Archaeology and History in Virginia City.* University of Nevada Press. 2005.

Fisher, Abby. *What Mrs. Fisher Knows About Old Southern Cooking.* Women's Cooperative Printing Office. 1881. Reissued by Applewood BookS. Bedford MA. 1995. (My source for Eddy's recipes—particularly the marmalade.)

James, Ronald M. and Raymond, C. Elizabeth. *Comstock Women: The Making of a Mining Community.* University of Nevada Press. 1998.

Rusco, Elmer R. *Good Time Coming? Black Nevadans in the Nineteenth Century.* Greenwood Press. Westport CT. 1975.

Smith, Grant H. *The History of the Comstock Lode.* University of Nevada Press. 1998.

In closing, I'd like to thank my editor, Erika Tsang, for her valuable insight and support. Her insistence that I dig deeper always makes me write a better book. Kudos to the great folks at Avon Art for another slamming cover and to everyone at Avon/Harper for twenty years of love. Many thanks to my agent Nancy Yost and her crew at NYLA. We've been together since 1995 and our relationship is still fresh and fun. And last but not least, to my dear dear readers. As I always say: when I count my blessings I count you twice.

See you next time,
B

Center Point Large Print
600 Brooks Road / PO Box 1
Thorndike, ME 04986-0001 USA

(207) 568-3717

US & Canada:
1 800 929-9108
www.centerpointlargeprint.com